Also by Catherine Mann

The Captive's Return
Code of Honor
Explosive Alliance
Pursued
Joint Forces
Anything, Anywhere, Anytime
Strategic Engagement
Private Maneuvers
The Cinderella Mission
Under Siege
Taking Cover
Grayson's Surrender
Wedding at White Sands

CATHERINE MANN

Blaze *of* Glory

HQN™

ISBN-13: 978-0-373-77118-9
ISBN-10:   0-373-77118-5

BLAZE OF GLORY

www.HQNBooks.com

Printed in U.S.A.

Dear Reader,

Captain Bobby "Postal" Ruznick's character flourished in my mind fully developed from the first time he stepped onto the scene in *Code of Honor*. Some characters do that, and it's a writer's dream to know the character so well from the get-go.

What surprised me, however, was how Postal lingered in my mind, nudging, making me think beyond preconceived notions of what "going postal" means. This quirky, free-sample-snitching character challenged me to look at the part of all of us that has a bit of "postal" inside, and therefore find an understanding for those with larger, more painful emotional battles to fight.

Not so long ago, people such as the character Matthias Lanier suffering from manic depression—bipolar disorder—would have faced a far more dire outlook long-term. Now, thanks to the wonders of modern medicine and compassionate psychiatric professionals, we can all benefit from their contributions and joy in life.

Thank you, dear readers, for following my stories wherever the next journey leads us! I very much enjoy hearing from fans, so please feel free to stop by my Web site and visit my message boards at www.CatherineMann.com. Or if you would like an autographed bookmark, send a self-addressed stamped envelope to Catherine Mann, P.O. Box 6065, Navarre, FL 32566.

Happy reading!

Catherine Mann

To those who fight a valiant battle against
life-threatening illnesses of the body and mind.
Your bravery is heroic beyond measure.

ACKNOWLEDGMENTS

Living in the Florida panhandle, my family and I survived a number of hurricanes in 2005 that made writing a challenge as we evacuated time and time again. Luckily, our home came through with manageable damage and our family is safe. However, I did have to call upon the help of dear and talented friends to bring this book to fruition on time. (Any mistakes or liberties with the research information are my own.)

Thank you to Senior Editor Melissa Jeglinski for her fabulous editorial insights, and to my agent Barbara Collins Rosenberg for her unwavering faith in my work. You both make my job a joy!

I owe huge favors to a number of friends who donated their time and talent with critiques and proofreading. Abundant appreciation to Joanne Rock, Stephanie Newton, Tina Trevaskis and Major Michelle Gomez, USAF Ret. I couldn't have made it to the finish line on time without you!

A special thanks to Dr. Henry Boilini, Major USAF, for information about the treatment regiment for Matthias Lanier's bipolar disorder. Thank you as well for all you do to keep our military members and their families together and emotionally healthy in these most trying times.

I've been blessed with the generous mentorship and friendship of two amazing authors, Suzanne Brockmann and Lori Foster. Thank you beyond words for all your help and support! You ladies ROCK!

And as always, thank you to my home-front hero, Lieutenant Colonel Robert Mann, USAF, who helps research military details. I love you, flyboy! And huge hugs and thanks to our four amazing children, who bring my heart and life such constant joy and smiles. My own dear "fab four," I am so very proud of you all. I can't wait to see what you accomplish next!

Blaze *of* Glory

PROLOGUE

Baghdad, Iraq

"I DON'T THINK we should see each other anymore once we get back to the States."

His soon-to-be ex-girlfriend's rejection rattled around in Captain Bobby "Postal" Ruznick's head as loudly as the echo of worn-out shock absorbers rattled along the dirt road. Dumped by a woman, in a crappy military bus, no less.

A first, but not a surprise.

He'd expected the heave-ho from Dr. Grace Marie Lanier—a profiler for the police when she wasn't called up for her Army Reservist duty—after their second date to a no-cover-charge bazaar festival in downtown Baghdad. Then she'd hung around for another date and he'd started to think maybe…

So yeah, this did sting a little after all. Not that he

would let on and launch into some major discussion when he had bigger concerns.

Such as the off-kilter sense he was getting from the desert town landscape outside the gritty windows. This should have been a simple bus ride to his plane, wrapping up a two-week quick gig in Baghdad. But then nothing around here ever turned out simple.

A Special Ops pilot, he had to trust his instincts or he could too easily end up taking the eternal dirt nap.

"Bobby, I know you're awake behind those sunglasses." Gracie's prissy tones contradicted her sultry, exotic scent. "Your boot's tapping so hard you're vibrating the floorboards worse than the potholes."

This didn't seem like an opportune moment to mention more than one woman had told him he twitched even in his sleep, so he kept listening to her ramble on like his third-grade teacher spouting the benefits of Ritalin for settling his ass down. Except his junkie ma never made it to the parent/teacher conference. By the time he'd gone to live with his grandma, he'd figured out to avoid raisins, grapes and sugar. He'd learned to concentrate hard and process those eight ka-zillion stimuli catapulting his way all at once. He'd fast figured out how to pick which one demanded the bulk of his attention.

The newly erected placards scrolled in local dialect along the dusty road won, hands down.

"Really, Bobby, I don't want to drag this out. Certainly it will be awkward during the flight home, but after we land tomorrow morning, we'll never have to see each other again. I'll return to North Carolina, you can kick back on your Florida beach."

He grunted.

What else could he say? She was right. A shrink and a psycho really didn't make for much of a match.

He figured he'd been lucky to get three dates. But holy hell, then on date three she'd flattened her hand to his fly during a lip lock behind a Humvee a second before the "time to leave" call from fellow CV-22 pilot Joe "Face" Greco. Face's sucky timing had cost Bobby's one chance at Gracie in bed. Sexy Gracie. Blond and busty and so smart he got off on the fact she couldn't string syllables together after their first kiss on the first date.

Now he wouldn't luck into a repeat.

Damn. Big-time damn. And so not anything he could think about now because holy crap something wasn't right outside the grimy bus window. He couldn't read the messages spray painted on plywood, and likely no one on the bus could read Arabic either.

Might just be signs for homemade fig preserves or "have you seen my lost goat?" Or it could be something else altogether—like a warning to locals.

Except these locals were in surprisingly scarce supply in the small village outside of Baghdad, not a kid in sight. He logged all textbook signs of an IED—improvised explosive device. The IED could be stored anywhere or strapped to anyone.

Inside the rusted-out jeep on the side of the road.

Buried under that leaning palm tree.

Perhaps stuffed in that dead cow carcass rotting in a ditch.

Gracie shifted in her seat, plastic crackling. Her soft curves pressed against his side and threatened distraction, no matter how adept he was at multi-tasking. More of her sexy scent mingled in with the pervasive military-bus smell—much like an old Boy Scout tent, not that he'd ever been a Boy Scout. However his buddy Face had, and vowed military gear carried the same musty stink.

Distracting thoughts whacked him from all sides. Shit. He was better than that now. Concentrate, and do not let emotions slither through to remind him how hell could explode in seconds.

"Bobby, you're a talented pilot and even a, uh, fascinating man. But we're just too different. That whole 'opposites attract' cliché is true, but not always healthy."

"Uh-huh." He shoved to his feet. *Fascinating? Cool.* He would process that later for sure. But first—

"'Scuse me."

"Where are you going?"

Her faint question tickled at the edges of his narrowing focus. He braced a hand on the back of a seat as he walked, then another seat, left, right, making his way up the aisle with slow deliberation while assessing that cow carcass in the ditch as the already creeping bus slowed at an intersection.

Plenty of carcasses decayed around this place for days, but that bovine gut offered plenty of room to hide a bomb. He suppressed nightmarish images of other IEDs strapped to women and children. His brain flashed with memories of bombs tucked beneath murdered American soldiers waiting to be retrieved and honored for their sacrifice. Instead their dead bodies in the field were rigged to devices and used as a tool by the enemy to blow up more Americans.

His gaze skipped ahead to the camo-wearing driver. The dude wasn't an Iraqi National since they didn't hire locals to drive buses. The burly guy was an Army Reservist like Gracie. Trustworthy.

But everyone was edgy and, well, Bobby had a rep for acting irrationally. This uptight Sarge driving the rattletrap bus already thought he was a loose cannon.

Usually they were totally correct. Just not today.

Still, there wasn't time for chitchat. Discussion would cost valuable minutes and he needed to get up front. Fast. Sprinting would get him tackled by any of the Army dudes packing the seats, rifles on their laps.

Of course a rifle didn't deliver much of a wallop against an IED. He made his way forward.

Slow. Steady. Focused. Almost there.

A hand snaked out, grabbing his elbow. Bobby resisted the impulse to draw back a fist—thank God, since the hand was attached to his crewdog buddy, Joe "Face" Greco who so wouldn't take well to a fistfight. "What are you gonna do, Postal, get off and walk? Sit down and catch some sleep. We've got a long flight ahead of us. Listen, cheap ass, I seriously doubt the driver has any complimentary pretzel packs and a soda cart."

Postal's parsimonious ways were legendary.

Bobby nodded toward the empty seats up front— let Face assume whatever he wanted—and kept on walking. Past "Vegas," a family man with kids.

Sandman, Padre and Stones, each of those gunners was a crew member with helmet bags and rifles of their own. His brothers-in-arms who didn't deserve to be blown to hell by a terrorist IED coated with cow guts. Nobody deserved that.

After dodging countless bullets on the street as a kid and even more bullets as an adult in war zones, he figured he was already living on borrowed time. Better to go down in a blaze of glory than let those bastards hurt a busload of innocents. Like Gracie, who, yeah, was always a little too perfect to hang out with a messed-up adrenaline junky like him anyway.

And if he was wrong about the IED? Well, they would just have another reason to laugh and call him Nucking Futz Postal.

Bobby stopped beside the driver. Focus. Adrenaline surge. Act.

He grabbed the wheel before the Army sergeant could do more than look up.

Bobby jerked the wheel left. Hurtled the bus off the road amid hollering from the back. The rear mirror showed slinging bodies too busy righting themselves to overtake him.

Excellent.

He slammed against the seat, clenched his hand around the steering wheel. The driver's shouts were lost in the…

Boom.

The explosion behind them rocked the earth, drowned out words but not the hoarse shouts. The rearview mirror filled with the image of flames splitting the road behind them, exactly where they would have driven.

Hands locked, he guided the wheel, plowed the bus through a piece-of-shit barn on the city outskirts. Chickens squawked and scattered.

The bus blasted out the other side of the ramshackle barn, into a ditch and up onto the road again. Safely. Although new shock absorbers were definitely no longer optional.

At least they were safe, and Baghdad International waited ahead in the stretch of desert.

Heated nerves chilled, settling in the stunned silence surrounding him. Sweat sealed his flight suit to his body, but more from the temp than from any stress, because he'd always known he would succeed.

Well, he'd been pretty sure.

He nodded to the driver. "Here ya go, Scooter. All yours again. But I'm thinking we need to get the hell out of here ASAP."

Bobby released the wheel and pivoted away. The swaying bus lurched under his feet before steadying again as the rows of passengers gawked and whispered.

Left hand on a seat, right, left, he made his way back down the narrow aisle.

Joe Greco shook his head and clapped him on the shoulder. "Thank you, crazy-ass bastard."

That he was.

Gracie stared back at him with eyes wide. Wary. Confused. But mostly wary.

Yeah, he was definitely too close to the edge for Dr. Uptight. That pissed him off, which was better than regretting the fact he would never get naked with gorgeous Gracie.

Without a word, he plunked in his seat, slouching. Boot bouncing a never-ending restless rhythm, he settled in for a few minutes' power nap before their flight out of this shithole and out of Dr. Gracie Marie Lanier's perfect world. She balanced it all, profiler for the cops, then racing to do her duty when called to her Army Reservist psy-ops job. All that and hot as all get out. Shee-it.

As still as she sat, Gracie fidgeted, causing too many damned tempting brushes of those lush breasts of hers against his arm.

With a final huff, she stilled. "Well, Bobby, you sure picked a hell of a way to avoid our farewell conversation."

CHAPTER ONE

Cantou, Asia
Nine months later

"AVOIDANCE," Lieutenant Grace Marie Lanier, Ph.D., sighed to herself with longing.

What a wonderfully passive-aggressive way of dealing with the uncomfortable moments undoubtedly in her near future. Not a particularly professional thought for a psychologist, but, well, professional objectivity checked out when it came to Bobby Ruznick. And she would be unable to avoid him for a full flipping week in their jungle mission camp in Cantou.

Grace Marie directed the unloading of her platoon's gear from the cargo plane for the joint Air Force/Army Reserves exercise in the lush jungle. A career coup that she had pulled strings to get. She wasn't here in Cantou for the job perk. Only one thing could have lured her here.

Rescuing her father.

And she could very well need Bobby's help, the reason she had by name requested his crew.

Grace Marie kept her eyes off the steaming expanse of sky where his CV-22 aircraft would crest the horizon any minute now. She'd arrived earlier today in a cargo plane with her equipment. Bobby's Special Ops craft would bring the troops.

Damn it, she needed to focus on her father, not Bobby. Yes, nuclear scientist Matthias Lanier touted more brain power than any Mensa think tank, but when it came to common sense, the man might as well still be in kindergarten on the buddy system for field trips.

A shadow stretched over her onto the tarmac, reminding her to get her head out of the clouds before genetics kicked in and she morphed into her absentminded old man. She pivoted to find one of the cargo-plane pilots rocking on his heels beside her…Rodeo, another Air Force flyboy. But this one was her friend, a very treasured and dear pal.

"Hey there, Flipper."

Grace Marie cringed at the use of her honorary call sign given to her by her Air Force buddies. Thank God, most of them didn't know the reason why and she sure wasn't sharing the details of that mortifying event.

My, how they loved their nicknames. She'd learned early on the different military services had different group personalities. Knowing that aided her in dealing with these people. Air Force service members tended to be more laid-back than their Army compadres, which wasn't a problem for her. She simply needed to understand how best to approach the different mind-sets, something she usually managed with ease thanks to her training, except when it came to Bobby Ruznick.

But Rodeo—Derek Washington—was a friend, easy to relate to. His Denzel-like good looks drew plenty of female attention, but for Grace Marie, Rodeo tamed any lady-killer tendencies in honor of their friendship.

She relaxed her Army stance for the less rigid Air Force at-attention. "Something I can help you with or are we just catching up on gossip?"

He gestured to the back hatch of the cargo plane, a military van rolling down the tracks with loadmasters controlling. "Just passing time while they unload. Did you bring any good shoot-'em-up videos for us to watch via your surveillance van?"

The equipment would also provide infomercial-type films for the camp and area military to teach ways to win over the hearts and minds of an enemy in the hope of avoiding war. Or, at least softening up some of the enemy to lessen casualties.

"Capture their minds, and their hearts and souls will follow." She winked. "My unit's motto."

Heart. What an interesting word choice. She knew she and Rodeo weren't interested in each other that way.

She'd gone out with him a couple times after breaking up with Bobby, only for Rodeo and Grace Marie to find after a few kisses—no spark. Definite friendship realm. Most likely because they were both stuck on other people.

And why did it seem the monkeys were cackling louder at her thoughts right now?

Rumor had it Rodeo's call sign had been earned because he always shouted the wrong woman's name during sex and one particular time got bucked off in under eight seconds flat, bare butt landing on tile.

Grace Marie didn't have any firsthand naked experience with Derek on the subject. However, according to a late-night drunken conversation between them in an Officer's Club bar, he confessed he always called out the same woman's name.

Since Grace still couldn't ditch thoughts of Bobby, she and Derek made a pretty good team. They offered each other a no-strings way to keep others from hitting on them until they could shake loose of the past.

Something she could really use this week with Bobby around.

Another shadow stretched overhead. An aircraft. Bobby's CV-22 had sneaked up without her noticing. Damn, she was off-kilter today. Derek seemed to sense that, sticking to her side like glue as if he understood full well how tough standing strong against temptation would be this week. God love him.

Whoosh.

The cutting-edge new aircraft shadowed over her simultaneously with the noise like the sensation of someone strolling over her grave. The mammoth gray tilt-rotor roared over the towering banyan trees, right on top of them, in fact, skimming so close the branches and leaves parted, almost bowing.

Or evading.

The new-to-the-inventory craft differed from any other, able to operate as both an airplane and helicopter. The propellers on the wings could pivot forward, airplane style, or rotate upward so the craft could fly or hover like a helicopter. When moving forward, it could nearly double the speed of its helicopter counterparts, inserting or rescuing troops in half the time while maintaining the ability to land in the smallest of clearings.

The craft was technically still in the testing phase, Bobby one of the hand-picked few to see it through until a squadron could be stood up. Hopefully within about a year.

Another *year* of Bobby flying insane maneuvers to test the craft. Her gut clenched. Derek's hand stayed steady on her back in comfort in spite of the ban on PDAs—public displays of affection in uniform.

Regardless of her fears, clearly this craft was well on its way to being a major asset in the Air Force inventory that would save countless lives. She could envision spouses who would have their military husbands or wives return home through the door after combat because of the risks Bobby had been willing to take to test his craft to the max.

An awesome test pilot.

And really unsettling dating material.

Some kind of funky cawing parrot joined the mocking monkeys.

The CV-22 had to be at full speed as it skimmed the treetops. Then in a blink, it pulled up, losing airspeed as it climbed. God, would it stall? It had to.

There wasn't a doubt in her mind who was flying right now, because conservative Joe "Face" Greco would never pull a stunt like that.

The craft seemed suspended in midair, in midtime. Even the birds and monkeys quieted. The wings transitioned from flight to hover as the nose swung around, pointing down and dropping toward the tarmac, swooshing like something from a war-movie festival Bobby took her to on one of their dates— probably because of the free admission.

Right now, however, no one could look away.

Impossibly close to the ground the nose came up and the aircraft settled down just as soft as you please. From the second she saw the airplane until it was parked and spooling down could not have been more than thirty seconds. The maneuver would counter threats around the airfield, but who had the *cajones* to handle an aircraft like that?

God, when she was around Bobby, turmoil roiled. She'd been right to break things off with him. Although at the time, she'd been half hoping he would argue with her. Then he'd saved them all from the exploding cow, a brave and fearless act.

She'd been totally wowed. Who wouldn't be? Except she'd noticed his pulse as he sat beside her, drifting off to sleep. For a full five minutes she'd watched the throb in his neck, slow, steady, when hers had been about to explode out her ears in hyperspeed.

Any need to call back her Dear John words had

evaporated, as she thought of life with her mentally ill father.

Bringing her thoughts back to the here and now, she readied to see Bobby again, CV-22 acrobatics apparently through for the moment. Grace Marie compacted her focus like a snowball in her fist, ironic since it was hot as hell out here on the runway. But she would manage as she'd done since she was four and her mama gave up custody in the divorce in exchange for big bucks.

That was a tough thing to live with sometimes, that her mother had sold her and without a second glance left her with a bipolar parent.

Still, all in all, it had worked out for the best. Grace Marie was used to taking care of her old man, who functioned thanks to the wonders of modern medicine and a lifetime supply of lithium.

His sky-high IQ brought him many exciting opportunities, such as participating in the nuclear-research project here at Cantou for the summer. But she hadn't heard from him in over six weeks and that scared the crap out of her. What if he'd ditched his meds? What might he do? He carried so many U.S. secrets in his head, what might the people here do to him?

She definitely didn't have time for romance with

anyone, most especially a guy one loose screw away from a breakdown.

Screw? Bobby? Ohhhh… Tingle.

Paging Dr. Freud. Paging Dr. Freud.

Screw? Yep. Interesting word choice considering Bobby's animal attraction brought that notion to mind every time he strutted right past her boundaries. And even when he was nowhere around.

But he would be. Soon. So she'd better shore up her defenses or they'd be in a lip lock against the nearest wall again. And again.

And next time they wouldn't stop.

"WELL, FUCK ME sideways." Bobby pitched his checklist against the control panel, plane parked and still in one piece. Thank God.

Of course, he knew just how far to push the craft. His gut talked to him in a way guys like Joe would never understand.

In the seat next to him, Joe "Face" Greco scooped the checklist from the floorboards by rudders. "Sideways? Sorry, pal, but I can't help you out there."

Bobby evened out his pulse and stared through the windscreen at the lush jungle surrounding the field, so different from the desert landscape last time he'd seen Gracie.

Here they were, together in Cantou. What a major thorn in the U.S.'s side. One minute the countries were best buds with lucrative trade agreements. Then the nuclear weapon rumors started, with hints of terrorist camps setting up in those jungles.

However, nothing could be concealed in the rotting vegetation from this plane and its infrared sensors.

Bobby twisted in his seat toward Face. "No worries. I meant it figuratively. I guess a more apropos request would be for you to kick me in the ass."

"Now that, I'm glad to do anytime. But, uh, is there a particular reason for the ass-kicking, so I'll know how hard I should apply my boot?"

"It's not like we were actually in danger, but I probably was a bit heavy-handed with the maneuvers."

"Uh, hello," the flight engineer, Shane "Vegas" O'Riley barked from the seat slightly behind and in the middle. "Don't the rest of us get a vote in this? I'd like to weigh in with my opinion."

Bobby bristled. "I had the craft under control at all times."

Vegas coughed once with theatrical flair. "As soon as I get over my testicles thumping my ribs I'm going to have some words for you, Captain."

Face started running the shut-down checklist. "So why show off for a bunch of— Ah. It's not just a bunch of support pukes. It's psy-ops, including Grace Marie Lanier. You were showing off for a woman."

Bobby unstrapped. "An A plus for our very own fucking Sherlock Holmes."

"A woman?" Through the headset, rear gunner Sandman chimed in from the back, so named because of catching a woman's eye and being in her bed when she woke up in the morning. He'd been teased many a time at bars when karaoke renditions of the song "Mr. Sandman" started. "Well, why the hell didn't you say so from the start, sir? I'd have been applauding."

Face finished running the plastic-sleeved checklist. "Consider your hindquarters safe, dude. Any of us would have done the same for a woman."

Swinging out of his aircraft commander's seat, Bobby made his way toward the hatch. A lot rode on his flying right now as Face came along as an instructor. Bobby hoped to soon complete his upgrade to aircraft commander, but had to finish the instructor evaluation from Face.

Bobby winced as he stepped outside. He shouldn't be pulling crazy stunts right now.

The world outside the aircraft filled with noise, screaming birds and monkeys mingling, nearly drowning out the standard flight-line mayhem. Nearly. Everything but a tinkling laugh he recognized immediately, thanks to his ability to focus on the one most important detail in the middle of a cacophony of stimuli.

Gracie's laugh definitely took priority.

His eyes followed the path directed by his ears, but he couldn't find her in the crowd of planes and troops transported in for this exercise, Cantou soldiers as well with their different colored braids and medals.

He'd brought Army troops in the Special Ops CV-22. Gracie had come along with the gear in the cargo plane for the exercise with the Cantou military. Both sides engaged in a "you show me yours and I'll show you mine" sort of deal.

Bobby stared at the cargo plane all rigged out for the psy-ops unit that had been sent along for this low-key mission.

Grace Marie Lanier was sitting inside. No big deal, since they hadn't spoken in months. They'd just shared a few dates and an expected breakup. A smart breakup.

A breakup that he needed to put behind him once and for all because crazy him and uptight her—oil and water—did not mix. He needed to get her out of

his head and move on, the reason he'd begged his butt
off to be a part of this week-long mission, only to be
surprised at how easily the assignment came through.

Must be fate—laughing at him, no doubt.

And yeah, there she was standing under the wing
of a C-17 cargo plane, sun kicking up sparks off
braided notches of her champagne-blond hair. She
could have been one of those WWII bombshell
poster girls—except in camo rather than a red dress.

Well, he liked life on the edge and Gracie certainly
set him on a razor's edge. She stepped from under the
wing toward the yawning opening at the top of the load
ramp.

Gracie.

Here.

Hell.

And ah… Nirvana.

THE HELLISH HEAT could have swallowed her ability
to concentrate, but Grace Marie forced her attention
off the heat—from the weather and thoughts of
Bobby—and concentrated on doing her job. Time to
quit relying on her buddy Rodeo. The C-17 contained shipping containers with dismantled satellite
dishes, printing presses, comm gear, all packed in
around her unit's specialty van and a Humvee.

A Humvee she would need for a quick spin of her own after sundown, *after* she'd seen Bobby.

She'd realized after a few dates that Bobby was crazy as a loon—okay, not exactly a technical description given her occupation, but then Bobby had a way of jumbling her intellect.

Like now, as he filled the open side hatch.

Dark glasses shielded his eyes, not that he let anyone peek inside even when the shades were hooked on the collar of his T-shirt. Nine months ago, he'd sat in that bus, knee jostling, as if he had better places to be than listening to one of the toughest things she'd ever had to say.

Not that she wanted to admit how difficult it had been to break up, but she refused to participate in unhealthy relationships. Of course, his insanely impulsive and dangerous save had wowed her and scared the pants off her all at once.

He jogged down the side steps and out onto the cement. His jet-black hair radiated heat as much from the man as from the broiling sun overhead. Her hands clenched against the remembered texture, thick, soft, with a hint of curl sneaking around her fingers, insidiously tempting her through temptation to throw away reason.

Grace Marie pivoted away. She couldn't do this

now, when her emotions were too close to the surface, worrying that her unstable father had gotten himself into God-only-knows what kind of trouble.

Derek stepped closer, shadows darkening his chocolate-brown eyes. "You okay, Grace Marie?"

"I have to be." She donned her Army stance again like a rigid armor. "Let's check the unloading of the printers."

Printers that would flood the area with leaflets, propaganda, anything to educate the other side. Hmm…maybe she should compose a few of those educational dialogues for herself when it came to Bobby.

BOBBY LET his dumb-ass feet keep carrying him right toward Nirvana.

Lord, that woman was hot and smart and had he mentioned hot? He could get off on listening to her recite the *Farmers' Almanac* as easily as sliding his hands up her shirt to explore the graceful Gracie bounty of her well-endowed chest. No avoiding her now. Might as well be straight up. He didn't know how to play life any other way, and this was his big chance to move on.

He stopped at the base of the C-17's load ramp, large crates littering the runway. "Lookin' good, Gracie."

"Bobby." Her eyes went wide, then shuttered as the chatter around her shushed a level. "Captain, thank you. Any kudos on the equipment go to those who work with me."

"Equipment?" Oh, he burned to check out her equipment, all right, just not the metal-and-bolts kind packing the hold.

"My van. My computers."

"Sure. Awesome setup you've got here." He ran his broad hands over the rough-hewn wood of rudimentary packing crates on his way over to where Gracie stood under the wing. This woman had everything she needed to probe the hearts and minds of the enemy.

A man stepped closer, a big muscled man. The dude moved closer still and—shit—had the guy actually put his hand on her back? PDAs in uniform were a no-no, for God's sake. That spoke louder than if the guy had engaged in an all-out French-kiss howdy.

Who was this guy? This big fella in a flight suit with pilot's wings and captain's bars standing mighty damn close to Gracie with a protective air.

He couldn't miss the body language.

Body language?

Shee-it. When had he started thinking words like "body language"? He was beginning to sound like

Gracie with the psychobabble. Regardless, the dude was sending back-off vibes louder than the roar of a jet engine.

Might as well get right to it. He thrust out his hand. "Bobby Ruznick—Postal."

"Derek Washington—Rodeo."

They crushed each other's hands. If he squeezed much harder, the Air Force would be short two pilots for about six weeks. Medical report? Cause of accident: Adolescent posturing over a chick, like with the show-off landing.

"You fly this puppy in?" Bobby pointed to the C-17 with a tail flash indicating it was based out of Charleston, South Carolina.

"That would be me and my crew." Rodeo gestured with a wave.

Even as good as Bobby was at multitasking, he really didn't need this woman and juvenile jealousy right now. "Looking forward to seeing you around the club—except wait, we're all in tents, like some Army grunt." He grinned at Gracie. "No offense."

"None taken, pampered Air Force baby boy."

The guy beside her still didn't move away. What the hell. He'd never played it safe. "I meant it when I said *you* are looking good, Gracie."

And, ah, her spine went so predictably straight he almost laughed. Almost, because, well, that Rodeo dude still had his hand on her back and he, the outcast Postal, was still toying in his pockets with some freebie leftover tea bags from his buds' in-flight lunches.

Joe Greco—ever the honorable gentleman—ambled over and hooked an arm around Bobby's neck. "Do you want me to gag him for you, Lieutenant Lanier? Or better yet, maybe I could stake him down on an anthill in the jungle?"

"Tempting, but no need, thank you all the same." Grace Marie smoothed back hair already perfectly in place in spite of the cranking temps. "He simply complimented me—and my van. Nothing wrong in that."

This woman always did have a way of surprising him, which he liked even when he knew they would make each other crazy. Of course, he'd never been good about making smart choices. "She dumped me, so she's being kind now. She's a nice lady."

And he so wasn't a nice boy.

No big deal, though. They would hang out together for the next week on this low-key operation that would give him a chance to forget all about this hot, nice lady and find…

Uh.
His mind blanked on what plan B might be.
But he had one laid-back, quiet week to find out.

CHAPTER TWO

Cantou University
Nuclear science retreat

FELICIA FRATARCANGELO NEEDED information and Dr. Matthias Lanier had the answers.

She took her time storing her lab supplies while other younger students bustled out around her at the end of a brainstorming session that had run until well after dark. A research group of a dozen worked late tonight, so it shouldn't take long for them to clear and her to be alone with Dr. Lanier.

The whole symposium of approximately two hundred were designated into research sections. Ultimately, all the information would be cobbled together in hopes of developing a cheaper, hybrid form of nuclear energy to provide power to parts of Cantou poverty stricken after a tsunami. Honorable. Good work. If that's what everyone was really doing.

Seeing Dr. Lanier hunched over his computer at his desk, she could almost feel sorry for the man. Almost. He was smart, genius level, and while he might appear the stereotypical absentminded professor, she'd learned long ago not to trust any facade.

After all, she wasn't who she appeared, either.

The other classmates at the science retreat thought she was a disgruntled new divorcée returning to finish her higher education, most recently through a student-exchange program between the U.S. and Cantou. In actuality, she'd completed her bachelor's degree and two more postgraduate degrees in nuclear physics and microbiology well over ten years ago.

She enjoyed the whole Mata Hari notion after so many years as a bedridden bald teen, a slave to doctors, meds and pain. Germs had been her worst enemy, an ever-lurking lethal threat that left her with nothing but books for friends for nearly two years. An eternity to a teenager back then who'd suddenly yearned for even the confines of the Catholic-school education she'd once griped about regularly.

Now, she enjoyed her health, and yes, her sexuality. Men checked her out, wanted her, and she liked it. She really liked it, especially after the way her ex-husband had made her feel like a dried-up prune because she couldn't have kids. The clothes also happened to give her confidence as well as offer a great diversion. No one ever suspected a ditz like her could be ferreting out secrets.

Although she had a slight caveat to that. All men checked her out except this one.

Evidence indicated Matthias was straight. He'd been married—at eighteen no less. He and his wife had a "preemie" daughter born six months after the "I do," then completed his divorce when the girl was four.

From beside her desk across the room from him, she shifted from one stiletto heel to the other, flipping her thick black hair over her shoulder. The wild curls had grown in after radiation.

Just flick the hair again and wait…wait…

No reaction. Sheesh. So what was wrong with her? She might be pushing forty but she still turned heads, apparently just not this guy's head, and that miffed her more than a little for some odd reason.

Her cover as a newly divorced woman set on stretching her academic wings put her close enough to his age range that he shouldn't be totally condescending. His file indicated he was forty-four to her thirty-eight.

"Dr. Lanier?"

He flipped a page, frowned, glanced at the

computer screen and back down again. Seemed like he looked everywhere but at *her*.

"Dr. Lanier," she called, hitching her purse up on her shoulder, a purse made of overlarge sequins that shimmered and jingled softly with her every move.

Still he didn't so much as peek up from his work.

Hmm. She needed a prop. Bustling out the door to the vending machine, she reached into her purse for change, rattling around in the bottom of her jingly bag, shoving aside a pack of gum, a miniature Rubik's Cube key chain, a tube of Cha-Cha Red lipstick.

Pay dirt. Change. She pumped the machine full and—oh yeah—java. No workaholic could resist coffee, even the crummy vending-machine beverage.

Juggling her notebook, purse and two foam cups, she made her way back to the lab room. The second cup would make her staying put seem natural.

Felicia edged closer to his desk, hitching a hip up on one corner, toppling a pile of his files with her notebook and sequined bag. And still no reaction.

Holy Sister Mary Discipline, how easy it would be to utilize her high-tech training and kill this man. He wouldn't be the wiser until the bullet popped behind his ear or a blade slipped between his ribs. He was so damn vulnerable and seemed completely oblivious.

Felicia placed the steaming coffee beside his screen while bringing her own cup to her face and simply savoring the smell. His nose twitched. His hand eased over and around the cup.

"Thanks," he said without once glancing her way.

Had he known she was there after all? That threw her for three clicks of the wall clock's second hand.

"I wasn't sure how you prefer your coffee." She reached into her purse to pull out a small creamer and two packs of sugar she'd shoved inside. She placed them by his hand.

Long fingers completely encircled the cup, skin dusted with light brown hair, a masculine-as-all-get-out hand with callused fingertips, scrapes and a suntan. Her eyes trekked up his arms under his lab coat, bulky, so she couldn't determine much. But for someone she'd seen as sedentary, those calluses and his time in the sun implied perhaps he had a physical side no one knew about.

Apparently she wasn't the only one with secrets.

He jarred from his stupor long enough to glance at her latest offering. "I, uh, take it black. Too much trouble to keep up with froufrou extras."

"Of course." A huge fan of froufrou herself, she pinched up one of the sugar packs, teasing it between two fingers.

Popping the lid free, he drank down a swallow while clicking along the keyboard one-handed. Another drink, and still he ignored her.

She waited. And waited.

His fingers on the keys slowed…stopped.

He glanced over at her. "Did you need something, Ms., uh…"

Great. She'd been working her slightly oversize tail off to get close to this man for over a month and he didn't even know her flipping name. "Fratarcangelo."

"Oh. Hell. Fratarcangelo, huh?" He grinned. "No wonder I couldn't remember. Your name's got like eleven or so vowels in it."

A sense of humor to go with that brain and those work-roughened hands? A dangerous combo, especially when he hadn't once glanced at the skintight sparkle tank she'd put on with her favorite martini-glass stretch pants. "Try spelling Fratarcangelo in kindergarten. I was already taxed to the max with Felicia Belladonna."

"I can see where that might be challenging for a five-year-old."

His eyes never once slid down, which should be a compliment, but dag nab it, she needed to distract him and men tended to babble when breasts were in sight.

She inched closer on the edge of the table so she could arch her back just a smidge. Patience. Wait for it…

Blink.

Blink.

Still his gaze stayed locked on her eyes. Was this guy gay, after all? Just because his file said he had an adult daughter didn't necessarily rule out anything. Or was he genuinely that nice and sensitive? The most dangerous option of all.

She sipped her coffee then with one finger traced the Cha-Cha Red stain left on the rim.

His eyebrows lifted as he nudged aside the half-empty cup. "So? Why are you here?"

To form a bond that will hopefully eventually lead you to spill the secrets stored in your billion-dollar brain and make me look good to my boss.

She straightened from the table. "Okay, I guess I should confess my real reason for coming to see you this late when nobody else would be around."

"That would be helpful, Ms. Fratarcangelo."

"I wanted to hear more about your theories on maximizing production of light-water nuclear reactors." She tossed a wide-eyed look of curiosity his way, even though she had that subject whipped. She figured it was better to ease her way into the info she needed from him than alert him by going straight for the punch.

"Oh. Well, why didn't you say so right away?" His green eyes lit up.

She pivoted on her spiky heels to snag a second metal stool to pull up to the raised counter. Scooching backward, she tugged the seat across the floor, the screech bouncing around the otherwise silent room. She stopped, glanced over her shoulder at the doctor to find—

No way.

No freaking way.

He was staring at her slightly abundant bottom in a most un-gay way.

Dr. Lanier jolted, then his face cleared, the professional professor firmly back in place. But she wasn't forgetting what she saw. He wasn't as immune to her as he pretended. She had to admire his restraint and professionalism.

But she also had to remember this man could be just like her—fake, secretive.

Dangerous.

STANDING IN THE outdoor shower, Grace Marie shivered in disgust and maybe even a little fear, which was so totally not her style. Lord. She was a profiler for the police as well as an Army Reservist, damn it. She could kick a linebacker's butt seven ways to Sunday.

However, even the strongest of hearts would falter at taking a nighttime shower in a poles-and-tarp stall with geckos and heaven only knows what else running over her feet while she soaped her oh-so-bare nether regions. She slathered up fast, hopping from one foot to the other on the small wooden platform, which probably had at least seven species of gross bug life beneath.

And Lordy, how she missed her Victoria's Secret scented bath products, but they simply weren't prudent in the field and maneuvers when stealth counted. Besides, the scents attracted insects as well as men. Backing to the corner, she could see the whole cubicle while she shampooed her hair.

Ick.

She'd accidentally stomped a frog while her eyes were cloaked with lather. Why oh why had she forgotten her flip-flops back in the Army TEMPER tent?

Duh. She wasn't concentrating because of *him*.

She was as tough as the next Army grunt and had the PT scores to prove it. But the whole showering-in-the-jungle gig was never cool. Call it her weak spot. At least for here, she had her bathing time down to ninety seconds flat. Of course that meant she might have to skip shaving her legs tonight.

No. She refused to face an old boyfriend with hairy legs. Some things even a warrior woman simply couldn't bear. She stretched her right calf out, used soap to cream it up and raked that razor across so fast she knew she'd pay later, but some prices were worth the pain.

She shifted to hike up her left leg and—

"Ahhh!" She swallowed a scream that would bring a stallful of soldiers.

Not in this lifetime, gentlemen.

Damn, damn, damn! Something thick inched over the top pole holding the tarp sheet. A thick reptile grew longer and longer by the slithering second, his slit pupil eyes glistening in the moonlight. And not enough illumination to ID Sergio the Snake.

To hell with baby-smooth legs.

Her left could just be hairy. Her BDUs would cover it anyhow, so no one would know since she wouldn't be getting naked with any man here.

Grace Marie snagged her fluffy robe from the hook and made tracks far away from Sergio the pervert snake slinking his way for a closer peek—or worse yet, a taste. She edged along the tarp stall toward the door, shoving her arms in the robe, achieving as much modesty as she could before she reached the door and bolted out.

And slammed into a rock-hard body.

She didn't even have to open her eyes to know. Bobby. She could smell him.

"Snake," she said.

"Gee, thanks," his voice rumbled all the way through her terry cloth. "But you already made my reptile status clear nine months ago."

"No. Really." She inched back, guilt pinching, because God, she hadn't meant for Bobby to think poorly of himself. The guy was great. Off-kilter. But great. "There's a snake hanging over the shower stall all—"

His hand whipped downward, smooth, fast, into his boot. His fist swept upward with a—

Knife.

He held a hunting-style knife with a big butt blade, serrated and glinting in the starlit night. He launched into the stall and sliced off Sergio's head before Grace Marie could complete her sentence, much less her thought.

The reptile—probably about six feet long—well, five and a half now—thudded to the ground. The tail flopped around with after-death muscle contractions while the head lay limp and useless and horrifyingly ugly at her feet. She wasn't a wimp, but now she could see the damn thing had been a brown tree snake. Strong and poisonous.

With a swipe of his boot, Bobby kicked the remains off to the side into the undergrowth. He sheathed his knife in his boot without missing a beat.

Okay, she knew the surges of arousal going through her were adrenaline-based because of his show of testosterone. She refused to be so hormone driven. Thoughts of searching for a *thinking* man shimmied over to a corner of her brain and let all the tingly want swell and fill her mind, her whole doggone body.

She clutched her robe close and wished again for hips slim enough that she didn't have to worry about the least wind whipping open what little robe stretched across her thighs.

"Hey, Gracie."

Keeping one hand between her breasts to squeeze the robe together, she eased the other down so her arm anchored the lower slit of fabric. "You know you really scared the crap out of me when I ran into you. I could have hurt you."

"You sure could."

Even if she could down a linebacker in workouts,

a naked lady wearing only a robe was at a distinct disadvantage against a fully armed man in a flight suit.

A hot man, with long lean legs and the grittiest dark five-o'clock shadow that howled testosterone. Bobby was just sweaty enough to smell sexy and manly, and now she looked closer and saw his shaving kit gripped in his hand. He'd been on his way to the showers.

He finished securing his knife and straightened. "You could have choked me with your robe tie. Or given me heart failure just by showing up naked in front of me—wait." He closed his eyes, shook his head. "Nope, I don't think even my imagination could do that image justice, so I'll have to live in ignorance."

His wicked grin lit the night as he continued, "Unless you want to thank me for saving your life."

A laugh burst free. How could she not? They both knew he wasn't serious. "I'd forgotten how funny you are."

"You think I'm joking?"

Her laugh fizzled while her skin tingled. "Thank you for saving my life. Tell me your favorite sports team and I'll order you a jersey."

"Whoa, those suckers are pricey." He leaned one shoulder against a towering tree.

"Well, I'm not much good in the kitchen, so baking you a cake is out of the question."

"I don't have much of a sweet tooth anyway. Sugar makes me go all ADHD and God knows I suspect *more* Bobby Ruznick is the last thing this world needs."

"A little Bobby certainly does go a long way."

Was he serious now or not? Before she could reason out the notion, he'd reached to wrap his hands around the clump of her wet hair and wring water free.

Her nipples tightened and goose bumps prickled over her skin in spite of the heat. Ohmigod, this had to be the sexiest moment of her entire freaking life and she wasn't even naked. How could that be, and why didn't she stop him? Or breathe? He was stepping over the line, but the way he had of just being outrageous somehow made the action seem natural.

She shook herself out of the sensual haze before he squeezed all reason from her waning self-control along with water from her hair. She stepped back, spine Army-rigid, with her best police-officer face in place. "If any other man had done that I would have flipped him."

"Even that big fella, Rodeo?" he asked, his voice a hint too calm.

Jealous? Not territory she wanted to investigate while her nerves were on fire from a simple touch to her hair. Time to divert the subject off Derek Washington. "I am a trained Army soldier, as well as a police profiler."

"And I'm a Chair-Force Puke. Yeah, I get the picture."

"A Chair-Force Puke with street smarts," she conceded, managing to relax at least a little since the moment had passed without either of them slamming the other against the tree for a quickie. "Maybe you Air Force fellas could win in hand-to-hand combat, but I sure as hell would have maimed you on the way down. So it's best we don't tangle or someone could break something."

Like her heart. She backed farther away from temptation even if it placed her closer to the dead snake. She nodded toward the hacked carcass in the brush. "Thank you for taking care of Sergio in the shower stall. And about the other, thanks, too."

"Sergio?" He chuckled. "Only you would name your enemy."

Her training led her to say, "It's easier for you if you don't, isn't it?"

His face blanked. "Don't pull that pyschobabble shit on me as an excuse to ignore this."

He palmed her back and pulled her close. Closer still until even humid air couldn't slide between them. Any concerns about PDAs were taken care of by their shadowy corner secluding them from any nighttime camp activity. And she wasn't in uniform so technically this wasn't a PDA.... Hey wait? Why was she justifying this moment?

Nose to nose, minty breath to breath, she admitted, "I didn't mean the thanks for the snake incident. I was talking about earlier."

His grip gentled. "Earlier?"

"On the flight line when we first saw each other again. You didn't have to tell everyone what I said in the bus. You could have let them believe you did the walking away and saved yourself an ego hit." Her hand flattened to his chest, but she couldn't bring herself to push him away. "To be clear, my ego's not so fragile that it matters to me if every one of those crew members thinks you dumped me."

Ah, his smile. "They're not crazy enough to believe a guy like me would make it long-term with you. They know me." His hands inched higher up her back, his thumbs on her sides, a flinch away from grazing her breasts. "It may have escaped your notice, but I come by my call sign honestly. Of course you dumped a crazy-ass bastard like me."

She shook her head silently. Words were kind of tough at the moment, anyhow.

Monkeys cackled. The camp rustled. Her heart stumbled over itself.

Bobby's mouth hovered over hers like his craft in flight, unpredictable, ready to land or fly away without warning. "Are you seeing him?"

"Seeing who?" she whispered then mentally head-thunked herself. So much for pretend relationships as protection.

"Rodeo."

"Derek?"

"Derek, huh? Yeah, him."

She stared into Bobby's eyes and saw such raw anger she couldn't believe— "You can't possibly be prejudiced against an interracial relationship?"

"Hell, no." His honesty was unmistakable. His arms went steely around her. "I'm fucking jealous. And if you're standing this close to me and having a 'relation-ship' with him, then I'm thinking you've been lying to yourself about how you feel for this guy, which is damn well not fair to him, and you're always fair."

She stopped his tirade with a finger to his lips, not her most brainiac of moves. "Derek and I truly are friends, keeping each other company through rough times in our lives."

"Uh-huh, now I get it." Bobby grinned, always too damned perceptive. "So you two are just faking it to keep someone away. You were worried what would happen when we saw each other again."

Ohmigod, she so didn't need the high-schoolish thrill his jealousy stirred. Okay, so high-schoolers probably had more dating experience than she did, but she had maturity and human behavioral training on them. "What makes you think that's any of your business?"

"This." He grazed his hand down her wet hair again, minimal water dripping into the spray of orchids behind her, the squat plant stalling any retreat. "It's not fair for you to see someone else when we're still this attracted to each other."

"You're very sure of yourself."

"Am I wrong?"

She couldn't lie to him. "He's the one who needed a fake relationship to scare off someone. Not me."

"Ah, Gracie. What the hell are we going to do about this?" He looped her hair around his hand, binding them together.

Her fingers gravitated to the tiny scar near his ear, her thumb flicking away a droplet of sweat. Why did this man hold such sensual sway over her?

She'd seen well how her father's life had been

sent into turmoil by an irresistible attraction—which she should actually be grateful for or she never would have been born. But she'd watched her mother try to yank her father around by the—uh—libido—even after the divorce. She wouldn't allow herself to throw away reason for hormones.

Grace Marie shimmied out of Bobby's hold and away from his allure, her arms locked around her waist to keep the robe from revealing any more inches of flesh. "It's good to see you again and know that you're doing well."

His eyes narrowed as if he might push the point and then he simply nodded. "You too, Gracie."

He was the only one who dared do that—call her Gracie—and it implied an intimacy she couldn't allow, especially not now, when her mission was so vital.

"Please, I prefer Grace Marie."

He nodded again but didn't answer, which of course didn't reassure her in the least.

She would simply have to shuffle aside that concern for now, because before sunrise, she needed to toss on some clothes over her clean body with only one shaved leg, gather up her Glock, snitch a Humvee and retrieve her father.

CHAPTER THREE

BOBBY SHOVED his head under the ice-cold shower and thanked heaven that Gracie—aka temptation personified—was now tucked safely in her Army TEMPER tent.

He swiped the soapy bubbles from his eyes. Shit, that stung.

Blinking his eyes fast against the shampoo, he lathered up his hands with a miniature bar of soap he'd picked up at a hotel in Guam.

This practice operation should be low-key, but his street-sense nerves were itching. Only a year ago in Cartina, South America, he'd seen how fast a simple practice op could turn into something more intense. The whole world was a hot spot for terrorists these days.

Finishing soaping up the rest of his body, he figured he should probably sleep. Drying off and yanking on Air Force jogging shorts and a T-shirt, he left the stall.

No hottie Gracie waiting outside with her exotic scent to tempt him, no perfumes or special designer soaps, just the one hundred percent arousing scent of *her.* He made his way through the camp to the tent he shared with his crew: Face, Vegas, Stones, Padre and Sandman.

He dropped onto his cot and stifled down the itchy bad-feeling jitters. His job worked on a need-to-know basis. So no point in firing himself up until necessary. Hopefully, he would be out cold in seconds like Stones, Padre and Sandman.

He rolled onto his side on the cot, fisting his pillow rounder. "Jesus, what are we doing in these crappy ass tents?"

Vegas disconnected his cell phone—a call to his wife, no doubt. "Don't let the Army grunts hear you since our Air Force Harvest Falcon tents are downright cushy up next to their stark Army TEMPER tents."

"I picked the Air Force so I didn't have to do this camping shit."

"Used to the good life, are you?"

"That's me." More like he'd spent enough time roughing it for three lifetimes. He rolled to sit up, reaching over to Face's cot and snagging a perfectly good packet of crackers Face was about to throw away. Hand arced, Bobby pitched it into the small box across the room.

Face gathered up the remains of his meal and started their Postal-instigated ritual of pitching their unused MRE parts into Bobby's perfectly labeled boxes.

Face lobbed a powdered chocolate-drink package. "What are you gonna do with all these scavenger items, make a salt, creamer and cracker sandwich later?"

"Ever tried one? They're positively exquisite." Bobby couldn't resist jabbing.

Face's smirk faltered. "Okay, you got me. Even you aren't that cheap."

Wanna bet? "Shh. Don't let word get out or my frugal reputation will be shot and next thing you know I'll have to pay for a round of drinks. Actually with the bananas around here, the peanut butter packets will really come in handy, adds some more taste."

"Consider my trap shut...*if* you'll let me ditch some of this crap."

"I hate waste." They had a perfectly good corner to store the condiments. Why not stash a box there?

Vegas ducked a whizzing peanut butter packet and sagged back on his cot, shaking his head as his eyes drifted closed. "God, Postal, we won't be able to move around by the end of the week."

"Fine. Whatever." He shoved to his feet again, restless from his confrontation with Gracie, and damn it, that's how he thought of her. Gracie.

Everybody else could call her the more uptight Grace Marie. He squatted in front of the row of small boxes containing the leftover, unused parts of the MREs—Meals Ready to Eat. Not much in there after a half day, but the stuff could really pile up in a week for him to take home. No need to waste it. "Don't come crying to me when you're looking for salt at two in the morning for your in-flight snack."

Bobby fished through a few more MRE reject pouches, too antsy to drift off like the others. Well, everyone except Face, who shifted to sit, as if giving up on sleep.

Face leaned closer into the space between their cots to keep the conversation private even with the rest of the room sleeping. "Everything cool working with Lieutenant Lanier again?"

Thank God the C-17 crew was in a different tent because, regardless of what she said about Rodeo being a friend, Bobby sure as hell didn't want the guy overhearing. "Why shouldn't it be?"

"She dumped your ass." Face scooped his hand-held BlackBerry from his open bag, thumbing a message across the keyboard while he spoke. "It blows carrying around feelings for a woman."

Face's thumbs continued to fly over the keyboard as he undoubtedly sent his customary ten kazillion messages a day to his wife, Brigid Wheeler Greco.

Everyone knew Joe had waited for two years while Brigid Wheeler grieved for her dead lover—Joe's best friend—only to discover the dude wasn't dead after all. Things had been rocky there for a while, but Joe and Brigid were solid, one of those rare meant-to-be couples. Finding that forever fit involved a hefty dose of dumb luck as well, and he'd already shot his wad in the good-fortune department.

He couldn't even sit still. What made him think he could settle down? It wouldn't be fair to the woman or any kids they might make together.

So why had he been playing with her hair like a totally whipped dude? "Gracie's a hot lady, no question, but she's also a very smart lady, wise enough to know when something isn't working."

"Fair enough," Face replied, still dorking around with his BlackBerry. "But second chances are a gift, you know? Maybe the timing is better this go-round."

"I'm still the same guy I was nine months ago. Nothing's changed." Except for the fact that for the first time since he was seventeen years old, he'd gone without sex for nine months. Longer that that, actually, since he'd been two months without when he'd met Gracie, and they'd never cycled around to the naked part.

What did that say about his messed-up head? He didn't let women get to him. "Come on, you remember the old bachelor days."

Joe shrugged. Didn't say anything, sure, but a half smile kicked up his face. Yeah, the guy remembered.

So did he. Except the memory wasn't as much fun this go-round. Hell's bells. Bobby dropped back onto his cot.

Joe's face cleared. "I have no memory of any woman before Brigid. Just ask her."

"She's not here." Bobby waved around the musty tent full of snoring crewdogs. "Remember those two French nurses in the Balkans?"

"Uh, no, dude." Face shook his head slowly. "I have absolutely no recall of that. Really."

"Oh, right." Bobby thumped his forehead. "That was a dream and come to think of it, you weren't there."

Falling back onto his cot with a belly laugh, Face tucked away his BlackBerry. "I swear you make shit up just for shock effect."

"What of it?"

Face stuffed his hands under his head. "Well, we

did talk to those two Israeli women in that bar in Tel Aviv for ten whole minutes before they walked away uninterested."

"You're not listening." Bobby swung his bare feet to the ground. "I'm having a serious crisis here. I need your help."

His pal stared back, his expression even more serious than normal. Everybody knew Face—Joe—was the best guy around, a man you could trust anywhere, anytime. "You don't need me to tell you that you're a badass in the cockpit. And you sure as hell don't need me to remind you of all the women who have pitched their panties in your beer seconds after whispering to a friend—" his voice shifted to Marilyn Monroe breathy falsetto "'—I can fix him.'"

Vegas snorted from the cot behind him, apparently not completely asleep. Bobby tossed a pillow at the guy's head, even as he laughed along.

Gracie had no interest in fixing him. Smart woman. Because damn straight, he was as broken as a guy came while still staying functional.

Antsy, he walked around the tent, checking the boxes, the door, the stakes.

All he could think of now was a workout to burn off pent-up energy just from touching Gracie's hair. Smelling her fresh-showered skin. Touching her—

Hour-long workout, here I come.

Kneeling, he tugged his bag from under the bed and unzipped it for a change of clothes, rifling around for his gym shoes to carry with him to the tent set up as a weight/exercise room.

Face clapped him on the shoulder. "It's tough knowing what you want but being certain it's wrong, isn't it?"

Sympathy stank worse that his flaming hard-on. Bobby tugged on his BDU pants, tucked in his black T-shirt then laced up his boots, complete with the knife he never let out of arm's reach. Ever. "Don't you have a coloring book to finish or something?"

Face raised both hands. "Okay, dude. You're not ready to think this through. Got it. I'll back off. Don't know why I'm wasting good sleep time anyway." He sagged back onto his pillow.

Bobby eyed the door, his mind mapping out the trail ahead. Yeah, he should probably sleep, too. But first, he would have to pump iron until his muscles screamed for mercy.

No DOUBT, he needed some sleep, because images of Felicia Fratarcangelo had his libido screaming for mercy.

Matthias had been awake for twenty-two hours

straight studying Cantou's light-water nuclear reactor. The hall could have been any of the numerous research facilities that had requested his input over the years. Nothing different, except for the young couple making out in a dark corner, in their teens or early twenties, but obviously not interested in the soda machine.

One of the local girls...he scrambled for her name, uh, Jiang, yeah, and an eastern European boy whose name he totally couldn't remember, only that the boy was on scholarship to work with security, currently with his hand up the girl's shirt and her chanting, "More, more, more."

No unwillingness there. He could be on his way, secure in knowing this was completely consensual, even if rather unprofessional out in the hallway. Although he suspected they wouldn't be in the corridor for much longer.

Youthful hormones. God, how his own teenage libido had changed the path of his life, landing him into fatherhood at eighteen. His footsteps echoed down the empty, antiseptic hall, past a water fountain, a string of framed local landscape posters between each room, each class emanating a different acrid elemental scent of that group's chosen experiment.

Cologne to a geek like him.

Even the professors, researchers, teachers, students all looked the same. Except for one.

Felicia Fratarcangelo. He deserved an Academy Award for how he'd pretended not to know her. Oh, he'd noticed her all right.

The scent of flowers emanated from the lady, tickling his senses usually saturated by chemicals. Chemicals didn't smell like foliage. Even when heated to boiling temps. He would guess Ms. Fratarcangelo preferred things hot.

What did she hope to gain by coming on to him?

He wasn't such a geek he couldn't tell when a woman was hitting on him. He rounded the corner to his dorm room. All right, perhaps he zoned out and missed the signs sometimes, but only a dead man would overlook the sensuality oozing off that woman.

A woman who waited outside his quarters.

What was Felicia Fratarcangelo doing outside his place?

She had a body guaranteed to stop a train, trim but also curvy, her head packing a mass of hair that probably weighed as much as she did. A man could lose himself in all those ebony curls while losing himself in her naked body. He really needed a long run.

He wasn't celibate, but his work didn't leave him much time for relationships. For the most part, he ended up sleeping with women like himself, over-worked and in need of a quick release without messy complications.

He didn't want anything "quick" with Felicia Belladonna Fratarcangelo. He very much wanted to loiter with her.

Linger over her.

Under her.

Behind her.

Except he didn't know her, much less trust her, and he'd learned long ago that an untrustworthy woman could mess up a man's life big time. "You have another question?"

"A gift."

Said Eve to Adam.

She extended her hand with a wrapped muffin rather than fruit, but her fingernails were candy-apple red. She clutched another cup in the other hand.

He had too much riding on his work here to take a bite of this apple from this pushy woman. Or would that be a bite of her? Mixing up his metaphors, but then he was a science genius, not a word whiz.

"I've already eaten and the other cup of coffee was plenty. I'll be up all night." Shit! He didn't want to think of how they could fill the hours. "But thank you."

"No, you haven't and I kept you in the lab with

my questions earlier, and you had classes all day today. I thought you might be hungry and maybe I should have thought of that the first time." She offered up the cup as well. "It's decaf. And black, without any sugar. Right?"

He did forget to eat sometimes and right now his appetite was returning ferociously. Rather like the stretches of sexual fasting that brought on a gnawing need...

Hell.

He snagged the muffin from her hand. He'd better feed one hunger before he succumbed to the other. He peeled off the plastic and stuffed half the muffin in his mouth.

"Sorry it's not home-baked, but I'm not allowed to mess in Genji's kitchen. I'm not much of a cook since my divorce, living on my own and on the road so much." She hitched her empty hand on her shapely hip, right over a martini glass on her pants. "Give me a Bunsen burner, though, and I'm killer."

He stayed silent and chewed. She'd been divorced? What idiot let this bundle of life and sex appeal go?

"Thank you for taking the time to explain so much to me earlier this evening. I know I'm not one of your regular students, so you weren't obligated."

Not one of his students, she was auditing in addition to her other classes. The implication was clear—and correct. They could have a relationship without fear of reprisal.

Still, he'd learned long ago that when it came to women, he was an idiot.

He'd been deemed the smartest guy in Harvard's Ph.D. program—at eighteen. Anita had seen him as her own personal Bill Gates in the making, sure to invent something amazing and skate her into a life of wealth. She hadn't been wrong in his abilities. He could do that. He chose not to.

So she'd left him.

He'd patented some of his formulas that were used in nuclear medicines to make enough money to buy her off so she would quit yanking him around when it came to custody of Grace Marie. He wasn't much of a father, but he was a helluva lot better parent than Anita.

Felicia Fratarcangelo didn't look like Anita but still stirred something inside him that made him want to forget about work and the political land mines of working *here*. "Good night."

"Uh, don't you want to take a walk or something, to stretch your legs after sitting at a desk all day?"

Actually, he planned to run himself into a stupor once he got rid of her. The sooner the better. "Walk, huh? Sure."

Huh?

She smiled.

No way. "To your room."

Her smile froze. Why? Wasn't that what she'd been hinting for all along? That they should go to her room together, even if that wasn't actually what he'd meant when he offered to walk her there.

Either way, this woman confused him, no surprise since he hadn't found a female yet whom he understood. All the more reason to keep his distance and his mind clear during this high-stakes research project that could provide nuclear power to multiple poverty-riddled areas like Cantou.

Matthias drained his coffee and pitched the cup in the trash can. "Let's get moving so I can drop you off and finish this damn long day."

DAMP HAIR now French braided to keep it off her face until it dried, Grace Marie made her way out of the tent, footsteps silent in the sand, then against the mushy decaying leaves. Thank goodness the dark covered most of her movements only a few yards away from the pitched tent camp. They would have more lights set up by tomorrow. But by tomorrow, she would have her father safely with her.

Hers was tinier than most of the other tents,

because there was only one other woman on this deployment, and luckily, her bunk mate slept like a log.

She only needed to use the Humvee tonight. Totally kosher, since she was the boss and the equipment therefore belonged to her. She could write off the whole outing as a "scout the area" drive around.

She was armed, in uniform with all the proper papers. She should have no concerns even if stopped before she could get to her father, or after.

Her stomach gripped at images of what might be waiting for her. Please God, let him come willingly.

A long shadow blotted the already murky night. Her hand slapped over her Glock. They weren't at war with this country, but there were still plenty of spies who would like nothing more than to infiltrate a U.S. military camp for intel or a hostage.

She unholstered her weapon, held it low at her side, ready as she pivoted to find—

Bobby.

"Going somewhere, Gracie?"

CHAPTER FOUR

"YOU'RE GOING to do what?" Bobby swallowed back shock and probably a bug or two in this insect-infested jungle.

He couldn't have heard what he thought as he stood beside Gracie, who was in the process of climbing into the Humvee.

Gracie clutched the keys in her hand. "My father is one of the nuclear researchers at the local university retreat. He's here on an exchange program. I'm going to pick him up and bring him home."

So much for a temporary hearing malfunction. He'd heard exactly what he thought. "I take back everything I ever said about you being a sane woman."

Even knowing he was teasing, his words still stung. She lived in fear of battling her father's mental demons, in fact subjected herself to rigorous psychological testing frequently—only to be told she was not bipolar or any other number of mental disabilities. Still, she wasn't sure there was enough reassurance in the world.

"Well, thank you very much for sharing, but I'm not concerned with your opinion." She tugged open the door.

He sidestepped, which blocked her entrance to the vehicle. "Don't you think that while you were back in the States a plane ticket might have been a little less trouble than hauling your fine ass across the Pacific Ocean? Or is this a last-minute impulse and you figured that while you're in the neighborhood you'll give him a ride?"

"Do you really think I'm the impulsive sort?"

"Valid point." He shifted feet, frowned, never taking his eyes off her no matter how much his body fidgeted. "What's going on, then?"

Hand on the dark green door, she sagged. "My father is, uh, eccentric."

"I'm still not following."

Grace Marie stiffened, straightened and opted for the truth. "My father is a genius with only one toe barely dipping in this world. I'm afraid he may have pulled even that out. Professionally, I know I have nothing to feel ashamed of, but the reactions and distrust of others still string me tight on a personal level."

Surprise sparked through him for a simple second

before he blanked his face. She'd trusted him with something huge and he needed to be appropriate—worthy of that trust. "Your father has mental problems?"

The strain on her face was unmistakable and damned heart-tugging. She should be the last person to give any credence to the stigma, but still he could see it was hard for her to say.

"Yes. I haven't heard from him in six weeks, and I'm afraid he may be off his meds. I need to see him, check on him and possibly—probably—take him home."

His hand fell on her shoulder, with a support he doubted she would accept for long. "Don't you think they'll notice around here at the camp if you suddenly show up with your old man?"

"Of course." She shrugged from under his hand. "But if he's not all right, nobody's going to turn him loose to roam the jungle. I'll get him on a plane home with a flight doc."

He quirked his eyebrow.

She sighed. "It may not be the best plan—"

"It's not a bad plan. Sounds to me like you're going for the General George Patton approach— 'A good plan executed today is better than a perfect plan executed at some indefinite point in the future.'"

"You've studied Patton?"

He stuffed down the resentment over her intellectual snobbery. "I've even read two books since college graduation. Or maybe it was three. I'm not sure."

She covered his hand with hers. Then her mouth rounded into an O. She slid her hand away as if trying to be unobtrusive, but the flame shone in her eyes. "I apologize for prejudging."

"I may not have graduated with honors, but I finished on time." He put his hand back over hers on the door. "Nice try diverting me from the subject. I feel fairly certain there's nothing I can do to persuade you this is an insane plan. And since I excel at the nutzo stuff—no offense meant to your father—"

"None taken."

"—then it only makes sense for me to go along with you."

"Now you've really gone over the edge. There's a solid chance I might be late returning and there's no need for you to get written up as well. I can do this, although I do appreciate your willingness to help out—"

Enough. He cupped the back of her head and kissed her once, closemouthed and for a mindblowingly long four count before he backed away.

"Damn it, Gracie, anybody ever tell you that you talk too much?" He held up a finger right over her lips. "Never mind answering that one. Just climb on inside and slide over, Slim. No arguing. I'm coming with you."

GRACE MARIE GRIPPED the Humvee's steering wheel as the fine-tuned machine jolted through the pocked roadway leading deeper into the jungle toward the university retreat.

With Bobby at her side.

His "slide over, Slim" comment had only earned him a place in the passenger seat. This vehicle belonged to her unit and she would take the hit for anything that went wrong. She'd let him come along because it really did make good sense. Two people were safer than one, and she might well be occupied caring for her father on the trip back.

Which meant she would have to acquiesce to Bobby driving, but she would deal with that later. Her father was at the end of this trail and nothing would stop her from getting there. She should arrive right around breakfast, which shouldn't make her appearance seem too odd and that would give her just enough time to return for her thirteen-hundred brief after lunch.

Memories of past incidents with her father scrolled through her mind...of taking him supper, forcing him to wake up and walk around when his disease lured him to sleep and sleep and sleep into infinity. Or polar-opposite moments when he would fly high and play with her chemistry set with her until three in the morning and her eight-year-old self would be struggling not to fall over on the lab counter.

Overall, she had little to complain about. Her father recognized his problem, stayed in therapy, took his meds. He told her after she graduated with her Ph.D. as a psychologist he'd taken the meds for *her,* so he could be the best possible father he could manage. She'd cried. How could she not in the face of such heartfelt, deep and difficult love?

Her life had had erratic moments, but all in all, she had developed into an independent woman. But now, he didn't need to do squat for her. She was a grown woman, on her own.

Her chest tightened at the thought. She breathed in through her nose, out through her mouth, over and over. She let herself soak in and search her surroundings for possible threats—and to keep her eyes off the hunk of a man beside her, his arms and pecs filling out that black T-shirt with such tempting muscles. Maybe if she and Bobby had had sex just once before she'd broken things off with him, then he wouldn't seem like such forbidden fruit. Perhaps then she wouldn't have felt so compelled to push for *his* crew to be assigned to this mission. But she needed to regain peaceful emotions, and quite frankly, her feelings for Bobby scared the crap out of her.

Maybe he was a crummy lover. Yeah, think along those lines. Captain ADHD could be a quick trigger. Or perhaps all that excessive energy would make the sex acrobatic or adventurous but not emotionally connective—and blast it, she had a hairy leg. Bleck.

Besides, hadn't she said she was going to ignore him and study the landscape around her, everything so deep jade-green?

"You didn't have to do this." Look at the lilies and orchids, not him.

"I couldn't live with myself if you ended up in the back of some sex-slave trader's bus."

God, he really knew how to send fear slithering down a woman's spine in the middle of the night.

"Okay, fine. You've already won so don't hammer the point to death."

"All right. What do you want to talk about?"

Small talk? How strange was that, such a bizarre

juxtaposition with their surroundings. "Seen any good movies lately?"

"I don't go to movies." He hooked an elbow on the armrest between them, sweat starting to trickle from the lack of AC in the Humvee. Much longer and they would have to roll down the windows and suffer the consequences of all the gnawing bugs in this jungle. "Too expensive."

A snort slipped free. She was surprised they hadn't given him the call sign Scrooge, except he didn't fit the grumpy part. He was good-natured, and actually fairly generous with others, only a tightwad about his own needs. And, hey wait, wasn't that a revelation moment? "I've never seen anyone who can stretch a dollar as far as you."

He eyed her up and down in a visual caress before winking. "Why go to a movie when I could spend the time talking to a beautiful lady like yourself?"

She should ignore the obvious suck-up but, hey, she was human. "You're sure not stingy with the compliments."

"I mean it, you know," he replied as if reading her mind.

The Humvee hit a pothole, jostling her almost as much as his words.

"Thank you." What else could she say? While the

attraction was undoubtedly there, the inside had to be in sync as well.

Bobby shifted in his seat, facing her, although his eyes were darting all around them for possible threats. "Why don't we talk more about your father so I have a better idea of what we're facing."

"If he's on his meds, all should go well. We'll have a nice little family visit. If not…" She cut herself short and steeled herself for the possibilities ahead.

"Your father has these issues and yet he brought you up alone?"

"My father did his best."

"Damned with faint praise."

Parrot finches cawed Greek-chorus echoes from the trees.

"Interestingly enough you said the same thing about your mom once."

He grinned, beautiful white teeth ever so crooked. "Hey, between us, we had a full set of parents."

"Actually, I have a mother."

"Oh." That seemed to shake the unshakable Bobby for a full second as she detoured around an especially large rut on the ground covered by moss spreading over roots and up trees. "I thought she died."

"Why would you think that?"

"Because you grew up with your unstable dad. Why didn't the courts give you to your mother?"

"What an un-PC assumption that only mothers get custody," she responded, sidestepping his actual question about her father. As much as she understood her dad's illness, for some reason she just couldn't go any further with the talk today.

"So there was a custody battle?"

"No battle, actually." She steered down the narrowing muddy path, trying to keep her voice as level as possible when her insides felt more like the rocking vehicle. "She knew Dad would make the better parent, so she did what she thought was best for me and left me with him."

"Bullshit."

"What?" She jerked to look at him and damn near plowed into a waxy-leafed bush.

"You're bullshitting me." His expression hadn't changed except for the sexy lift of one dark eyebrow slashing his forehead.

"Is that a technical term?" She steered the Humvee back on course. If only predicting Bobby could be that simply accomplished. "Or are you just playing with me?"

"Actually, that is a game, too, you know, 'Bullshit.'"

Huh? How had they gone from her mother pitching her out with the trash to playing some bizarre game? "Are you smoking the hippie lettuce? Because I can't follow your train of thought for beans."

"Good luck. Nobody's figured it out yet, least of all myself. I've learned to just hang on for the ride." His exhale rode long and hard, hinting at deeper depths and concerns than his simple blow-off. "Anyhow, back to bullshit. I'm talking about that game where you bluff and folks shout 'bullshit' if they think you're lying. Well, you suck at bluffing. How you manage to make a career out of psy-ops is beyond me, with a crystal-clear face like that."

She jammed the Humvee through a right-side rut guaranteed to jar his teeth. "Are you trying to piss me off or is this just a natural gift you possess?"

"Touché." He braced both hands against the dashboard.

What did it matter if she told him the truth? It wasn't her shame, but rather her mother to whom she owed zilch in loyalty. "All right, you want the truth. Fine. Mom did know Dad would be the better parent because what kind of parent sells her kid in the divorce settlement? It was like she hung out just long enough for Dad to hit the big time, moneywise, with some of his nuclear-research patents. Then, so long family life."

He reached to cover her hand with his. "Oh, hell, Gracie—"

She smacked his hand away, while keeping her left on the wheel. "Do not call me Gracie and definitely do not pity me. It was a long time ago. But yeah, in exchange for a kick-ass seven-figure divorce settlement, she signed away her rights to me. She still had visitation. We saw each other maybe once a month to do mother-daughter things. I was luckier than most kids."

"What things?"

"Pardon?" How could he shift moods so easily? She was still stuck in mad and he was ready to play twenty questions. But of course that beat the whole mad thing.

"What kind of mother-daughter things did you do?"

She searched her mind for memories she rarely visited. "Shopping, theatrical plays, visits to salons."

"Salons?"

The memory flowered in her mind, bringing the acrid smell of polish remover. "This one time she took me to get a manicure right before school started. I was maybe ten? I had my nails painted blue with tiny whale tails airbrushed in white."

"That sounds like a good memory."

She nodded. She glanced at her bitten-to-the-quick nails.

"But what?"

"But nothing. It was a great day. I had a very lucky childhood, no money worries, two parents." She understood the reality, had even studied these situations in grad school. She wasn't a genius like her dad, but she was damned smart, even graduated a year early from high school and a year early from college. "Divorced parents, sure, but plenty of children come from broken homes."

He stayed quiet. He had a gift for that, sitting silently. Of course, his knee still joggled at the speed of light.

Slowly the smoke cleared on the rest of the memory. "Except every time I looked at the fingernails I wanted to cry. I kept thinking how she paid for those airbrushed whales with money she'd gotten from giving me away." She paused, resisted the urge to chew on her fingernails and continued, "I hated crying so I figured I had two choices—feel sorry for myself until I turned into some screwed-up troublemaker. Or I could figure things out and make the best of the situation."

"So you started your psychoanalyzing young."

Hmmm...interesting insight and entirely on target. She admired his perception. "Understanding helps keep me from getting blindsided as often."

Blindsided by disappointment when her father faded to his other world. It was better to cast herself in the role of caretaker.

Or blindsided by hurt because her mother forgot about one of their spa sessions. So Grace Marie learned not to count on her showing up. She was an expert at low expectations and evading possible pain.

Hey wait. Could she have been running from Bobby back in Iraq? A horribly unsettling thought if she'd hurt them both needlessly.

Except she hadn't heard one word from him in the past nine months.

Her conscience forced her to admit she hadn't called him, either. Not even a little howdy-do e-mail.

She gripped the steering wheel tighter and stomped the accelerator. The sooner she dealt with her dad the faster she would get a reality check on why she and Bobby were a toxic mix as lovers.

Lovers?

Sheesh, could somebody shut Freud the hell up?

"Gracie!" Bobby shouted, loudly, jarringly, the erratic shout scaring her more than his deep silences.

She looked away from the road at him. "What?"

Already he reached to take over the steering wheel. "Hit the brakes. Now!"

She didn't even hesitate to obey the order in his tone, the surety in his order. Her foot ground the brakes to the floorboards.

Too late.

Spikes spit upward from the earthen path, puncturing their tires. All four. What the hell? An overlong branch swung toward the windshield. She flinched instinctively.

The spikes resembled types used at U.S. military gates to control traffic.

What was going on here, and did anyone happen to have a paper bag handy for a little deep breathing? Even a cop profiler and Army Reservist would have a racing heart after that. Only an idiot didn't recognize fear.

Embrace it if necessary, just never let it control you.

She turned her head to check on Bobby—fine, thank God. Okay, but dark and mighty darn pissed looking. Now she really needed that bag to contain all her relief.

She started to speak, only to be interrupted in the distance by—

Boom.

She jerked toward the noise. Holy crap, toward the research facility, where flames were shooting from the east wing.

CHAPTER FIVE

THE CAFETERIA WINDOWS still rattled in the research retreat center. Or was the ringing in her ears?

Felicia peered through dust and debris around the overturned table. At the first blast, she'd hit the floor hard, Matt's hand on her back shoving her down, safe, which would have been an arousing thought if not for the frightening reality around them. The smell of smoke. The blare of fire alarms in her ears. And what about Matt?

Matt?

When had she started thinking of him as Matt instead of Matthias?

Well, shit—she paused, crossed herself—she had other things to think about than her sudden machoing up of a guy's name. They shouldn't have even been in here. He was going to walk her to her room, after all, but next thing she'd known they'd both decided the snacks and coffee weren't filling and they wanted a midnight meal at the twenty-four-hour cafeteria.

Had the kitchen stove exploded? Fire alarms still blared. Screams echoed from students, interns, teachers…workers from every part of the research facility crawled around on the floor under the tables amid spilled soup and fruit, the late-night meal of workaholics. One of her lab partners—Jiang Lee— had all but disappeared in the embrace of her oversize boyfriend with a goatee, Rurik Zazlov.

Kinda romantic.

Okay, really romantic since it was so obvious they'd just been together. Felicia inched closer to Matt and holy Sister Mary Christina there were mighty taut muscles around his rangy body. She snuggled a little closer even though she wasn't afraid. She had training out the wazoo to take care of herself. She wasn't a dependent teen or weepy wife any longer. "What was that noise?"

"An explosion."

Duh. It took a Mensa IQ to come up with that? And he hadn't even asked her if she was okay. Definitely unchivalrous and, given all the hours as a teen she'd spent reading romance novels for fear she might never live long enough to experience the real thing, well, she knew what romantic should be.

But doggone it, she needed to get her head back to reality here.

What had caused the explosion? A test gone wrong? Or a bomb? As much as she knew about the safety precautions in place for the nuclear experiments, there was still the off chance that at any second she could be standing in a shower for a chemical removal spray down.

Not the kind of shower she would like to take with Matt around.

While Jiang might have lucked out in the sensitive-male department, Felicia had to admit Matt's hand still resting on the middle of her back felt mighty darn nice. Warm. Broad.

Big.

The alarm stopped. Her lungs deflated and Matt's hand started to slide away—only to have a second pitched alarm start.

The kind that meant go to the bomb shelter. ASAP.

Matt hooked his arm around her waist and hoisted her out from under the table. Jiang was romantically cradled in Rurik's chest, and Felicia was jostling along with Matt's one-armed hold as he slung her over his shoulder, fireman style, butt in the air.

Death might be staring them all in the face and there was nothing she could do about that at the moment.

MATTHIAS HADN'T had breasts against him in quite a few months, and these were mighty nice ones to break his fast.

Too bad he could be in the middle of running for his life. Felicia's life, too, and damn but that affected him more than thinking about any of the other students running down the hall, bumping and pressing, the stress of fear already sending up a stench of sweat.

They cleared the kitchen, rounded a corner then filed into the small square room that served as a bomb shelter, with one wall full of shelves packed with survival gear and a small curtained portable-toilet area. They'd run drills many times before—minus the explosion and smoke and real fear that they could all be nuclear-filled glow-in-the-dark ghouls within seconds. He eased Felicia back to her feet, enjoying the glide of his hand along her body just a little too much.

With so many people in the room, there wasn't much space left. Apparently no one wanted to walk the extra length of a hallway to the other shelters.

Matthias had to admit he would have preferred the privacy of another shelter, and even would have risked the extra seconds to get there. But with Felicia's safety in the balance, he'd simply acted without thinking.

An oddity for him.

He always thought first, logically. He'd prided himself on that as a parent, reading every book he could, keeping his child safe, like now, by limiting contact during this controversial study program. He didn't want to worry her, and yes, he simply forgot to call sometimes.

However as he stood here in this press of people, he couldn't help but think of when seven-year-old Grace Marie had fallen off the swing and broken her arm, bone protruding. He was a logical man, by God, but he hadn't been able to think to call a cab—they'd lived in a condo downtown and had no need for a car. He'd just scooped up his daughter and run the five blocks to the nearest hospital. Totally scared shitless the whole time. Like now.

Except his feelings for Felicia Fratarcangelo bore no resemblance to fatherly sorts.

Felicia stood face-to-face with him, noses close, which made lips close, too, her bright red lips. There must be a name for that particular shade he'd never seen anywhere before, but how could he explain asking?

"Thank you," she whispered.

Someone jostled against his back, ramming him closer, leaving Matthias no choice but to wrap his arms around her waist.

Holy crap, there went his entire blood supply surging south. "Shit."

"Shh." She crossed herself before draping her arms over his shoulders.

A puritan with a Jezebel body? Heaven help him, because it seemed he might not be able to help himself. Still, he felt compelled to apologize for his foul language.

"Sorry. Just worried about this mess," he bluffed rather than acknowledge his raging hard-on begging for release from his khakis.

Felicia's hands moved along his neck, one long fingernail gently scratching. Deliberately? "The alarm should hush up soon."

"Probably just a test. If so, we shouldn't be in here much longer now."

"Uh-huh," she answered with a little wriggle of her hips as if trying to find space away, which made it blatantly apparent she must be aware of his discomfort. Now he had his chin resting on the top of her head, her abundant black curls teasing his skin.

Discomfort? Uh-uh. His outright mind-exploding, agonizing need to be inside this woman.

Talk. Discuss normal, bland subjects so no one else would guess. "Do you know of any tests scheduled for tonight?"

"No. But that doesn't mean anything, right? There are always things going on around here that nobody else knows about, especially at night when there are fewer people around."

He tensed in a totally different but no less uncomfortable way. Was she probing him for information? And speaking of probing.

"Hell."

Her lips pursed and she crossed herself a second time.

All right then. What kind of spy crossed herself when a man cursed? Just to test her—and maybe for a little fun because there hadn't been any fun in his life for...well...pretty much never—here went the test. "Shit, it's hot as hell in here."

Her eyes narrowed, although still she crossed herself twice, which rubbed her elbow mighty close to his source of discomfort, damn it all.

Alarms still blaring in the compound and his body, he gripped her shoulders. "Be still."

"Uh, I am. I mean, I'm trying, but these high heels hurt so I can't stand in one position very long."

He understood well the concept of pain and the

need to fidget and smell her hair with its floral scent. "Keep trying, unless you want to embarrass us both a lot more."

Her voice lowered to a husky whisper, her hair tickling his shoulders as she brought her lips close to his ear and out of hearing of the two data programmers beside them. "Can you imagine how many students are making out right now?"

"You're not helping my current situation."

"Sorry." She eased back. "Sorta." She grinned. "Okay, not at all. It's just that while, well, this may be a bit weird and so embarrassing, it's also a lovely compliment."

"Lovely?" He leaned to whisper in her ear, making sure to brush his five-o'clock shadow across her cheek in what he hoped was a mimicking torture. "I'm not so sure I like you calling my d—"

Her hand reached for her forehead in the start of a cross—

"Catholic schools?" he said.

She nodded.

"Then could you think of another word for my manhood?"

"How about if I admit it's a *huge* temptation?"

Huge? "Better." Much.

Although he couldn't believe they were having

this conversation. Sheesh. How old was she again? His photographic memory cited her at thirty-eight but she could easily pass for thirty. What was she doing flirting with a balding old dog like him?

And that brought his suspicions to the fore again. There were many around here he couldn't trust. For now, he could do nothing more than play along. "So should I start reciting the periodic table?"

She grinned with those kissable red lips. "I don't think that will help."

"Do you have lots of high-school memories of under the bleachers? Or locked in a broom closet with your boyfriend?"

"Do you?"

Not hardly. "Considering I graduated high school at twelve it would be pretty perverted if I did."

"Your parents must have been proud of your graduation day, taking rolls of cap-and-gown photos."

He didn't want to think about those days of freakdom. At least now as an adult people didn't see him as quite an oddity. "What about your graduation day? I'm guessing your parents were just as proud of you at eighteen."

"They were proud—" her smile went slightly sad "—but I was, uh, sick on graduation day."

"That's a shame." He skimmed her hair back

behind her ears as if to clear it from his face, while actually enjoying the silken, soft texture of those curls twining around his fingers. "You deserved to celebrate."

"I did, in my own way." She let her arms linger on his shoulders. "What about you? How does somebody celebrate graduating high school at twelve?"

"My dad took me to drive go-karts and then we went shopping for my first skateboard." His parents had done their best to let him be a kid, but then he'd left for college and they weren't there to suggest carnival rides any longer. Vacations were packed with more of the kid fun, but by then it was almost painful in comparison to his daily routine of freak-show Matthias in college.

And damn it, he didn't do this self-pity routine. What was it with this woman?

She continued to scratch her nail ever so lightly against his neck. "Sounds like the perfect way for a twelve-year-old to cheer on a landmark."

Yeah, except there hadn't been any friends to take along. Everyone his age thought he was a dorky geek—which he was. And their conversation bored the sh— uh, dickens out of him.

This lady, however, with her hot body and quick mind, was anything but boring.

Suddenly the loudspeaker crackled. "Everyone return to your daily business. Only a small explosion in one of the labs, no toxicity."

Relief swept away concerns in a heartbeat, leaving him with nothing to think about but the woman in his arms.

Maybe it was time he found out if Felicia Fratarcangelo enjoyed go-kart rides, or was she one of those other-side spies in hiding?

THROUGH THE Humvee windshield, Bobby scoured the surrounding undergrowth, mangrove trees and limestone outcroppings for possible danger in hiding, while keeping Gracie damn close to his side.

He knew she wouldn't go for the he-man "cover her body with his" gig. She'd likely flip him on his ass. He kinda enjoyed that about her, all spunk and softness at once. And speaking of that spunk, they could well need it if any real hazard lurked out there.

Flames lit the dark in the distance, but so far he hadn't noticed anything imminently threatening other than an exceptionally odd but cute rodent the size of a large house cat, with long, flowing, silky black hair, known as the Luzon bushy-tailed cloud rat. Since the beast wouldn't hesitate to sink its teeth into anything that looked like dinner—especially hairy-as-hell legs—he would have to let fly with his knife if it didn't scurry off once they left the Humvee.

Still, his street days instincts blared: Danger.

The spikes that had punctured their tires could be new or old. This area had been in battle mode for centuries. The metal stakes poking from the ground now could be a mere coincidence if perhaps this wasn't the main path to the university.

But hell's bells, he didn't believe in coincidences.

Why such stringent security around a simple university retreat? Reasonable protection for their students was nice and all but this went beyond the campus cop in his little cart cruising the grounds.

He had a bad feeling, and knowing that Gracie's old man was at the end of this booby-trapped road made his pulse slow to the predator level.

Protector.

"Are you all right?" he asked.

Gracie stretched each part of her body slowly, with a sensualist's grace that fit her name in spite of her uptight attitude. "I think so. Yeah. I'm all right. And you?"

"Nothing rattles me, remember?"

The canvas seat rustled with the shift and shuffle of Gracie moving. Movement was good. Alive. God, he didn't even want to think about Gracie dead.

She and he may not be a couple, but she was still…well…Gracie. She would always tickle at the corner of his brain and make him think about what if he'd been a different sort of man….

What-ifs were a waste of time and he considered "waste" an eighth deadly sin. "Seems a strong possibility that somebody doesn't want us inside that place."

She swept stray strands of hair back with hands as steady as his pulse. Maybe they had something in common after all. "Jesus, Bobby, thank goodness whoever it was sucks at putting together booby traps or we would both be dead." Her face tilted toward the puffs of smoke rising skyward in the distance. "I just hope…"

He covered her hand with his. "I know. Hang in there. It's probably just a routine test around here."

She nodded without answering, the worry still staining her sky-blue eyes, so pretty he could swim right in. But they had more pressing matters first. Focus.

Actually, now that he stopped to consider, his thoughts had been clear and steady all evening. No working to juggle all the sensory bombs heading his way. Must be because of the dark and not because the woman beside him had a crazy way of stirring his libido while soothing his mind. No way was any woman having that much control over him.

Period.

"Guess it's time to assess the damage." He slid his knife from his boot while she unholstered her 9mm. He kept his eyes on that semi-charming rat animal. Yet Bobby couldn't resist thinking if he could cage the thing it would make a helluva fun house pet.

Bobby swung open the door with caution, on the lookout for snakes. His boots hit soft ground of decaying undergrowth.

Circling the vehicle, he found four very flat tires.

They were in a shitload of trouble if help didn't arrive soon since they'd already been cutting the timetable close as it was. Of course there was always the possibility that the owners of these particular spikes might not be too happy to see them.

"I guess retrieving your dear old dad is on hold."

Grace slipped into the Humvee, slammed her door and reached for the two-way radio controls. "I'll call for someone to come pick us up."

Bobby launched back into his side as well, closing the door, while Gracie finished her SOS call. He slung his arm along the back of the seat.

"So, Gracie—" he eyed her hot bod, slipping into far safer territory than wondering why she calmed him "—what do you suggest we do to keep ourselves occupied while we wait?"

CHAPTER SIX

HOW EMBARRASSING.

Gracie shifted in the driver's seat of the crippled Humvee, sweat sealing her uniform to her body after two hours of waiting. Her great plan to liberate her father was seriously kaput. Here she sat with four flats in a hot, bug-infested jungle waiting for the equivalent of an Air Force tow truck.

All of which was nothing in comparison to how wretched things could be if her father ditched his lithium. The fear built the longer she waited to lay eyes on her dad and look deep in his eyes to see if *he* was really still there. Would the university facility lock him up in some institution where she couldn't even locate him? Or would they pick up his impaired brain? Her chest tightened at the horrific possibilities even as she tried to think positively.

Bobby seemed more concerned about her getting in trouble. But the Humvee was a part of her equipment and therefore she had every right to sign it out. She should be fine. Not that it would have mattered to her either way with her father's life at stake.

Her breathing grew faster until she realized she was beginning to let that fear conquer her, something she refused to allow. Ten slow, deep breaths later, she was under control and determined to keep her mind on the here and now with Bobby and their SOS.

That had been a mortifying call to make on the radio. Now everyone in the camp would think she and Bobby had slipped off for sex, which beat having to explain the truth. But still. She hadn't been that embarrassed since her father caught her in the driveway making out with her senior-prom date, his hand up her dress.

Of course, in hindsight, most of her acting out her senior year in high school had been to catch her father's attention, or somehow pay him back for having to be his caregiver every time he went through a depression cycle. She was lucky she hadn't actually hurt herself, physically anyway. Emotionally, she still had her fair share of baggage.

Staring through the broken windshield, she watched the fractured image of Bobby climbing a tree to find their midnight snack—mangos. Food hung and flowered lower to the ground, but when she'd accidentally given a simple soulful look up at the mangos, which seemed so much more appealing than bugs or roots…

Wham.

There went Bobby up the tree. His whipcord athleticism was a total turn-on, as much as his consideration. He had charm down pat. For a second she decided not to think about the "Postal" side of him, because, hey, she had her issues, too.

She inched to the edge of her seat. Please Lord, don't let any of those snakes languishing on the branches decide to wake up and make a snack of him. He was so fearless. And what about other "surprise" security measures? Were there cameras? Trip wires? Pits with thinner spikes to spear trespassers? The possibilities were endless. She was willing to bet his pulse wasn't even up a notch. Which made her memory swell with just what *did* make his pulse ratchet. Her fists clenched to will away the phantom memory of touching him.

Or was she trying to capture the sensation that lingered after nine months?

Lingered?

Hell. Loitered. An unwelcome, wrong, wrong, wrong feeling.

He didn't need someone like her, either. If he ever decided to commit, he should have a free spirit who could fly through life as he did. Sure, she'd been wild in high school, which scared her badly enough that now she was wrapped tight for fear she would unravel like her father.

Although holy guacamole, what a month it would be.

His muscles bulged as he scaled down the tree, mangos and bananas stuffed in the pockets of his BDU pants and one piece of fruit between his teeth. He straddled the last limb. Other branches had broken on his way up, which left him with a much higher perch.

Yet, he simply flung himself forward airborne as if his plane would carry him safely to the ground even if he happened to not be inside it at the moment. With the grace of a panther, he hit the ground in a low crouch. The only sign the landing may have been at all teeth-jarring was that the mango fell from his mouth into his hand, a large bite chunked out.

Five seconds later, he swung back into his Humvee seat beside her.

"Wow." She took her mango from his outstretched hand. "That came with everything except the Tarzan whoop."

"I was thinking more along the lines of *Jungle Book*," he replied between bites of mango. "The big ol' bear was always my favorite, and here I am with the bare necessities."

She swiped her wrist along the side of her mouth where juice trickled. "I like your humor."

"Thank you, babe." He carved his mango with his hunting knife. Had it been cleaned since the Sergio the Snake incident? "I like you, too."

Watching that knife so ably wielded in his large hands was a serious turn-on, too, and the turn-ons were accumulating with manic speed. Their attraction had never been in question. How easy it would be to make true the rumor of them sneaking off for sex.

Finished with her mango, she peeled her banana and gave up tamping down sexual thoughts. Thinking of bananas in a sexual manner didn't even really qualify as subliminal. It didn't help matters that her mama had taught her to use condoms in the ninth grade by practicing on a ripe, firm banana. Of course her mama had expected her to be sexually active very young as undoubtedly her mom had been.

Yet in her first three years of high school, Grace Marie's curves were far more generous, not what boys were looking for when their eyes gravitated to the teensy cheerleader types. Then her senior year, she'd joined Jr. ROTC, and the extra pounds melted off. The popular guys started circling, but she couldn't forget that those same boys hadn't looked twice before when she was crying her eyes out on prom night with a box of Twinkies while watching the video of *Sixteen Candles* for the twenty-seventh time.

Instead, she picked her date from pretty much the same pool her father would have run in during his younger years and whoa Nellie, wasn't that a factoid for the psych books? They were wilder than some would have expected.

All right, enough traveling down memory lane. She wrapped her mouth around the fruit and to hell with phallic symbols, because she was still hungry.

Bobby slouched in his seat, chomping away on his third mango. "This kinda reminds me of our first date the week before we left for Iraq, when our teams were briefing together."

She choked on her bite, pressed her wrist to her mouth and struggled to recover her composure. "Um, because you're snitching free food?"

"Good parallel, but not the one I was shooting for, thanks." He opened the door a crack and pitched out the pit. "I was thinking more of how my truck broke down on our first date the night before we deployed to Iraq."

"I'd forgotten about that."

She'd cracked her heel on the walk to the gas station, but laughed when Bobby responded by scooping her up into a piggyback ride. He'd worn a sports jacket and tie and she'd chosen her favorite little black dress—which ripped halfway up her leg when he'd hauled her onto his back for the rest of the walk.

She'd been too busy laughing to notice.

Too turned-on to care.

Then they'd both gone to Iraq after that weekend for a short stint. Their next two dates had been widely spaced but progressively intense. Deeply scary, because Bobby was a man without boundaries and she desperately needed her space. "Do you still have that beat-up old piece-of-crap truck? What was it you called her?"

"Sweet Thing? Of course I do. I dropped a new engine in and she runs just fine." He kissed his fingers. "Truly a suh-weet thing."

"Hmm." She had to admire his thriftiness and seeming lack of concern for what anyone thought of him, but also couldn't squelch her curiosity. What did he do with the rest of his money?

He'd once told her since he was TDY or deployed

nearly ten months out of the year, he didn't even have an apartment of his own. He and three other thrifty fellas rented a small place to stow their stuff.

Finished with his supper, he swiped the knife flat side down his thigh to clean it, then the other side before sheathing it once again. "Don't tell me you're the vanity-car sort."

Her? Not hardly. Her car was every bit as staid and beige as she was these days. "No, it's just that you have such amazing transportation at work with these cutting-edge aircraft. Other flyers I've seen really enjoy speed, horsepower when they're on the ground, too—new trucks. And the number of motorcycles among Special Ops guys is astounding. I can't figure out why you would choose to drive something that's borderline unsafe."

"And this Hummvee here is working any better than my truck?"

"Spiked booby traps will do that to anything." She stated the obvious.

He tapped her nose and grinned. "I'm just yanking your chain. I actually bought a nice used truck a couple of weeks ago—Suh-weet Thing Two."

She really was uptight if he could "yank her chain" that easily. She should be able to follow the train of his thinking, since she was a pro, after all.

However all professional training seemed to go out the window around this guy.

"Used, huh?" She tipped her best flirty grin and decided to play along, because it was fun and too often she starched the fun right out of her life. "A nice fifteen-year-old model, gently used, with only a dented front fender and strategically sprayed bondo?"

He clapped a hand over his heart as if mortally wounded. "Three years old, thank you very much. Still has a new-car smell as far as I'm concerned."

She shared his laughter, the sounds twining to bounce around the inside of the vehicle and, damn, that sound felt good seeping into her skin.

He settled back, hands on his knees that were of course bouncing since he never sat still. "Actually, there's no need for me to keep a great car around. I'm only home a couple of months a year these days."

"That doesn't leave much downtime for relaxation." She'd seen plenty of combat stress over the past few years.

So much, there were days she exercised herself into oblivion to work through all she'd heard from these men and women carrying burdens in their heads and hearts. They needed more vacation time between deployments, but she didn't have much sway over that.

"Downtime?" He scratched his head. "I vaguely recall taking a Caribbean cruise with you …no…wait…it was just a dream one time when I fell asleep in a hotel hot tub."

Night sounds from outside still seeped in, muffled but intimate, reminding her of their first date, which ended with a beach walk. She'd been TDY down at his base in the Florida Panhandle, Hurlburt Field near Fort Walton Beach, preparing for a two-week-long training swing through Kuwait and Iraq.

Hurlburt even owned its own stretch of sand along the Gulf of Mexico. They'd walked, and he'd taken her there for a first kiss as well before the truck incident. "The date was really nice, though. You took me out to a great restaurant."

"I seem to recall you didn't think it was funny when I put a bread stick in my pocket."

Her lips twitched. "It was a *little* funny."

He'd made her laugh plenty that night, a memory she'd apparently buried in lieu of all her fears about other aspects of his personality. Of course, that first kiss had drawn her in with a burning need to come back for more. That he hadn't pressed for sex on the first date had surprised her.

And impressed her.

He thumbed some fruit from the corner of her

grinning mouth. "Ah, so the disapproving school-marm gig is all an act."

It worked well putting most men in their place, but then Bobby wasn't most men. "Maybe, maybe not."

"A woman of mystery."

She snorted. "Yeah, right."

"You are."

Really? What a heady thought that she might shake his world as much as he did hers. "Right?"

"Mysterious."

"You're full of crap. I thought we'd already turned this page, Bobby."

"You're right." He cupped the side of her face, thumb brushing her cheekbone. "I wanted you to know I took you out for that dinner to impress you, because you sure impressed the hell out of me the second I saw you."

He dazzled her. Still. It was all she could do not to nip his thumb with her teeth and then suck on it in an unmistakable message of sensuality. Instead, he brought it to his mouth and sucked the fruit off his own skin.

Even more sexy.

She shivered. Wanted. Wondered why she couldn't urge herself to lean just a hint forward and she could have it all, another Bobby Ruznick kiss that stirred a tornado within her. An out-of-control tornado that would swirl everything inside her until the Humvee would be their whole world, nothing outside.

Her mind stumbled on that last thought. Her ears perked just as Bobby looked up. A roar swelled outside, a stirring of grass and dirt around their vehicle that made it almost impossible to see outside.

Bobby shook his head. "Face always did have the crappiest timing."

"Face? Timing?" Her mind was still back on thoughts of licking mango juice off each other.

"Looks like my buddies have arrived, undoubtedly with a mechanic and a new set of tires."

The dust spiral slowed and thinned to reveal the CV-22 landing in the clearing beside them. Bobby left the Humvee, tugging Grace Marie along with him.

The crank of the rotors slowed, quieted enough for speech. Bobby shouted to his pal Face as he and the spare copilot stepped out of the craft. "About time y'all turned up."

Face shook his head. "And what dipshit-bad timing for you to snitch a vehicle to go make out in the woods." He paused, winced and gave Gracie one of his affable smiles. "Sorry. No disrespect intended."

"None taken." She would rather he think she was sharing mango-tasting kisses with Bobby than explain the debacle with her father.

"Thank you, Lieutenant," Face continued. "The base camp is in an uproar over our surprise visitor."

"Visitor?" Bobby frowned.

"General Hank Renshaw just landed all stealthy like and has called a meeting. Pronto. So we need to haul your asses back before he realizes you're gone."

A general? At their little encampment? Her thoughts too quickly flew back to her father's silence in the nuclear think-tank retreat. Please, please, please don't let these two events be connected, especially since she'd lost her chance to get to her father first.

SPRAWLED IN Jiang's tangled bedsheets, Rurik ran his fingers through the length of her ebony hair. Incense hung in the air. He touched her naked body, sated and half-awake. Ebony swirls of hair covered her new dragon tattoo she'd gotten on the small of her back to commemorate the fierceness of their love.

The explosion scare during their midnight snack had been nothing more than some idiot youths playing with chemicals without approval. The program for university undergraduates was a mammoth waste of time in his opinion. They didn't understand the importance of this project. They only saw things at face value. However, a few of the graduate students grasped the full breadth of information available here.

He worked in security and even *he* understood. He envisioned so much more. Immortality through creation. And soon the world would see what he saw. Soon, but not yet. Timing was important. He would prove to his father he could be someone special.

For now, he would lose himself in Jiang's lithe body so he could forget for a moment that the world was changing. People had to watch out for themselves and their interests and principles. Old avenues of effecting change folded daily. Things that never would have crossed a person's mind now became the norm for survival. He was only twenty, disowned for not living life his father's aristocratic way.

He'd studied to receive a place on this security team. It must be divine providence that put him here, giving Jiang and him the chance to be a part of the famous Dr. Lanier's discoveries.

Times had changed. Brawn no longer ruled the world. Brains won.

Years of being teased in school for his weakling

appearance and geeky ways had finally paid off. Now he had the brain and brawn, thanks to a surprise growth spurt at sixteen, combined with some minor steroid use. Not too much, though, because he refused to let anything drain his ability with women.

Something he was grateful for now more than ever as he sought to impress Jiang with his performance. And power.

Jiang stroked him even in her sleep, always giving. He hated that her reputation could be sullied with his presence in her quarters, but he couldn't stay away.

She rolled onto her side beside him, rustling the sheets still damp with sweat from their vigorous lovemaking. Shy virgin-no-more Jiang had surprised him. She would do anything he asked in bed, on the floor, against the wall, on her hands and knees.

Anything.

"Tell me again," Jiang Lee asked in his language, surprisingly awake and alert.

He didn't have to ask what she wanted to hear. He knew. Their dream future, where they would be free to settle down. The specifics of that they played around with and changed each time of telling.

"Your country or mine, this time?"

She placed her hand on his bare chest, scratching

her painted nails gently through the mat of hair. "I would miss my homeland, but if I am with you, none of it matters. Tonight, let us plan for your country. Tell me more."

Why not fantasize for her? Let her keep her emotional innocence about the world a while longer.

"Mountains," he answered, mentally transporting them from this stark room and silence outside the door and windows, "much like the landscape here, except the greenery and foliage is much tamer, smaller roses rather than flamboyant orchids."

Yet Jiang was more like a rose. Perhaps that was why he felt so drawn to her. She was a mix of his country and hers—a unique, one-of-a-kind rose. *His*.

She would have enchanted their neighbors with her whimsical generosity. He let himself seep into that imaginary world, envisioning her even starting her own shop of incense, spices, meditation tapes and classes. She would bring peace with her wherever she went.

She hooked her slim, cool leg over his, her knee brushing against his replete penis. Jiang kissed his shoulder. "We will settle in a small town where we can make lifelong friends."

"There are plenty of villages to choose from." Part of him yearned to turn on the steel bedside lamp so he could see her body better, but then the light would likely pull them into the reality of the here and now.

He listened and pretended for the moment he could give her those dreams.

CHAPTER SEVEN

STILL FIRED UP from moments alone with Gracie that had affected him far more than they should have, Bobby jerked on a clean flight suit, yanking the zipper up and damn near catching his penis. After the Humvee debacle, military humiliation, libido agony and now a surprise visit from a general, which rarely boded well, this day couldn't get any *fucking* worse.

Why did General Hank Renshaw, the PACAF DO—Pacific Air Forces Director of Operations—want special time with them? He was only supposed to be here for a routine inspection. No biggie. Low-key.

The last thing *any* captain wanted was some good old-fashioned face-time with a general, for crying out loud. Especially a captain renowned for shoving his size thirteen boot in his mouth on a regular basis—when he wasn't busy pocketing free pens.

What a really rotten time for Gracie to be wriggling around with the regs by commandeering a

Humvee for her personal use. She hadn't technically broken any rules. She was within her right to scout the area, not that anybody bought that. They were both getting ribbed for trying to sneak off for sex and ending up with four flat tires.

So not cool.

If Gracie's Humvee SNAFU—situation normal all fucked up—slid onto General Renshaw's radar and it seemed she might catch heat for it, Bobby would fall on his sword in a heartbeat and do something to distract the old bird, like ask if that hot youngest daughter of his who flew cargo planes was still single. Rumor had it she was married to some secret-agent dude, but hey, who says a fella couldn't play dumb to save his own woman?

His own woman? Gracie?

Dr. Uptight would bang him over the head with an MRE for his tremendously un-PC thought. Except hey, why should a dude be convicted for what was in his brain if it didn't fall out of his mouth? Especially when not fifteen-and-a-half seconds ago he'd been willing to make an ass of himself in front of a general for Gracie.

Ah crap. He glanced at his watch. Eight minutes and forty-seven seconds left until this bizarre surprise meeting. He needed to get his butt in gear or he would be late, and by God, if he was gonna fall on a sword, it would be deliberate, not because of some punctuality problem.

Hopefully General Renshaw had bigger things on his agenda than Gracie's little jungle mishap. Undoubtedly so, since generals had packed schedules.

Tying his boots with record speed, Bobby hauled out of the tent and over to the lumbering C-17 cargo plane where the meeting would be held for security. He took the steps on the side hatch two at a time and launched inside.

Uh-oh. The guest list was small on this one, which meant spooky shit. With years of studied practice, he narrowed his focus to the moment.

Only his crew. Rodeo's crew. The commander of the Delta unit.

And Gracie.

She sat in a chair at the long stretch of red seats lining the C-17 cargo plane Rodeo flew, a larger craft than Bobby's CV-22.

Yep, this definitely showed signs of being much higher on the totem pole of importance than her Goodyear tire flats, which made him all the more determined to keep his attention dead on the moment. He wasn't sure what role Gracie would play in this but he surely intended to find out. Bobby dropped into the seat by Joe rather than add fodder to the getting-busy-in-the-Humvee rumor.

The back hatch was sealed tight, only fluorescent lights inside and a side hatch open, then filling with the general's aide. "Ladies and gentlemen…General Renshaw."

Boots hit the floor and spines went stiff in unison, salutes popped tight and steady, eyes unwavering.

"At ease," General Renshaw barked from the front of the craft, "and be seated."

A large screen in front of the bulkhead beside him fired to life in two-image split-screen style, one side stacked with photos, the other with a detailed floor plan of someplace.

Apparently his and Gracie's transgression was in the clear for now, but that didn't relax him in the least. He still had this briefing to get through.

General Renshaw was an old bomber pilot with military bearing bred in his bones for generations, something he'd passed along to his three children, all currently USAF aviators in different airframes. Their family name was well-known.

Hands behind his back, the General strode toward the screen, his salt-and-pepper hair buzzed short as always.

Bobby couldn't think of a time he'd seen the man

with anything but an impeccable haircut. Did he have a permanent barber on staff? Or hey, maybe he had a beautician lady friend he kept with him—

And damn it, there went that ADHD out of control again. Focus on what the man had to say. It had to be the gut-twisting instinct he'd learned was always right, the intuition telling him now this meeting would put Gracie in danger.

Renshaw took out his laser pointer and aimed it toward the screen. "Ladies and gentlemen, this is your lucky day. You just happened to be in the right place at the right time to make your mark in the fight against terrorism."

Lucky?

"It seems our little exercise here has put us in the vicinity of an active terrorist cell." He pointed to the face at the top of the screen.

Nobody Bobby'd run across while picking up groceries. Too bad. Life never did make things easy.

Even with the generator and air-conditioning cart hooked up to cool things down, sweat still melded his flight suit to his back. He stole a quick glance at Gracie—cool and blond and sending those red-alert vibes through him.

"The terrorist leader seems to have a dual plan here. Screw up a democratic process already weak in its infancy. And make sure the candidate sympathetic to the U.S. loses."

Well, hell. Hadn't the recent German elections had major repercussions for U.S. relations? This terrorist's method of thinking certainly could work and was far more devious than the rat bastards who went around strapping bombs to their chests to take out the nearest American.

Renshaw shifted his pointer to the floor-plan model. "All signs indicate one of the cell's operatives could be working or studying in the nuclear-physics department at the University of Cantou."

Ah, crap. The bad feeling was getting worse. He glanced across at Gracie.

Really, really pale Gracie.

"The CIA hasn't been able to contact a United Nations representative sent in undercover to monitor possible leakage of nuclear data. The U.N. agent has gone totally silent, without sending even standard covert tracking signals for satellites to pick up. Either the agent is in trouble—or has turned."

Yeah, he got that. Those spikes into the tires *had* seemed a bit excessive for security around a university lab. These dudes were serious. Just how many of them in that facility worked for the bad guys?

"Delta will be dropped in to extract the agent.

Since we already have a Special Ops aircraft in
country, they will fly the infiltration. Your psy-ops
exercise offers the perfect cover for us to trot all
around this country speaking with people from both
sides of the political fence. From there, we hope to
learn enough to eliminate whatever this cell has in the
works."

And if not?

Gracie shivered almost imperceptibly across
from him, but he was too in tune with this woman's
every move to miss it. And no wonder she was
shaken. Hell, even he was sitting stock-still which,
like, never happened.

This wasn't an exercise at all. They'd been
brought in for a specific purpose, none of which
promised to be in the least low-key. What the hell was
Gracie's old man messed up with? Or had he aligned
himself with the other side?

And what might Gracie know about her father's
situation that she wasn't sharing?

SASHAYING OUT of the cafeteria and into the gardens
to check out the lay of the land with some exercise
tossed in, Felicia ran her thumb along the waistband
of her stretch pants. She really should have skipped
the slice of pineapple cake at dinner. But sheesh, she

was hungry. She popped another fried-egg noodle in her mouth.

The workout room in this place stank. You'd think with all the money they put into building this facility, they would have some decent exercise bikes or weight machines. Maybe they didn't see the need since apparently once these folks' brains were sucked dry of information, they would get the great honor of blowing up their under-exercised selves in some terrorist's bomb.

She wound her way around a plum tree, too fired up to sleep more than a couple of hours. But God, she loved her job and how it made her feel alive.

Matt sure seemed to have found a way around the place's lack of a workout area. Having spent approximately a half hour pressed up against a man's muscles and that surprisingly impressive erection could stir some frustrations in a girl and, well, she was feeding hers full tilt right now.

She pitched another fried-egg noodle in her mouth as she strolled through the gardens after dark in the vain hope of meeting up with her contact. Something had to have happened to him. Undercover as a vending-machine supplier, he'd simply disappeared. The job should have given him flexibility to come and go.

He'd been replaced six days ago and that scared her. She'd sent other messages through radio transmissions but couldn't be sure they'd gone through. Certainly she'd received no answer.

Leaving would arouse suspicion, even if she could manage to get out. Roll was taken obsessively. This week, they were all supposed to be participating in some big meditation project—led by Jiang Lee—that would free their minds to conceive of higher-order thinking.

Quite frankly, she didn't like people tinkering around in her brain so, thanks to the training she'd received for her undercover assignment, she'd learned to drown out Jiang and dream of other things.

Like a pedicure and manicure—paraffin dip, too—she was so due once she wrapped up this assignment. And ohhhh, most definitely a hot stone massage for good measure. She wound along the path by a line of perfectly trimmed bonsais.

Throughout Jiang's latest session, Felicia couldn't help but notice Matt's mouth moving silently the whole time. She began to realize he was reciting equations.

Apparently he didn't like the idea of anyone poking around in his mind, either. And speaking of Matt, holy Sister Rebecca Margaret, was that Matt in a tank T-shirt enjoying an evening jog around the perimeter?

Yum, and then some.

Those whipcord muscles she'd felt against her were not the result of any cable sweater. Those were one-hundred-percent grade-A *M-A-N*. Sure, he wasn't all big-bulk buff like a football player. He had a runner's grace and strength.

And presumably endurance.

So what did she intend to do about it? She didn't really know how far she could trust him, but trust and raw sex were two different things. And these were dangerous times.

Damn, damn, damn—she crossed herself, because there went Sister Bertha Jeanne in her head reminding her of the sins of the flesh and using foul language. How odd that the more she wanted Matt, the more her Catholic schoolgirl side resurrected.

Anyhow, while surely someday she might give her body to a man again, it should be out of commitment. Except she'd tried commitment and it was crap and she did *not* intend to cross herself for that curse. As a matter of fact—she dug deep in her purse past her miniature Chinese triangle puzzle—where was her lipstick? Just because she wanted to practice control didn't mean she couldn't look her best. But she had to be honest with herself. The clothes, the bold walk and look were all bravado. She'd been with one guy—her husband—and he'd trounced all over her already tender heart and self-image.

Day by day this job gave her little victories. In his face. In the world's face. She won. She was alive and vibrant, and if she died tomorrow she'd lived a day longer than anyone ever expected during her teenage years.

She'd just finished slicking on a fresh coat and smacking her lips together when Matt rounded the corner that would lead him right to her path. Brazen it out.

Deep breaths, girl.

"Well howdy flipping do to you, Dr. Lanier. How's it shaking?" She chomped another egg noodle for restraint, bravado, anything so she wouldn't pucker up for Matt and offer him the lipstick print of a lifetime out of goofy nerves. "Thank goodness those alarms were nothing. Those dang undergrads shouldn't be left unsupervised."

He slowed his steps to a jog over to her, stopping. "Always good to practice emergency procedures."

"I have to confess." She ran her hand along a stone bench in a gentle let's-sit hint. "The first time I heard a chemical siren go off, I snagged my chem suit, like a good girl, because of course I'd kept it right there by my side at all times."

Oh, what the hey, she might as well sit. She plopped down onto the bench which would conveniently give him a peek down her favorite Blondie T-shirt. He leaned down to grasp his knees and rest his fine butt against a tree as he sucked in slow, cool-down breaths and just listened.

She placed her snack beside her, no longer in need of food for bravado. "I shook the thing out to put it on, counting the seconds before I was radiation toast. I shoved one foot in and the other, and I jumped and jumped and jumped and doggone it but the thing wouldn't go on. Finally some kind soul told me I was trying to shove my feet through the armholes."

Chuckling, he straightened, still resting against the plum tree. "I assume it was a false alarm."

"Yes, but all the same, thank heaven and the saint of fools."

The corner of his mouth tipped up. "And who might that be?"

She clapped her hand to her chest. "You're kidding, right? I actually know something you don't?"

"Appears so. Although you can educate me. The saint of fools is…?"

"Saint Harin, I believe, is the patron saint of jesters, simpletons and fools, but we digress."

He crossed his arms over his chest, eyes narrowed as if taking in the whole of her. "So you really are a good Catholic girl."

"Not so much these days." She shrugged nervously. "I've got a divorce behind me, which for quite a while didn't put me in good stead with the church."

"I'm sorry to hear that."

"I'm not. He was a jerk. Our annulment should come through soon. He refused to have children with me and in the Roman Catholic Church, that's a big no-no." Of course, she couldn't bear children—a by-product of her cancer—but her ex refused to consider adoption. Slowly the marriage fell apart because he considered her a dried-up prune. The damn jackass.

No crossing herself required.

And suddenly her need for bravado faded.

She rested a hand on the bench and let herself enjoy the view as well, the dappled moonlight giving the hard planes of Matt's face a mysterious air. She could have sworn she saw his fists clench on her behalf when she spoke of her scum-sucking ex.

Yeah, she was liking Matt more and more every second. "Actually I figured a better saint to thank for ridding me of my ex would be Saint Martin de Porres."

"Ah, and your vast knowledge continues to

outstrip my humble self. This saint would be appropriate because?"

"He would be invoked for protection against rats."

Matt applauded lightly. "Very nice."

"Thank you." She tipped her head regally. "Actually, in honor of the good Catholic schoolgirl I once was, I should probably also educate you with some of our kinder images, like Saint Albert the Great, the saint for scientists such as us. He is said to have tutored Saint Thomas Aquinas."

"You have a wide variety of knowledge stored under all that hair."

"You like my hair?"

All sound stopped. Or maybe that was just because she couldn't think of anything but that he really may have noticed her and apparently the notion sent him equally silent for a second before he gave her a nod in return.

"It catches the eye."

"And your attention?" She clenched the edges of the stone bench.

"Maybe."

She crossed her ankles under the bench with glee, so silly because this was dangerous considering she wasn't even certain she could trust him. "I think definitely."

Finally, he straightened, all playfulness gone as he brought them closer. "What do you want from me?"

Sex?

That didn't sound quite right and she did have her job to think about. Her hand slithered into her purse to work the miniature Rubik's Cube absently while she measured her words. "I just wanted to talk to you. You're an intelligent man, near my age. And not to sound arrogant, but there aren't a lot of people out here I can talk to who can keep up."

"What color lipstick is that?"

That sure stunned her silent. Where had that come from? He looked horrified to have blurted the words, so if she didn't do something fast, they would never have another conversation like this again. The distance between them would be metaphysically continents wide instead of the mere inch right now.

Time to act.

She stared straight into his amazing emerald eyes and said, "Cha-Cha Red. It tastes like berries."

And without bothering to ask for permission and risk rejection, she leaned forward and kissed him.

CHAPTER EIGHT

HOLY SHIT, this woman could kiss.

Matt palmed her back to keep them both from tipping off the bench into the flower bed—which actually didn't sound too bad but wasn't particularly prudent. Her arms twined around his neck, all the enthusiasm that shimmered from her body like a splitting atom poured into Matthias as he tasted Felicia right there in the garden.

Out in the open where anyone could stumble on them.

Unable to stop, he stood with her clinging tight and showing no signs of letting go anytime soon. He backed her toward the building, toward an outside door that led into his lab office. They stumbled inside, the perfume of the garden fading until he could only smell the floral scent from her hair, her skin. *Her.*

Not one flower in particular, but more like a mixed bouquet that always kept him guessing, roses one second, then lilies, then perhaps a carnation or lilac. Not that he was a flower expert, but he could sure see working at being an expert on what made this lady writhe.

He kicked the door closed behind them and reached to fumble with the lock.

Click.

Alone.

Her soft, sweet arms looped around his neck, slowly loosened for her hands to slide, glide, entice. Apparently she liked her kissing intense and a little rough, as her long nails dug into his shoulders, his hair, his ass. Her hands and his were everywhere while their tongues met and soothed, explored.

He backed her against a lab table for balance because, yeah, he could still stand, but he would far rather put his energy into leaning against her. He skimmed his hands down her sides to dig his fingers into her hips for a second before roving again. And hey, there were breasts up there. She mewed like a happy kitty cat when he found them, massaged them into taut tips, plucked.

She bit.

Gently, she nipped his bottom lip as she writhed against him. More of this would definitely be a good thing.

He hooked his hands behind her knees and lifted her up to sit on the table, which made things a lot more convenient for him since he didn't have to crick his neck downward to kiss her. Hot damn, he could rub his erection right at the juncture of her sweet thighs. He could swear she was already damp for him, the vague scent of pheromones in the air, the feminine perfume of desire.

He wanted her, here, now. And apparently she wanted the same. Technically there was nothing stopping them. The door was locked. She wasn't a student of his. Their ages were close enough that he couldn't be considered a COG—creepy old guy.

So why not go for it?

Because somewhere in his too-damn-smart mind something niggled. There was something off when it came to Felicia, and he was too damn smart to be wrong. Ms. Felicia Cha-Cha Red Fratarcangelo was lying to him about something, and even with their tongues stoking a fire that should have burned away any facade, still the secrets of her soul stayed shielded.

Even as a teen, he'd been hit on by a number of women who thought his brain and money would offer them an easy life. Hey, he was nuclear research's answer to Bill Gates.

At eighteen, he'd been idiot enough to believe one of the women and he'd paid a helluva price. He couldn't regret the result, his Grace Marie. But God knows his daughter had deserved better than she'd gotten out of her childhood.

He refused to screw up again.

Regretfully, painfully, he pulled himself away from the willing woman in his arms. Her tempting, stretchy pants he longed to peel off would have to stay plastered in place until he learned more about the secrets held by the elusive Lady Cha-Cha Red.

HOLY GUACAMOLE, what had she done? Or almost done?

Felicia adjusted her pushup bra on her way back to her room. Her whole darn face was probably blushing Cha-Cha Red right now after that royal rejection. They'd been playing tonsil hockey like there was no tomorrow and she'd been thinking wow-oh-wow that brain of his makes him intuitive at the speed of light as to just how to turn her inside out with want.

Jeez, did she *want*. A glimmer of Sister Esther Regina's voice whispered through her head then, almost drowning the sound of a door opening down the hall. Now, the nun was yacking away at how loose girls could get in trouble if they ditched their knickers around a boy.

Matt was *so* not a boy.

Footsteps drew closer, and she quickly looked down so her blushing face wouldn't show. Her tender skin hinted she might have rub marks from whisker burn.

She peeked up and said, "Have a nice night."

The young man—Rurik Zazlov—nodded back on his brisk way down the corridor. "Good evening."

Whoa, hold on just a hinky second. What was this boy, maybe twenty, doing in the women's quarters so late? Could be nothing but a simple romantic tryst with Jiang. Could also be a covert meeting that boded ill, as her instincts insisted. As much as she wanted to run her embarrassed self to her room, she needed to speak to this guy.

"Wait," she hollered at his back. "Do you have a minute? Mr. Zazlov?"

Slowly, he spun on his heels to face her, his shirt-tails untucked, his rangy body loose with that just-had-sex relaxed air. His soul patch was a bit thin with that look of a young boy trying too early to be a man—a bit endearing. But his eyes were sharp. She needed to remember that.

Still, she could play dumb and assume he was

here for professional reasons. She hadn't spent much time chitchatting with this boy, and maybe focusing on work for a second would help calm her.

Running the two-hundred-person roster through her head, she recalled he worked security rather than testing. "Is everything all right back here? Has someone breached the perimeter?"

He blinked once, twice, a third time before answering, which seemed to Felicia he thought a little too hard about his answer. "I'm only doing a walk-around. All's in order."

"Glad to hear it. There are too many whack-a-zoid rebel factions in this country for my peace of mind. But hey, academic environments need to spread their wings and thanks to good folk like you we have the freedom to work together in safety."

"So it would seem."

This was getting her nowhere fast. Maybe she should try some subtle flirtation just to see if he was a dog of a man willing to go from one woman to the next.

She inched closer and reached to smooth his collar, folding down the corner sticking up. "I'll just have to trust that folks like you can keep our info inside these walls."

"Apparently so," he answered in his slightly accented English, not even nibbling on her flirtation.

If anything, he backed up a step, his gaze betraying him by flicking ever so briefly to Jiang's dorm door.

Apparently somebody was getting a little. Or were they meeting for another reason as well?

He nodded coolly, still backing away. "Good night."

His footsteps echoed, growing softer as the distance grew between them. Hmm…she scratched her itchy nose. That couple definitely deserved closer observation. A simple romance was fine, but there were so many politics and agendas here, she couldn't discount anything.

Sex always messed everything up.

She'd known it wouldn't be wise to sleep with Matt, but with an attraction like theirs, she had to be prepared and safe. She'd started carrying a condom in her purse, for crying out loud—she winced as Sister Esther Regina shrieked in her mind.

She so didn't know what to do about this enigmatic man. This was a tough world to be living in for a thirty-eight-year-old divorcée. Healthy and so very needy for the man down the hall, but wincing at sex without commitment, sex with lies between them.

She should call a priest real quick and say please, please marry us ASAP before my body implodes and then I won't be able to complete my mission, which could have *huge* world implications. But she didn't love the man, either, so a marriage would be a sacrilege.

All of which wouldn't be a problem if she could just have one hour of wall-banging sex with the surprisingly hot Dr. Matt Lanier. Too bad she only had her instincts to rely on that he wasn't some maniacal terrorist enemy.

CONTROLS IN HAND as the craft lifted off the ground, Bobby let himself merge with the craft as the sun beat through his windscreen. He wouldn't admit something so whoo-hoo-ey out loud, but when he flew, the experience was definitely otherworldly.

He could "feel" the plane inside him, therefore he knew the craft and exactly how far he could push. Most people already thought he was crazy and he wasn't about to prove it by explaining his secret to kick-ass flying. Even when it came to test missions like today, he gave his all.

Bobby flicked the controls that would move the propellers from the upward, helicopter style for takeoff, to forward facing on the wings for fast moving, straight-ahead flight over the dense green jungle.

Flying. Precision.

He had to keep his mind and body in the moment, not thinking about Gracie and the implications of the General's visit. He had a job to do and if Gracie's dad was in deep caca with the terrorists, then the man had to pay.

Bobby skirted the edges of life, but never crossed the line.

However, he damn well would do his best to keep Gracie's father alive. That much he could do for her. Other than that, though, he would be wise to keep his distance. Finishing this demo mission for the General's observation would carry them all one step closer to plugging the spy leak and shutting down another terrorist cell.

The staccato thump of the CV-22 winging through the midday sky echoed off the green hills masking the direction of approach from those in their Army/Air Force tent camp. The first purpose of this flight? To demonstrate the CV-22's ability to deliver psy-op leaflets into a target village. They used their own camp today, but the real deal would be over a nearby village, with political flyers supporting the democratic process.

Normally they performed this maneuver at night so the noise of the CV-22 added to the psychological effect of the messages soon to be fluttering to the

ground. But since they were on the General's timetable, a late-afternoon flight worked best.

Through his windscreen, Bobby could see everyone standing around in the tree-surrounded tent camp
turning and searching the sky for the aircraft as the
rumble grew louder. Inside the CV-22, Bobby enjoyed
circling the camp while staying out of their view.

God, he loved to fly, and this cutting-edge new
craft offered him the chance to stretch his skills to
the max for some mind games with the folks below.
He cranked the stick, turning and driving directly at
the target area, then wheeling the aircraft into a tight
turn to point away. The acrobatic jolts threw sound
so it should seem to those below that there were
aircraft surrounding the area.

The appearance of more power.

Head games.

He had to admit, Gracie's line of work helped.

"This is my favorite part," Postal said over the interphone. "Padre, crank up the music."

Bobby could envision Padre in the back playing
DJ as he flipped the switches on a box strapped to
the floor of the aircraft. "Music is on and the
volume is up all the way. Get ready to rock and
roll, sir."

Bullhorns strapped to the landing-gear blisters

blasted "Ride of the Valkyries" adding to the effect on the target village. Soon the noise of the aircraft mixed with another sound. The intimidation factor doubled the power of psychological warfare on the target.

Textbook perfect. But a person could read about it all day long and not get the full impact without experiencing it firsthand.

Gracie knew her shit. They'd run her plan as ordered and he could feel the ripple effect. He definitely believed in mind games. He just didn't like the idea of someone being able to pick around in his brain.

Bobby guided the aircraft toward the camp but this time didn't turn away. This may seem like a simple demonstration for General Renshaw and local military and political figures. But their small group, along with the General, understood there was a secondary, underlying mission as well. This was also a practice run for the real deal, when they would deliver flyers to cover dropping Army soldiers in to retrieve the agent—and hopefully Gracie's father.

Normally, the leaflets contained info such as rewards for handing over wanted individuals, instructions for surrendering, political messages, details on where to tune a radio frequency.

For now, focus remained on working out the bugs

so things went picture-perfect when it counted most. When lives were at stake.

Bobby dove down to treetop level and spoke to the crew over the headset built into his helmet. "Let's get this done. Get both packages ready. We are sixty seconds out of the first drop."

Gunners would unload the two batches of leaflets out the back hatch. Then while everyone was distracted with the floating leaflets, the Army Deltas would unload just minutes away.

Since these leaflets would just fly out over their own camp, Bobby wondered what Gracie had printed on them and then he wondered why it even mattered to him what Gracie did, damn it.

"Roger," Stones responded, a fearless fella who'd earned his call sign for his large *cajones* in combat. "Ready when you are, sir."

"Stand by in the back," Bobby ordered. "Fifteen seconds and counting…ready, ready…now."

"Off and away," Stones answered in back as the three gunners would begin tipping the boxes aft.

Leaflets flew off into the slipstream, filling the air and falling into the tent camp, some catching in the trees. The CV-22 roared over the lines of tents, engines howling, music blaring, with paper streaming out and as suddenly as it appeared, it was gone.

Bobby worked the rudders at his feet, banking the plane left. "Clear of the camp. Music off. Ready with the second package?"

"Roger that, sir," Sandman answered this time. "Standing in the door."

Face sat in the copilot's seat while watching over and grading Bobby in the aircraft commander's place. "Come twenty degrees right. The clearing is five miles away."

"All right, start transition." Bobby jockeyed the controls to begin slowing the aircraft down while Face leaned forward, looking for the landing zone.

"I got it visual," Face confirmed with his typical calm. They made a good team that way, balancing each other out. "Get ready in back."

Bobby settled the big aircraft into the opening in the trees until it was just a few feet off the ground. Now time to practice the rest of the mission—off-loading the troops. In the back, a team of twelve Special Forces soldiers launched themselves off the back ramp and flattened into the elephant grass. These same men would bring out the U.N. spy and Gracie's dad—saving or condemning him.

Stones shouted, "Go, go, go, everyone is clear."

Bobby climbed the aircraft over the treetops and

began the transition to forward flight. Soon they were at full speed, leaving the landing zone far behind.

"That went pretty well," Bobby said over the interphone. "Did we get most of the leaflets into the camp?"

"Yes, sir," Stones answered. "Some went out the end, but most got in there. We succeeded in doing our part to get SpongeBob SquarePants elected as the next president of Cantou."

"Suh-weet." Bobby laughed with the rest. Apparently Dr. Gracie had a sense of humor after all. "Nice job, everyone. Let's get this sucker home." Bobby put the aircraft into a climb. "Give me a steer point back to the camp, Face."

His buddy punched buttons on the navigational panel. "There you go. Heading to our parking spot." Soon the tents of the camp became visible again on the horizon. "Prepare for landing, crew. Start transition to hover, Postal."

"Roger that, starting transition." Bobby began the steps to slow down the aircraft and move the propellers to the helicopter configuration when suddenly...

Red. One of his displays began blinking a malfunction message. Shit.

"Well, look at that." He regulated his breathing in spite of the potentially deadly malfunction unfolding in front of him. Steady. In. Out. Breathe. "The engines won't transition up. I seem to recall that is a not-so-good thing."

The whole craft went darkly silent while he thought....

"Going to backup mode," Bobby decided and mentally crossed his fingers—wow, wasn't that a personal vote of confidence?—pushing more buttons only to see the red malfunction light remain blinking. Definitely not good. "Face, we got nothing here. That is supposed to be impossible according to the tech order."

Face's usually calm expression appeared a bit too pinched for Bobby's peace of mind, but still Face left him in control. "Start over and check all the switches and circuit breakers. And hey, guys in back, scan the circuit-breaker panels."

The headset crackled to life from a gunner. "Everything is nominal back here."

They couldn't land with the propellers pointed forward. With the rotors forward, the props would tear into the ground before the landing gear touched down, ripping apart the plane and likely exploding the whole damn craft—turning the six souls inside quite crispy.

This definitely sucked.

He refused to injure anyone on his crew, much less

die or lose his plane. And even though he and Gracie weren't an item, he knew her well enough to realize how traumatizing it would be for her to watch this explode into a flaming hell.

When had he gotten to a point where her hurt became his hurt? Somewhere along the line they'd become friends. A female friend. A first for him and something he didn't know how to deal with yet. And definitely couldn't deal with at this particular moment.

"Well, we can't land with those props pointed as they are, so I guess we better try some more crap." His mind raced with options, training taking control over emotions. "Pull and reset all the circuit breakers and see what happens."

Flight engineer Vegas began pulling out breakers and pushing them back into place. "Damn, this one is freaking hot." He yanked his hand back, a blister bubbling. "It burned through my gloves."

Bobby jumped in on the interphone, mind racing with a plan, risky, but better than tooling around with their thumbs up their noses. "It burned you? Don't push it back in yet. Let it cool off. If we set up for landing, push in the circuit breaker at the last second and we might have a split second to transition the rotors. Face, does that work for you?"

"Beats any plan I've got." Face shrugged, a hint

of defeatism not quite disguised. "If it doesn't work, we can just keep on going and set up for the next idea."

Bobby turned the aircraft back toward the camp and began a landing profile. "Get ready with that circuit breaker on my call, Vegas."

"Standing by," the flight engineer answered, mouth pinched tighter together than a nun's knees.

Bobby descended toward the open patch of field stretching through the dense trees, working the mental math to figure out when to call for the breaker. "You ready to run the transition faster than ever, Face?"

"I was born ready."

"All righty then, Vegas, push it…in— Now!"

Bobby's hands raced over his controls and displays and the engines began to rotate. The sound of the gears moving broke the relative silence of the aircraft.

"Music to my ears." Bobby lined up on the landing area while the aircraft slowed.

"Full transition, ready to land," Vegas prompted.

Pop. The overheated breaker exploded this time, but it had held long enough to get the rotors pointed upward again, thank God.

Bobby exhaled. Hell, even he'd been tense and

he'd surely seen rougher situations in training and combat. He couldn't avoid the reason.

Damned if all he could think about was finding Gracie and kissing his new *friend* until she melted into his arms.

CHAPTER NINE

GRACE MARIE SIGHED her relief as Bobby's hovering aircraft landed with the slight "poof" of flying debris on the runway. The aerobatics of the flight indicated Bobby was the one at the stick. He'd told her Face was riding in the copilot's seat as an instructor. Once Bobby passed all the training and tests, he would be an aircraft commander of his own crew. It seemed strange to envision the six of them splitting up.

Standing by the observation bleachers in the whirlwind stirred by the slowing propellers, she thought of how she'd only known them all a short few weeks nine months ago, and a handful of days now. These were memorable men, pioneers in their test world, strapping themselves into a plane still in the design works, so much unknown.

Every flight was a life-and-death matter to a test crew.

But she couldn't forget the more important part,

the more immediate problem. Her father was in that compound with spies and terrorists.

Her father battled his disease with a fierceness she admired, but she couldn't ignore reality. Her father was bipolar, a lifelong mental illness that required constant medication and monitoring. Without proper maintenance, he could grow overconfident and adjust to smaller doses, lose his edge and delude himself into going off the meds altogether. She'd seen it happen twice and it had been nearly catastrophic. Once he'd become a near hermit, the other time suicidal.

He was too vulnerable in that state to the suggestions of those well-versed in brainwashing.

Already she'd been told her father would be brought out in two days, but she wanted to be there when it happened. She knew how to handle him at his worst. As much as she admired her workmates, she couldn't escape the fear they might hurt her dad to subdue him.

She prayed he was simply hanging out enjoying his test tubes and equations. If not, at least she could ensure he spent a lifetime in a psychiatric prison rather than a penitentiary or, worse yet, receive a lethal injection for treason. She could be his advocate until he was hooked up with a psychiatrist and lawyer.

Everything inside her rebelled at the notion. God. She understood him, thanks to all her training. Which didn't make it hurt any less.

He was her daddy, the same man who'd bought her a skateboard at six—he was all of twenty-four—and they'd ruled the condo parking lot. With all his painful mental struggles, he'd worked so damned hard to be a good father.

The CV-22 came to a stop, bringing her back to the present, engines quiet, the hatch door opening and filling with Bobby, silhouetted by a sunset. She couldn't deny the flip-flop in her tummy. She wasn't any more immune to this man now than she'd been before. Sometime soon, she would have to make a decision about whether or not to be with him. Dating?

If he agreed and if she could keep her fluttering nerves under control.

None of which she could finish thinking about, because Bobby strutted toward her with all that lanky, indolent style that made thinking damn near impossible.

She steeled her spine and her will before she jumped in feetfirst without thinking. "Bobby, that wasn't the music I gave you for the exercise. This is about winning over the enemy, not scaring the crap out of them."

"Yeah, but you're not my enemy." Wind whipped dust and leaves around his big, booted feet. "Today's selection brought a smile to the face of all of us who cut our teeth watching *Apocalypse Now,* and dreamed of one day shrugging into the uniform, flying the craft so low it spread the water while that song played."

"You dreamed of that?" She couldn't resist edging for a peek into what made Bobby tick. He seemed so antiestablishment she often wondered why he'd chosen a military career.

His wicked smile shone brighter than the setting sun heavy on the horizon. His crew obviously picked up on the mating-dance vibes and steered clear of the two of them, granting a modicum of privacy. "Did you rat me out to the General?" he said, ignoring her question.

"Hell, no." She wasn't a tattletale.

His megawatt grin broadened as the outdoor sensor lights clicked on in the darkening night. "Because he liked it."

Busted. "Apparently he's a big fan of the movie *Apocalypse Now,* too."

"I've always been a lucky bastard."

Lucky? Uh-uh. She suspected he'd done his research. She was learning Bobby sported more of a brain under all that jet-black hair than he led people to believe. "Or you read his bio online."

"Do you expect me to play a freaking lullaby next time?" He'd shifted gears in the conversation so fast the ground rocked under her.

"Not a lullaby per se, but we should keep in mind in *this* situation we're trying to win people over, not scare them spitless."

"Damn." He snapped his fingers, stepping closer. "I guess that rules out any songs alluding to the end of the world and feeling fine."

"Most definitely." Had she brushed her teeth before coming here?

"That's too bad." He'd definitely brushed his or popped in a mint, the peppermint scent filling the scant space between them.

She considered backing away, but with bleachers behind her, she only had about two inches of space and the movement would reveal her vulnerability. "I'll have the new CD for you tomorrow."

"I'll be waiting." He braced a hand past her on the metal seat.

"Not that you intend to use it."

"Now why would you say that?"

"Because you don't take orders well." She admired the rebel in him even as it frustrated her.

His face went as still as the air. No expression, but a definite chill. "I always do my job and I do not break rules."

Her professional instincts told her he fuzzed the lines. "If that's what you want to tell yourself."

His hand fell away from her and he straightened. "Get the hell out of my head, Dr. Lanier."

She blinked back her surprise at yet another quick shift. "I'm not trying to psychoanalyze you."

"The hell you aren't." His face closed, he stepped back in an unmistakable no-trespassing air.

"I'm sorry if you felt I wasn't respecting your boundaries."

A corner of his mouth twitched.

"What?" she asked, indignant.

"There you go getting all prissy again, and somehow that's still sexy." He drummed his fingers against his thigh in his typical constant motion. More predictable than that strangely silent, still second of his.

Grace Marie accepted the normalcy with a regret that unsettled her. "Are you all right? Did everything go okay up there?"

"Yes."

"To which question?"

"Does it matter? I'm here."

Yes, he was there with eyes on fire and an edginess

that had her longing for peppermint kisses and breathing in some of his endless supply of energy. He seemed to have enough spare sparkle to send them both crackling.

And then—

He stepped back, tapping her nose. "Thanks for worrying about me, Gracie."

As he strode away, she couldn't even contradict him with a reminder she was only doing her job. Because, damn him, he was right.

She would have been out here waiting for him regardless.

JIANG RACED through the retreat compound gardens in the early sundown. She had limited time to reach her contact before Rurik would be looking for her.

She hated to go behind his back, but she suspected he might be getting in above his head. No doubt he was keeping secrets from her. She could sense it as she sensed many things. If only he would trust her instincts, they could have so much. Everything.

She understood so much more about the infrastructure of her country. And on a more intrinsic level she understood a deeper rightness. But he had his plans. They all did. Everyone in this place worked for some agency or group—good, bad, silly, selfish, altruistic. No one came here without an agenda. She only wished she and Rurik could be completely honest with each other.

Silken clothes whispering over her skin that already longed for his touch, she rounded the maze path until she located the bench where her contact would have left the contact pouch beneath a bench. She sat as if to meditate, her hands clutching the edges…feeling…searching…until yes, there it was.

Covertly, she placed her disk of information in place and finished her meditation in case anyone watched, all the while grieving over the lost time with Rurik. They had such little time alone together she treasured each moment they could steal. Not just for the sex, but to share their dreams for her country.

Rising, she made her way back inside toward the sleeping quarters. Finally, she had a chance to set things right for her slaughtered family killed simply because of their differing political beliefs.

Bitterness seeped through her veins like meditation smoke. Ten-year-olds and babies did not have political beliefs.

Zipping past cookie-cutter generic doors, she finally made it to her room. Ducking inside, she searched—empty. She squelched her disappointment and used the time to set the scene instead, lighting a candle, shedding her clothes and crawling under the covers to wait for him. Her soul, dry and thirsty for love, soaked up all Rurik so generously offered.

Her photo mural on the back of her door stared back at her—a picture of her grinning with her arms wrapped around his waist on his moped, the two of them at target practice. An image of the seedling they'd planted in the gardens here to commemorate their love.

Her head sagged back into her pillow.

She hated the forces that made her lie to him, but in the name of all that was right, she had no choice.

THREE HOURS LATER, Bobby didn't consider himself a coward, so he decided running from Gracie right now was simply prudent. Yeah, that sounded better as he strode through the camp that evening, waiting like the rest of the gang for Gracie's brief inside Rodeo's overlarge cargo plane. They would learn more about their part in her psy-ops side of the mission.

Seeing her there on the runway after he landed felt right. Too right, when he couldn't decide whether to forge ahead with her as friends or cut ties for good.

On the one hand, he saw Rodeo over with his crew doing a postflight walk-around. The guy was perfect for Gracie, levelheaded and a genuinely nice guy that Bobby wanted to slug for even standing beside Gracie.

Not a mature reaction, but there all the same.

On the other hand, he saw Vegas fishing out his cell phone as he did after every flight to call his wife, talk to his kids and try to keep the peace on the home front.

Quite frankly, this way of life sucked monkey for building a family. He would never be home, miss out on eight kajillion milestones, not to mention the hellish pressure on the wife to be all but a single parent.

Wait now. He'd gone from worrying about the F word—friendship—to being spooked over thinking the *M* word—marriage.

He definitely needed to lighten up, another reason to keep his distance, because Gracie so wasn't the "lighten up" type. Anybody with half a brain could see Grace Marie Lanier did not do flings.

Which made his original idea to date her one of his more insane moves.

Ah, but there she was stepping outside of the van with her curves filling out those BDUs in a way that made him long to peel every stitch of her clothes off and find out what sort of lingerie she preferred underneath. Not that it would matter, because if he got her that close to naked, he would be tearing her undies off with his teeth in ten seconds flat.

So what to do?

Then it hit him as *she* returned to the van. She was an adult. She could always say no. Where did he get off thinking the choice was all his? That shrieked of an overblown ego. He might be "nucking futz," as his buds often said, but he had a fairly good sense of himself and his limitations.

Why not go ahead and just talk to the woman?

He dodged and wove through the camp full of aviators and army dudes. Bobby ducked inside the van and pulled up short behind Gracie. "Looking for more music to play on the real flight two days from now when we get your dad and the agent?"

She startled, glanced over her shoulder and grinned. "Any suggestion, since you seem to have such a hotline to the favs of those on the ground?"

"I'm a fan of Sugar Ray's old tune 'Fly.' Light, fun, just what we're looking for in winning over these folks to our side of the fence."

"Good point."

"So? Are you music hunting?" he asked.

"Actually, I'm movie hunting." She flipped through a book full of compact discs. "I thought everyone could use some downtime before the big show, as it were. I can rig a screen with a white sheet."

"The shrink's two cents on making us more effective by some enforced relaxation time?"

"Perhaps." She smiled over her shoulder.

"What kind of movies are you looking through?" he asked, living in fear of some "get in touch with your sensitive side" flick.

"Mostly John Wayne oldies."

"Really?"

"You don't have to look so shocked. It's my job to understand the people I'm slated to work with every bit as much as I need to understand the enemy." She cocked her head to the side. "Am I right that you would enjoy a John Wayne marathon?"

"Almost as much as sex." He pressed for a reaction.

She spluttered, an encouraging reaction. "Okay then, let's hear it for the Duke."

"So we're going to watch movies." He angled his head sideways to read over the DVD titles she was carrying, and yeah, sneaking into her personal space for a body brush across her breasts. "Do you have a seat beside you saved for me?"

"Sure." She answered without hesitation—how

about that? "We'll also roast hot dogs and marsh-mallows."

"How did you find all that over here?"

"There's nothing you can't buy in the wide-open-air market in downtown Cantou." She stared then finally said, "You're a classic-movie buff, then."

Face facts, bud, if he wanted to get up close and personal with the woman, he had to play by the chick rules and offer up a piece of himself. "Old war movies played a big role in my childhood." He fidgeted from foot to foot, more restless than usual and wondering why he'd let himself get sucked into this subject when there were other ones that would have sufficed. "My mother wasn't the superattentive type and I didn't live in a playground kind of neigh-borhood. If I went outside I would likely get shot, beat up, raped or roped into selling drugs. John Wayne flicks seemed like a safer alternative."

She stayed silent for a minute—thank you, God—and she didn't even try to pat his back in some solic-itous pity-party fashion. Then she asked, "Which was your favorite movie?"

Not what he'd expected her to say, but exactly what he'd needed to hear after being stupid enough to bare a piece of his fucked-up past. "You'll laugh."

"I promise. I won't laugh."

"It's a tie between *She Wore a Yellow Ribbon* and *The Quiet Man*."

Her whole body softened. He knew that was a nebulous kind of description and probably borderline sensitive enough to get *him* beat up in a bar fight, but he could swear she went mushy-sweet.

Her soft smile shone. "You're a closet romantic."

"Shh!" He played along, even as he ached to keep her like this. Approachable. "Don't out me or I'll have to do something really macho like fling you over my shoulder and take you behind that tree and kiss you like you're Maureen O'Hara drooling over the Duke."

"No outing. I think it's sweet."

"Shit." Can't have her thinking he's got too much estrogen pumping through him. "It wasn't just the John Wayne military flicks, either. I watched all the Jimmy Stewarts and Audie Murphys. You get the idea. There was so much order in their world and the power to make things right. I wanted that and was determined to get it."

"You had a mission young. That's amazing and admirable," she acknowledged.

"Why, thank you kindly, ma'am," he said with his best John Wayne imitation, then shifted back to Bobby. "I figured I would enlist right out of high school. There certainly wasn't any money in my family for college, even when I went to live with my grandma. She did have a playground, though, and man I loved to fly on the swings."

Things went quiet between them. The camp buzzed with activity—MREs scenting the air along with the sounds of showers and all-around breeze shooting. Gracie just waited for him to continue. He'd never met a woman who could let five seconds go by without having to fill it with *something*. He appreciated the chance to sift through his ten kajillion thoughts and pick the one he wanted to focus on and tell her.

"Anyhow, I expected to enlist and work through the G.I. Bill. My high-school grades were decent, but they weren't through the roof. This ADHD brain of mine wasn't quite so in control during those days."

"You're in control now?" She clutched the DVDs to her luscious chest.

So much for his silence theory. "Do you want to hear this story or not?"

"Do."

He tapped her mouth and the softness made up for—what was it that torqued him off? He couldn't remember anymore, not with her lush lips under his touch.

"Then shush, Dr. Gracie." He lingered on her lips a second, two, three longer, then continued. "In one of those flukes of fate that makes you realize there really is a God, my high-school counselor heard about this scholarship. It was kinda bizarre, offered by an Air Force Officer who'd grown up in the inner city—L.A., I think. Anyhow, he was some supergenius whose grades and ACT score got him into an Ivy League school. He then decided to donate funds and set up a foundation for underprivileged dudes like himself who wanted to attend college."

She went back into Gracie quiet mode, waiting, eyes never wavering from him. He liked that about her, too. Never once did she look away from him while they spoke. So many folks were always too busy checking to see if someone more important might be walking onto the scene. He'd never been much for the ambitious ass-kissers.

"I didn't think I had a chance. My grades really weren't the best in the application, even though I made it to the final-ten cut. This dude, every year, meets with the final ten himself and talks to them. He was a captain then, with odd questions you wouldn't expect, and from that, an amazing man named Lieutenant Colonel Lucas Quade gave somebody like me the chance to go to college. No way in hell could I let him down."

He finished his ramble, surprised it hadn't killed him to share that after all. Now that he thought about it, Lieutenant Colonel Quade deserved to have his story shared. He'd never thought about it that way before, but there weren't enough stand-up men in the world, so it seemed like a civic duty to sing the praises of at least this one.

And he—Bobby—pinched pennies hoping to save enough to set up something similar for some other scared and crazy teen only a hint away from jail, but yearning for the sky.

"Oh, Bobby." She cupped his face in her hands and stretched up on her toes to kiss him. On the lips, closed, but sentimental and hot, and he could even tell she'd already snitched a marshmallow. The taste would turn him on forever, reminding him of sweet Gracie totally concentrating on him.

He wanted more, yet knew better than to press. Because now, he was damn certain that at least once in his life, he would make love with his friend Grace Marie Lanier.

CHAPTER TEN

THE NEXT EVENING, Gracie parked the van in the tiny village of Lipah near their camp. Yesterday's movie night had gone so well at her own camp, they were taking the same concept over to the nearby village. General Renshaw deemed it a goodwill gesture and superior excuse to check out the lay of the land. When she'd packed back in the States, she'd included movies with subtitles on the off chance they would have time for just such an opportunity.

Movies were a universal language, a modern art form that spoke to the masses in the way that sculpture did in the Renaissance, and van Gogh's paintings did at the turn of the century. A lot of power rested in the hands of Spielberg and Scorcese, but in a crazy world with so many disparate views, Grace understood the value of using any tool at her disposal to create a connection. A sense of common ground— that wasn't blowing up under their feet.

She wished she could find that common ground with Bobby. Or her father. Sometimes she feared she didn't share common ground with anyone.

Meanwhile, she needed something to keep herself occupied until the flight tomorrow night to pull out the gone-silent agent. She'd managed to wrangle herself onto the flight roster. It had been humiliating to explain to the General about her father, but once she had, he agreed it would be best if she went along tomorrow to ID the renowned nuclear scientist potentially valuable to the U.S.

She searched the faces of the villagers and not surprisingly found wariness but no open hostility. This village, at least, seemed to support the Cantou presidential candidate the U.S. hoped to see elected in a few more days.

Still she couldn't shake the sense of what if…

All it took was one person. One terrorist, one individual bent on killing other people simply because they wanted chaos to erupt. She searched the crowd again, but there were so many faces and rusted-out vehicles.

Arms slid around her. "No dead cows."

Bobby.

And somehow he'd managed to read her thoughts and fears. "Better yet, no IED cows."

His hands slid to rest on her hips in a major PDA for the troops that had accompanied them to Lipah. And of course to all the locals, which right now consisted of a couple of grubby barefoot boys pushing toy dump trucks through the mud.

"That near brush in Iraq left its mark on me, Bobby. Realistically I understand that when I'm home, I'm safe. But yeah, when a car backfires or I'm driving out my frustrations along a deserted road and I see a dead deer, I remember." She shrugged. "I guess we're all a little postal."

Almost immediately she wanted to recall the words. He'd made it way clear how he felt about her digging around in his head. Had she trod into forbidden territory? Except she'd meant her message wasn't so much about figuring him out, but that she understood him—sometimes, anyway.

Something flickered in his eyes, a... She struggled to put a name to it and could only come up with gratitude.

Gulp.

She'd never even considered until now what it might be like to get into his heart. And wasn't that a scary notion that had her wishing for simpler days when she was a kid playing in the mud or riding skateboards with her dad?

Leaning against the bumper of her souped-up van, Bobby crossed his legs at the ankles, randomly passing out candy bars and small wooden toy animals to kids while he talked. "Hard not to be, after all the shit we've seen."

Her eyes skirted over his crew and her Army comrades standing guard, unobtrusively but right there with them in Lipah, located about twenty miles from their tent camp.

How many of these men and women carried around residual effects from the wars they'd participated in over the years? All of them, most likely. The powers that be only tapped her to help the ones ready to eat a gun.

But what about the people getting by through grit, by gutting out low-level pain from what they'd seen or experienced?

There wasn't enough of her to go around to fix the wounds she saw in so many eyes for that flash of a second when they'd thought the vehicle might be rigged. Or those who wondered if the child taking candy had a bomb strapped to her little chest.

Nobody should have to question those things. It tore her apart and *she* had professional training in dealing with such horrors.

This stank. Plain and simple. And nothing could

be done but to forge ahead, because the enemy would never surrender.

All the more reason for her to take what happiness she could find. A restless man like Bobby would break her heart eventually. She didn't have what it took to keep someone like him interested long-term. But then, while contemplating the horrors of exploding cows, cars, people, she thought perhaps short-term had value as well.

Across the crowd, Rodeo cupped his hands to his mouth and shouted, "Are you ready to fire up tonight's movie, Flipper? Or are we going to stand here all day twiddling our thumbs?"

Nice to think that they'd enjoyed the first movie night enough to be cool about this encore.

She inched away from Bobby. "One John Wayne movie coming up, Rodeo."

As she cranked up the film for the locals—a different show with subtitles—some of the Delta boys served up more hot dogs and marshmallows. Watching Bobby teach a little boy all about roasting marshmallows turned her heart as goopy as the sweet treat swelling on the end of the stick.

Then he sent the little fella over with a marshmallow for her, crispy burned on the outside, just as she liked it. He'd noticed her preferences, sweeter than even a marshmallow. A man who took note that every woman was different…wow.

For a second, she could almost forget that in places like this, even little boys couldn't be trusted.

She needed to have at least a pinch of faith in human nature, trust that this child's innocence was real and would stay so. She took the marshmallow into her mouth all at once, some oozing out the sides. The cherub-cheeked tiny guy giggled at her and she laughed right back while sucking in the yummy treat, all the sweeter because of this child.

Because of hope.

This was the reason she gave up vacations and even put her job at risk so she could serve in the reserves. She reached into her backpack and found a candy bar and a coloring book packaged up with crayons. Such a small thing for a tiny child who would one day be a man. Would he be brought up to hate her country or could the ties be forged for peace? She reminded herself winning over the hearts and minds of enemies took time.

Grace Marie offered the boy his prize. His grubby little fingers grasped it from her cleaner hands with gnawed-to-the-quick nails.

He tore the candy-bar wrapper off with his teeth, his other hand clutching his coloring book fiercely.

He bit the chocolate-covered granola in half, his cheeks puffed from so much food. He could have been any child, from anywhere. A smile curved her lips, making it halfway up her face before—

A scream tore through the camp.

Followed by a masculine shout, hard and loud, authoritative, Bobby in a way she'd never heard before. "Everybody down!"

"MIND IF I sit down?"

Matt felt the heat of Felicia's breath more than he actually heard the whisper of her words. "Why should I mind?"

The university retreat used their lecture auditorium to play movies each night to provide brain breaks for those in need. Felicia nudged the hinged seat down and shuffled into place. Everything about her rustled.

Her sequined purse. Her mass of curls. Her dress— Lord, that woman had a set of legs.

Movie. Eyes front, buddy, and watch the old classic, *Casablanca,* or he would be back in Cold Showersville. He needed to remember his reasons for staying away from her.

Not that she had protested in the least. Once he had broken their kiss, she'd looked as shocked and horrified as he'd felt.

Uh, hey fella, his subconscious nudged, watch the damned movie.

He partook of these flicks not so much because he enjoyed them but because he understood the benefits of letting his mind air out. Besides, Bogey knew sometimes the high road was the only safe path, the one without the ever-tempting Ingrid Bergman. Not that he was drawing any parallels or anything.

Felicia settled her bag on the floor, then hitched her elbows on the armrests, both armrests, which meant he had to touch her or find somewhere else to put his right arm.

She cocked her head toward him and said in the worst stage whisper ever, "Mind if I have some of your popcorn?"

With Felicia around, he had no trouble at all for-getting about work. Most likely not what the board of directors had in mind when they advocated relax-ation.

"Sure." He passed the bucket to her, his whisper considerately low, damn it. "I'm done, anyway."

"No, no," she gasped. "I don't want to take all your popcorn. Besides, it's more fun to share."

He usually had no problem understanding people. Age brought wisdom. Right? Apparently life also brought curve balls, like Felicia.

"Fine." He jammed his hand into the cardboard bucket and grabbed a fistful. Yet, they had to know that with all these adult men and women confined together, pair-ups were bound to happen.

"I didn't want you to feel bad or obligated to sit with me because of what happened between us on your lab table."

"Felicia," he hissed. "Can you keep it down please? I'm not a fan of having everyone know my personal business."

"Sorry."

She pouted damn well, movie lights and shadows flickering across her pixy, pointy and cute features. His ex-wife used to pout and it didn't faze him, because he knew a check would shush her up.

Little Gracie used to pout as well, with her bottom lip out boo-boo style, but hers had more to do with anger over being grounded or sent to time-out. He'd learned to ignore those temperamental displays and she got over them faster.

But this pout. Shit. It tugged at something inside him. He *had* been the one to push her away. Then there was the fact that trusting folks didn't come easily to him in a regular situation, and this place was rife with potential liars.

However, on the chance she was on the up-and-up, he owed her an explanation or apology. Both, most likely.

"I'm sorry for how things turned out earlier. I prefer not to mix business and pleasure."

"I agree." She chomped a mouthful of popcorn, her lips all shiny from the extra butter. "That kiss we shared was most definitely pleasurable."

A buttery-flavored encore sounded mighty tempting. "We're both healthy adults."

"That's exactly the point I'm making. We're attracted to each other. It was inevitable something would happen since we were trying to ignore the feelings. Now that everything's out in the open, it should be easier to control ourselves, right?"

"Of course." Although his libido didn't seem to agree with either of them at the moment and kept hollering for him to kiss all that butter right off her lips.

"We could be anywhere in the world, right? This is such a universal moment enjoyed by people everywhere."

"I imagine so."

She settled deeper into her seat, her legs crossed, foot swinging with her high heel dangling off her toes, her eyes rapt and ahead. Apparently conversation time had ended, her attention totally wrapped up in popcorn and Bogey.

A normal moment that could be experienced anywhere, hadn't she said?

She thought of things he would never consider, a strange notion because he knew that intellectually, while she challenged him, his IQ was higher. How strange to realize he'd never considered folks could have a "people skills" IQ. Something like an EQ— Emotional Quotient—that enabled them to assess situations in a way that far surpassed his ability. What if Bogey's need to release Ingrid really did have more to do with EQ? Sophisticated, emotional intelligence that was altruistic in putting other people's needs first.

Guilt pinched hard as he thought of all the times he ignored others' needs. His EQ stunk. Especially when it came to his daughter. How many times had he simply allowed her to run the house, bring him food, remind him of appointments, because he assured himself his experiments on things like maximizing control-rod production or spent-fuel safety were of world importance?

What could have been more important than letting his kid be a kid? Or at least reassuring her she mattered to him? How long had it been since he called her? Damn. He couldn't remember when. A couple of months, maybe.

And what about Felicia's needs? He figured a woman had to be damn close to him before her emotional needs even crossed his mind. All these thoughts made him feel like crap and left him thinking how self-revelation might need to have him check out his medicine cabinet and adjust some levels before he sank into a serious blue funk.

He forced himself to watch the movie, still unsettled by the thought that other people had the EQ thing figured out while he was struggling like a freshman taking pre-algebra. How odd to realize that other people, not just Felicia, but Grace Marie, too, and even the freaking silver-screen characters understood a big human truth that he'd been missing.

Well, hell, talk about knocking him out of his ivory tower. He may have been the one to pull back, but apparently he wasn't in control of shit around this intriguing woman.

ROLLING OFF of Gracie, Bobby sheathed his knife in his boot.

The scream had been from a woman who'd spilled a boiling pot of supper on her foot. Painful, but not deadly. Yet, the whole village had dropped to their stomachs as if expecting worse. This place was primed for trouble for a reason. Not just PTSD from a few folks, but a whole town of people braced for terror.

He checked out Gracie releasing the two little boys she'd grabbed at the first sounds of trouble. Kneeling, she checked them over with maternal concern, dusting them off.

She even spit on her fingers to clean off a smudge on one boy's cheek and that universal motherly act just about did him in. Not that his mother had ever displayed any concern such as that for him, but he remembered sheepishly ducking his grandma's spit cleans. "Are you all right? I didn't crush a rib or anything, did I?"

Breathless but steady, she shook her head. "I'm fine. The boys, too, I think. Thank you for worrying."

He reached to skim his knuckles across her cheek. "You're going to have a bruise."

"Hey, at least it wasn't an exploding cow."

"Yeah, right." This time.

How many of these people already knew about the local terrorist cell? Had they been threatened? Or were some willing participants?

Regardless, he knew one thing for certain. He didn't care if Gracie had a black belt in every martial art known to mankind, he wasn't letting her out of his sight.

CHAPTER ELEVEN

HEADLIGHTS STREAMING ahead, Grace Marie gripped the media van's steering wheel while Bobby rode along beside her in the passenger's seat. His crew rode in back with a low buzz of conversation that reminded her things were not private here, even though the darkness hinted at an intimacy.

Leading the way, the rest of the Delta boys were traveling in the Humvee—tires repaired now, thank goodness. They would all be back to their tent compound and ready to hit the rack by eleven.

Nerves had hung heavy in the air after the scream for help, but everyone still watched the movie and at least pretended to enjoy the event. Of course she suspected no one could forget that nerve-blistering moment. No doubt about it, this group knew there were rumblings afoot. Some of the terrorist cell members could have even been in the crowd. They had their own forms of psy-ops—methods that usually involved threats and pain.

How could she combat that with cartoon flyers and a few movies?

She knew her job had merit and in the long run worked, while keeping her honor in place. Still, on days like today, she felt a bit like they were David fighting Goliath without even a slingshot.

Then there was the whole attraction to Bobby. She didn't know what she wanted anymore, except that when he'd been covering her body with his after that scream, she'd felt both protected—and weak. Very strange, because she was used to taking care of and protecting people, not the other way around.

Was she really up for a short-term fling with this man? She could so easily fall into something intense. So she'd learned early to count only on herself.

She'd been reassured by psychiatrists that she was not bipolar. She wouldn't spend a week staring at a wall, unable to make herself get out of a chair for more than a trip to the bathroom. She wouldn't seclude herself in a lab for seventy-two hours straight, unable to sleep or unwind.

Still, she feared that a host of other problems might genetically swing her way, and yes, perhaps that was a bit paranoid, a problem in and of itself, but Bobby was just so much man she could totally lose herself in the sheer magnetic essence of him. And more than anything, she feared losing control of herself like her dad.

Also, what if Bobby couldn't be there for her in a crisis? As much as she and her father had managed to forge a relationship, she'd never truly been able to count on him—or anyone—for support. When it came time for a permanent commitment, she needed an equal partnership.

Bobby shifted in his seat, stretching back, foot jiggling while the console illuminated him and the cab in a ghostly green. "Flipper as your call sign, huh? There's got to be a story behind that. Because I can think of a thousand natural puns off your name that would have come to mind first for a call sign."

"Such as?"

"We can get to that later. I don't want to risk pissing you off."

Wise move, bud. "I'll share the story of my call sign. But, in return you have to watch one of my movies and really freaking pay attention."

His twitching boot stilled for a second. "You noticed, huh?"

"The snoring gave you away."

He tutt-tutted. "I knew I should have brought those Breathe Right strips."

She couldn't see any real harm in telling him. The story was embarrassing, but it would give them something else to talk about besides the unshakable attraction between them.

"Okay, you want the whole sordid tale about how I got dubbed Flipper." She kept her eyes forward, on the road, ever aware of him staring at her and the men in back likely listening with avid ears. "I was in this bar up in Norway, and I may have been a little over-served with the local brew. But we were laid-back, having fun on a stopover coming home from a rough stint in Iraq. There were other countries' soldiers there from countries who refused to support U.S. action."

"Shit, Gracie." Bobby straightened. "You're damn lucky to be alive."

"Moot point now. Back to the story. I'm dancing with my buddy Rodeo here and this asshole says, 'Fuck the U.S.A.'"

Silence weighed heavy. Blasphemy like that wasn't unheard of. In fact, they put their lives on the line daily so rude jerk-offs like that around the world would have freedom of speech without fear of their tongues being cut out. But to say that to a woman, even a soldier, damn it, that was crossing a line.

Padre cracked his knuckles. "Bar-fighting words if I ever heard them."

Gracie grinned, tight and deadly—and mischievous? "That's pretty much what I was thinking. I was also thinking how really ugly that fight could get, as wired tight as we all were and world politics in a mess. So, I dredged up all that training I'd received for the best possible way to defuse the situation."

"And that would be how?"

She couldn't stop the full-blown smile at the memory, embarrassing and yet somehow totally the sort of thing long-ago, "Un-Graceful Gracie" dreamed of having the guts to do. "I flipped up my brown T-shirt and flashed them my sports bra and said, 'Fuck this.'"

Laughter exploded throughout the van. Stones started a round of applause. "You are definitely okay—for an Army grunt. I think we'll have to dub you an honorary Air Force Sky God."

Damn, it felt good to embrace that daring side again. What had happened to make her so uptight? The urge to live a little sparked to life inside, quickly fanning to a cracking fire.

"Why thank you." She glanced back quickly to toss him a wink and smile. "As you can imagine the story made the rounds, and flipping up my shirt turned into 'Flipper.' Bottom line, using my brain pulled our asses out of the fire rather than resorting to fists, and that's what my job's all about."

Bobby shook his head slowly. "Pardon me, sugar, but I would say your magnificent rack pulled your asses out of the fire."

Gulp. Awkward-moment alert, with all those guys in the back. Brazen it out. There was no other way. "Magnificent, huh? Sounds like you may be playing some mind games with me yourself, Captain."

Bobby leaned to whisper, and, Lord, he was the best whisperer with those puffs of heated breath against her ear, which made her hormones sit up straight and assert, *Short-term affair works A-okay for us.*

"Those aren't the only games I'd like to be playing with you, Miz Gracie."

RURIK, HIDING in the far corner of the meditation garden, clutched his cell phone. Voice low, he checked in with his contact. "Something is not right. I can feel it. We need to move up the date."

"Explain, please, beyond this feeling." The person on the other end, his connection, would then pass the message up the chain. It was almost impossible to construct the whole network just from speaking to one person. Unless somehow someone infiltrated the very top echelons, there would always be branches of their cell that would survive to fight on with their cause.

It pained him to say the words that would cut short his time with Jiang. He loved her as he had loved no other in his life, but their cause was bigger than love. It had to be.

Their love could be logged in history as they changed the outcome of the election. That would have to be enough.

"Security devices have been sprung left and right of late. Spikes activated on a dirt road rarely used. Minor trip devices snapped, indicating someone's very interested in spending time just outside our boundaries— someone smart enough not to get caught on tape."

"Hmm. I can see your concern. Give me a few days to investigate—"

"I don't believe we have days. I think perhaps we should simply bomb the laboratory now instead of the whole public show. We have everything we need to know and all the supplies stored away," he insisted. "This will warrant news coverage and rid the country of much of its brainpower, who seem to have such 'scruples' about how to use their nuclear knowledge. This is war. We should fight however we can."

The People's Revolutionary Council had all the information—a lead that he had squirreled away for years, the past months more than ever.

"This is not your decision to make. Be patient."

"It is not a matter of patience, but rather one of ensuring we do not miss the opportunity."

He saw Jiang round a sculpted tree, her whispery loose pantsuit caressing her gentle curves with provocative hints. She smiled for him, only him. She would have made a good wife. Biddable, sexy, devoted. She must have slipped responsibilities to be with him now.

Her satiny long hair hung all the way down her back, swishing forward like a curtain when she knelt to snap an overgrown branch on a miniature bonsai.

"I still am not completely convinced," his contact said, "but I will pass your concerns up the chain and get back to you by tomorrow with your orders."

"Thank you." Rurik extended his hand to her as he finished his conversation.

He clutched her fragile bones for their short remaining time. In actuality, he didn't need anyone's permission to carry out his revised plans. Jiang definitely would not agree, which left him no choice but silence.

She slid into his arms in a perfect fit. "Who were you talking to?"

"Regular business, working out details, nothing we need to worry about now." He wrapped her tighter. "What do you say we skip this afternoon's lecture and make love under the trees?"

Her eyes went wide. "Outside? In the open where anyone might find us?"

His body went hard at just the thought, but then he lived his life on the edge. "The risk will make the pleasure all the sweeter."

Her smile matched his as she sank with him onto the mossy green grass beneath the trees. He welcomed the chance to clear his mind of what would have to come soon, because he did not doubt for a second that his instincts were right and he'd been trusted without fail in the past.

Therefore, he figured at most he would have only one more time after this with Jiang. He had to make it count for an eternity.

BOBBY WAVED to the last of his crew to leave the van after an eternally long drive to their camp. He made his way into the back of the vehicle while Gracie restored perfect order to the DVDs and other gear. The interior carried a uniquely sensual mix of the scent of Gracie and popcorn.

Hell, he would never be able to go to a movie

again without getting aroused. He would spend the rest of his crazy life keeping the popcorn bucket strategically placed in his lap in theaters.

He plunked down in a swivel chair in front of a console. "Flipper, huh?"

She glanced over her shoulder, her hands pausing while closing the DVD cabinet. An overhead dome light provided the only illumination, the tinted windows and nighttime casting the rest of the world in pitch-black darkness. Parked at the edge of the camp, he and Gracie were as alone as they'd ever been except for two hours in the jungle with a broken Humvee. His craving for popcorn quadrupled.

What did *she* want? He didn't have an answer for that one, however, he did know she deserved better than a wham-bam-thank-you-ma'am from a guy who'd been a long time without sex.

The tail of her braid, normally tucked up, had snaked loose and brushed between her shoulders. "Are you asking for a 'Flipper' demonstration?"

"I wouldn't say no."

She laughed and went right back to restoring order to her psy-ops van packed with computers, printers, monitors and, yes, the projector. "Bobby, I never thought our paths would cross again until this op came up."

He stretched his legs out in front of him, ankles crossed. "Oh, Miz Gracie, there you thought wrong."

Now didn't that startle her quiet and still.

Slowly, she turned to face him. "Pardon?"

He leaned forward, elbows on his knees. "Do you really believe that little brush-off in Iraq would send me running for good? We have unfinished business. Who knows where it will lead, but we never had the chance to find out. I made damn sure our paths crossed again."

She dropped into another swivel seat beside him, their knees brushing, upping the temp in the van at least ten degrees. "You chose to be a part of this operation?"

"No. I begged." He wanted honesty between them and he wanted her to realize how much she'd haunted his thoughts these past months. "Once I learned you would be a part of this operation, I pleaded my guts out to the original aircraft commander who was slated to fly the mission. I had to buy his whole family tickets into Disney to get him to agree—and he's got seven kids."

"You paid all of that money just to spend time with me again?"

"Yes, ma'am, I did." God, he'd missed talking to

her, and yet, she'd only been a part of his life for a short time before. When he'd first met her, he'd immediately broken things off with his other girlfriend. But it had taken him six weeks to get Gracie to agree to go out with him on those three fateful dates—one in the States and two overseas in Iraq.

She laughed. "I wrangled you on this op so I could finally get you out of my head—and you happened to be the better crew for the job, in my not-so-humble opinion."

"You're kidding, right? You didn't actually set this up?"

She shrugged. "My dad has some connections and I made use of them."

Bobby cursed. "That damn other pilot knew he was off the op and still scammed me out of Disney tickets."

He shook his head, chuckling along with Gracie, unable not to admire the man's ingenuity until finally they both went silent.

She stared into his eyes for an extended second before asking, "Why didn't you just drive up to North Carolina?"

"Whenever I was home at Hurlburt, you were in another country. I saw this as my one and only chance. Well worth the cost of some Disney tickets."

"And risking your tush."

"No risk." He shrugged. "We're just that damn good."

She stayed quiet, staring at him until his boot started bouncing again, which made their knees rub. Crap. He wanted her in his bed, but he still preferred people—Gracie in particular—keep out of his brain. "What?"

"You do have the most interesting way of stringing words together in a fashion that I know wouldn't come out of any other individual's mouth."

Her smile went whimsical and just thinking that word—whimsical—was so un-him he almost fidgeted right out of the van. Except he really wanted to hear the rest of what she had to say.

"If someone relayed the conversation to me, I would know Bobby Ruznick said that."

She'd put that much time into studying and thinking about him as something other than a freak to check out under her psychologist microscope? That sent a heady rush through him.

He reached to take her hand, smoothing his thumb across her wrist. "Don't you find it interesting you know me that well?"

"You're that memorable."

She squeezed his hand and, damn, it was more

erotic than a full nude stretch with any other woman. She embodied subtleties that stroked his exhausted, over-reved soul.

He took her other hand so their eyes had to meet. "I appreciate the compliment but I do believe you overestimate me."

"How about we give that a test run and see how you measure up?"

She couldn't actually mean…she wasn't saying…his brain stuttered over even the fan-fucking-tastic possibility.

Sex?

He held tightly to both her hands and the possibility. "You mean now? You want to have sex now?"

"Sure. Why not?" She leaned closer until she knelt in front of him. "We both want it so much our toenails ache and we obviously haven't forgotten each other, so let's give that wild-monkey sex—as you call it—a chance and see where it leads."

"O-kay. Uh." Way to go with the smooth talk, Romeo. But he wanted her so much even the notion of having her actually initiate the encounter scrambled his brain like Sunday-morning eggs. "I would have liked to give you a more romantic setting. This is a bit, uh, high schoolish, doing it in the back of a vehicle."

"It's adventurous," she insisted. "I would think you would be an outrageous lover."

Ah, hell. She had high expectations going into this. He had the confidence he could come through, but still... He would just have to work all the more. No great hardship. "So you think you have me all figured out, do you, Doc?"

"Somewhat, yes." She nodded, a stray strand from her blond braid slipping free to caress her jaw. "Although you do tend to surprise me occasionally."

He released her hands and stroked upward to her hair, tugging apart her braid, each strand of gold over his hands a sensual experience all its own. "Well then, prepare to be surprised."

CHAPTER TWELVE

GRACE MARIE'S MIND raced with endless possibilities of how Bobby could surprise her, all the while knowing she probably hadn't even come close to whatever this outrageous man might have in mind.

"Stay put." Bobby dropped a quick yet intense kiss on her mouth. "I'll be right back."

As she watched him leap out of the van to collect heaven only knows what, she kept her mouth closed and tipped in her chair. A warm burst of air from outside gusted in along with silence outside. Bobby shocked folks on a regular day. She could only imagine what he would have in store if he worked overtime on the stun effect.

And to think it seemed he planned to put all that creative energy into making love to her. Gulp. She felt a smidge outclassed here given her own limited knowledge. Her past couple of relationships had been satisfying but by no means fireworks-provoking.

Bobby seemed to be the fireworks sort.

She stuffed down her insecurities. This could well be her only chance with Bobby, since who knew what she would face in taking care of her father. How would Bobby feel about her father at his worst? Certainly her last serious relationship had broken up because the rat bastard had made it clear he didn't want her crazy genetics mixing with his.

For nine months, she'd regretted not making love to Bobby, even if their relationship couldn't have gone anywhere. How atypical for her to want a fling. Right now was even a stretch for her, but she wouldn't run from him this time.

She looked around at all the technical equipment, computers, screens and printers. So not a romantic setting, but this was about the two of them.

The front seat had possibilities. And thank goodness for tinted windows and the front windshield cover.

Grace Marie passed the time by taking off her boots. She wore the clunky leather combat gear, comfortable in her own femininity, but they weren't exactly do-me pumps. She wriggled her bare toes. What was he doing outside? And, sheesh, if he didn't get back in here soon, she would get cold feet.

Okay. Not. She'd waited nine months for this moment. She could wait nine minutes if necessary.

The side door slid open again with another burst of muggy air, Bobby's lean and hot form filling the opening, his arms full with a wadded blanket. "Did you lock the doors?"

"Oh, uh, no, I didn't think. Can't think." She risked and admitted, "Because of you, this, what we're finally going to do."

"I like it that you can't think right now. That's a real rush."

He locked the doors. Committed.

Brushing a quick but no less sensual kiss across her lips, he reached to drop the blanket on the bench seat along the back. No cold feet on her part, she watched and waited. The military-issue blanket blossomed open, booty tumbling out.

"I just want you to know I was careful and stealthy about returning to the van. I would never want anything you and I do here to be fodder for gossips, and God knows we guys are the worst gossips."

He won her over so totally with his thoughtfulness her eyes teared up. What a sweet and deep gesture she never would have expected from him.

Hands on her shoulders, he urged her down to sit in the front seat.

"Uh, Bobby, about the front seat?"

"Not the seat. Trust me."

Nudging all the contents to the side in a pile she couldn't quite distinguish in the dim overhead lighting, he spread the blanket along the long center-aisle floor.

At the head of the makeshift bed, he placed two water bottles, both purple. "Kool-Aid added. Manna from the gods."

She giggled. Giggled? She hadn't indulged in the teenage-style giggle, well, ever. But Bobby encouraged uninhibited behavior.

He spread a bounty of crackers, Kool-Aid drinks and a pineapple with his knife beside the fruit. She searched the back seat and found nothing more. Her brow furrowed. She'd almost expected "toys" of some sort, but then Bobby never did anything the way she expected.

Then he knelt and unfurled his finger to place one, two, three condoms beside the bottles.

Three? Hmm… Yum.

He held out a hand to her. Such a simple gesture, but one of commitment to the moment. He was giving her all the power by having her come to him, rather than scooping her up and kissing, stroking away her inhibitions as he undoubtedly could.

She rose, extended her arm and fit her hand in his. Hers wasn't a pampered hand, not with her chewed nails and calluses from working out to keep in shape for her regular job as a profiler for the police department and her reservist position in the Army. She could hold her own in physical training with men in both professions.

But somehow her paler skin and rough hand eclipsed by his much larger one seemed feminine at a time she wanted so much to be one-hundred-percent woman for him.

The heated gleam in his eyes reassured her he found her brown T-shirt and BDU pants as sexy as any slinky, sparkly evening getup. Definitely. Because he was looking at her.

Holy crap, he was already seeing her naked.

She smiled. A laugh bubbling. Because yep, she was already seeing him without his clothes, too, and so it was all okay. And she had a feeling the reality would be even better.

She reached for the hem of her T-shirt and he brushed aside her calloused hands. "No way, lady. I've been dreaming of unveiling you since the first time I saw you."

Having him undress her felt more…well…intimate somehow, especially when she'd expected a more frantic first joining. Slowly, his hands bunched the cotton fabric of her shirt, inching upward ever so slowly, as if he were savoring each patch of revealed skin illuminated by the overhead dome. No outside halogens pierced the tinted windows.

His dark eyes flamed hotter. His knuckles against her flesh burned a path she would feel for hours. Then the shirt was off and over her head. She shook her hair loose, looking at him looking at her. She still wore her bra, pink lace, thank goodness, instead of her sports bra. She'd been ready, just in case....

From the obvious appreciation in his gaze, apparently he was a breast man. Thank goodness again, because her thirty-four-C size sometimes made her feel a bit, uh, "out there." Clothes didn't glide over her. They stretched and outlined, which wasn't exactly how she wanted the world to see her. She was a brainiac, after all.

Sexy felt good right now and somehow Bobby had a way of making her feel beautiful *and* respected.

His hand fell to her waist, the BDU pants buttons. The van was tall enough for her to stand inside, but he had to lean down, which put his mouth conveniently on her shoulder for nips and kisses and more of the same up her oversensitive neck.

She smiled her acquiescence and, before she could blink, the pants were pooling around her bare feet. She kicked them free and stood before him in her pink bra and matching thong, the set see-through-lacy enough for him to view the proof of her true blond status.

She tapped the tab of his flight suit zipper. "Your turn. Or rather *my* turn to torment you."

He spread his arms. She tugged the torso-length zipper down, trailing her other hand behind to feel the tensing of his muscles as she made her way, down, down, down…yes. Right there.

Carefully, she eased the zipper over his boxers-covered erection. Yep, he most definitely wanted her. He shrugged his shoulders to hasten the falling away of his flight suit.

She pushed him to sit on the back bench seat so she could rid him of his boots.

He whistled long and low as he looked down at her. "If I live to be a hundred and eight, I'll never forget how magnificent you look right this instant."

She tossed his boots and socks aside. "I never would have pegged you for a romantic."

He stood and pulled her against him. "I think I may be insulted."

"I didn't mean to. Only to say you seem more the fun-and-games type."

"Lady, ensuring that I bring you to a screaming orgasm is serious business."

Oh my.

And then their underwear was gone. Poof.

Disappeared, thanks to their faster-than-the-speed-of-light hands, and now they were finally, finally, oh yes, thank you, naked. She couldn't writhe hard or fast enough against him.

He lowered her to the blanket and covered her body with his. Skin to skin in the ageless, traditional position. Not acrobatic as she expected, but from the look in his eyes the moment seemed so very intimate. Something she hadn't expected from him, this openness of emotion. Feelings and flesh and a slight slickness of sweat from the warmth as well as the need.

Then, he kissed her.

Gently, a brush across her lips, so slow and sweet her heart squeezed. This wasn't how she'd envisioned being with Bobby, yet it was far more arousing and maybe a little frightening because it was all very…she searched for the right word and could only come up with…

Real.

This was *real.* Bobby took his time to let them find their familiarity in kissing each other, because they had moved rather quickly from a couple of quick gropes in the past to *this.*

She whispered against his mouth, "Slow is sweet and good and sexy—" she traced his lips with the tip of her tongue "—but more would be even better now."

"That's just what I was waiting to hear, because this is all about making sure you're comfortable with what comes next. It's about making this as pleasurable for both of us as possible."

In case they never came together again.

The rogue thought smoked through her brain without warning, threatening to chill the moment. Something she refused to allow.

Her hands slid around to his bare back, muscles bunching under her fingers as she urged him closer. "More would pleasure me much."

He met her mouth open and hungry, the kiss as personal as any she'd ever experienced because of that realness, mumbled words of want and reassurance and worship of how damn hot he found every curve of her body.

Speaking of finding her curves…his hands cupped her breasts in a gentle massage that tingled to her toes. Again he took his time, no bebopping around from body part to body part before she had a chance to fully enjoy that…

Yes, more of that.

His fingers circled and teased the peaking buds until she wanted to scream, stopping only a second short as she realized everyone outside might hear. At least no one knew they were inside.

His mouth replaced his hands, moving from breast to breast while his hands moved down, his finger slickening the dampness and sliding inside. A low moan ripped free from her throat along with the notion that she needed to be a more active partner. She was usually more active than this, but he stole her reason.

She dipped her head to tease his flat round nipples into a hardness echoed by the rigidity she was about to learn more about. Her hand traveled south to test the length of him.

She didn't have enough hand.

Uh-oh. And maybe ouch.

"Trust me." He blew the heated words against her breasts as she stroked the length of him again and again.

"Oh, I trust you. I just don't trust the laws of physics on this one." There was only so much of her and there was so very much of him.

"No worries, lady, we have all night and many ways to bring each other pleasure." He spoke each hot word lower down her body. "Your choice." Pausing, he huffed a breath against the golden curls between her legs. "Your comfort level."

Her knees fell apart as quickly as her concerns.

He pressed a kiss as slow and gentle against her nether lips as he had in their earlier kiss. Taking his time. Drawing out the pleasure and making her yearn for more suckling kisses until she begged.

Something she'd never, never done before but found it in no way demeaning. Rather arousing, because he could make her want more than she'd ever felt or needed before.

"Please," she begged again.

In answer, his mouth grew bolder with the stroke of his tongue parting her lips, seeking, caressing, exploring until she writhed against the blanket suddenly itchy against her oversensitive skin. Her knees clamped against his shoulders, her feet swinging up to rest on his waist. She reached to twine her fingers in his short-shorn hair, holding him in place even though he seemed in no hurry to leave her until she…until she…

Spasms of pure pleasure squeezed through her, arching her back upward, her hands squeezing tighter in his hair relaying her intense need to wring every sensation. She bit her bottom lip to keep from screaming out. Her spine curved upward twice, once more and held with her tightly restrained moan until she finally collapsed back into a muscleless mass on the blanket.

Bobby pressed another of those gentle kisses to her intimately, then to her stomach, easing the dampness from his face before he stretched over her, reaching for a condom.

She tried to string words together—not very successfully. "Wait. I want. Give you." She gasped for breath. "Same. Let me."

"Later. Definitely," he promised while sheathing himself. "Right now with my entire self full of the scent of you, I *have* to be inside you."

Thank goodness, because she felt the same, a bundling mass of nerves tingling from the amazing orgasm and greedy for more.

He braced on his elbows, the head of his penis just touching between her passion-swollen lips. Her treacherous mind chose that second to re-engage and remember the size and feel of him in her hand earlier.

"Shh," he soothed against her ear.

Wild and rowdy Bobby, so focused on this moment she lay amazed again. He eased his way into the clasp of her body—no rush, no push or pain, just a slow and sexy stretch as she accommodated, accepted.

Welcomed.

Eyes open, he stared down into her eyes, connecting emotionally as well as physically, boundaries dropping in a way she never would have expected but embraced all the same. All the intensity she'd seen lassoed inside himself poured into her stroke after stroke after soul-rending thrust.

How could she have been so wrong about him? She'd expected shallow and fun sex without any true connection. The realization of how she'd misjudged him shook her as deeply as the driving force of their bodies rocking together, harder, faster. And, oh, she was going to finish soon, too soon after being so long without the real deal.

He smoothed her hair back from her face. "Shh…it's okay. We'll go again. And again. You can let go now. There's more."

"More," she breathed into his mouth, urging her hips up to roll against his, finding just the right angle to wring…

More.

She arched, the power of so much more searing through her, pulling a gasp, a cry from deep inside her.

He sealed his mouth to hers, swallowing the sounds into himself as she took him inside herself, throbbing, his growl of completion mingling with hers as finally, finally after nine months of waiting, release tore through them both, leaving her shaking in the aftermath, trembling with aftershocks.

He rolled onto his side, gathering her close as they both panted. Hot and oh-so sweet. She would certainly need a few minutes before she could go for more. Right now she could barely breathe, just tingle.

And realize she'd deluded herself. This wasn't a fling. So much more emotion swirled through her than she'd expected, more than she could handle, turmoil that threatened every orderly corner of her life she'd structured in a desperate, driving need to be the opposite of her father.

She was scared, flat-out terrified to wade deeper into these waters with Bobby, that could be beautiful or lead her into a loss of control, a pool of liquid nails if she fell apart. What she'd planned to be a wonderful release to bolster her for the stress of tomorrow's mission had only served to make her all the more shaky.

Now she could only lie in Bobby's arms.

And shiver with the knowledge of time ticking until tomorrow, when she would have to face whatever waited at the end of the flight into the university research center.

NIGHT-VISION GOGGLES heavy over his helmet, Bobby scanned the jungle ahead, looking for trouble.

This was a mission, not a test run. The stakes

were higher, their options limited. Aborting the flight would be far too costly. With only a short time to plan the ingress route and pick a drop zone, things were bound to go, well, not wrong exactly, but not to plan.

Quite frankly, he didn't trust himself as much as usual tonight. Being with Gracie had shaken something loose inside him the night before and he hadn't yet figured out how to realign the crazy-ass parts of himself again.

Beyond the mind-blowing orgasms—and yes, he'd used all three condoms, while adding some inventive other means of release as well—he'd enjoyed sharing the pineapple with her afterward. Okay, Dr. Priss wanted to make sure he'd washed the knife since he killed the snake, because otherwise she wasn't having anything to do with his carved fruit.

They'd laughed together afterward as they lay tangled and sweaty in each other's arms. That was huge for him. So damn intimate it screwed with his head and that wasn't good right now.

Would his risks be the correct ones? Or was he too off-kilter to make the wise decisions? He thought about turning over the controls to Face, but then that posed a problem. Face had prepped to ride copilot and Bobby knew this part of the mission. Sure they could fly for each other, but they would be most effective in the preplanned roles.

Hang tough and keep mind-blowing thoughts of naked, pliant Gracie tucked away.

Tough to do with her sitting in the back with the Delta boys, slated to sneak into the compound and retrieve the secret agent and her father. Once Gracie explained her father's possible emotional meltdown, General Renshaw had agreed they needed the American brain out of there and Gracie could make the positive ID.

Great.

Could this night suck any worse?

How would he keep from worrying about her in there while he tooled around the skies waiting to pick them up and hoping he wouldn't get his butt shot off while waiting?

His edgy crew scouted for what he liked to think of as derailers, events that would derail the plan and make them pull their butts out of the fire. He knew it was coming. No plan ever survived first contact with the enemy. Seemed that he'd had to memorize a quote like that in some military-education class he attended at some point.

"Keep an eye out, boys, my spidey sense is tingling," he said over the interphone.

On cue, a bright light flooded the cockpit from the left side. A voice in the back, Stones, yelled out, "Incoming, break right."

Bobby yanked the plane into a hard turn as a flash passed in front of the windscreen and out of sight. "Simple university retreat, my ass."

No university kept security like that around.

Sandman in the back hollered, "Heads-up, rear gunner. It came from a bunch of rocks by a stream."

Rear gunner Stones responded, "I got the rocks and some hot spots in my goggles. Oh yeah, I can see where the shot came from."

"You are cleared to engage if you have a threat back there, guns," Bobby said from up front.

"Roger that, I have a target. Fucker is reloading an RPG. Engaging."

The minigun on the open rear deck spit flames and 7.62mm rounds into the night, a tail of fire. The sound of the two-thousand-rounds-per-minute minigun always reminded Bobby of the old Bronx cheer. "Target down, pilots. Press on."

Well, that little engagement was a pain in the butt, but not really a plan-changing problem. Just a reminder that things in that compound were every bit as treacherous as they'd suspected.

Bobby paged through screens on his multifunctional displays. "All systems green and still on time, everyone. Get those snake eaters in the back ready to go, Chief. We are about five minutes out of the landing zone."

He glanced over his shoulder and saw the snatch team in the back standing up checking their equipment. Gracie looked so small compared to the badasses they were getting ready to drop off in a jungle clearing.

How in the hell could they let her go with them? Probably thought that they would eventually lose the argument or she would stow away in someone's ammo pouch. He turned his head forward again and got back to business, his mind clear and focused.

Yeah, right.

"Two minutes out. Get ready. Start slowing down. You should see the road at twelve…right— Now! You got it?"

Face leaned forward and peered through his night-vision goggles. "I got the road in the NVGs. Looks clear. You got anything on the infrared?"

"The road is clear. We are in transition." The craft slowed down as the props rose from airplane to helicopter mode. "This is the place."

Shifting the wing rotors from forward to upward, they settled helicopter-style onto the road and slowed the props to lessen the blast on the exiting soldiers.

"Get them out of here, Chief," Bobby said to the crewman responsible for taking care of the troops until they were off the airplane.

He could almost feel the lightening of the craft as he watched them stream out, as Gracie left, and yet he knew that was impossible. Maybe it was some funky woo-hoo sense within him that wanted to send a part of himself with her. She was a trained officer, sure, but this was Special Ops shit beyond her level of expertise. Those Delta dudes had better stick to her like glue.

Both pilots scanned forward of the aircraft while the gunners searched the jungle on either side.

"All clear, sir," Stones said, calm as you please, like always. "You can get us out of here."

The CV-22 lifted off the ground and rose above the jungle, slowly transitioning the rotors to forward flight. Postal punched up their next destination on the MFD. "Come right to two-three-five degrees. Keep your eyes peeled, boys. We have three more landings to make. Hopefully that will mask where we dropped off the team."

He had a job to do. Emotions had no place here. He couldn't think of Gracie inside that compound. He needed to keep his crew and craft safe so they could get her when this mission was complete, because damn it, she was coming out of there alive.

CHAPTER THIRTEEN

NIGHT JUNGLE SOUNDS all around her, Grace Marie stuck close behind the mountainous man in black, her protector on this mission. She was having major doubts about the wisdom of following her heart into this place. No wonder it took years to build those special operators with ice water in their veins.

Her veins were pumping lava-hot fear and she was a seasoned combat vet, yet in a different field. An experience like this made her all the more determined to make the most of her skills to soften the enemy.

The soldier in front of her halted and held up a clenched fist. The signal for stop. She stood as still as the ten others in the wooded area outside the perimeter walls of the compound. Grace Marie gripped her M-4 Carbine so tightly in her bloodless grasp she thought it might snap in half. The soldier worked some kind of electronic magic and a small back gate swung open. She held her breath.

No alarms.

No dogs.

The team leader's arm came down and they began to move again onto the grounds of the campus. They crouched behind service vehicles, altogether forming a circle with everyone facing out from the middle. The point man slipped away toward the set of buildings that intel said held their targets.

Fifteen heart-pounding minutes later, the point man returned from his recon but to Grace Marie it seemed more like fifteen hours.

Finally, the point man slipped back into the circle and whispered into the team leader's ear while gesturing toward a building. The team leader's voice carried through the earbud secured into Gracie's ear. "All righty, we have a way in. No hurry and be smart. Lots of good shadows to work through on the way there. Ma'am," he addressed Grace Marie, "stick tight to Smitty until we call for you to come forward and make the ID."

Grace Marie clicked her talk switch twice to signify she understood.

The group of twelve worked their way over to the door that the point man had managed to finesse open. The team slipped into the building and established a small perimeter near their entrance. The troops pulled out handheld sensors that could see heat—body shapes—through walls and began to search for rooms with people in them.

Each device was interfaced with a small computer that would give information about the target heat source such as height and weight of a target, male or female. The snake eaters had all the cool toys. She would have to mention that to the powers that be once she got out of here.

And she *would* get out of here, damn it, and promptly haul Bobby to the first private place she could locate and let off some steam with screaming sex.

Her microphone clicked, and she heard one of the soldiers reporting that he had found a room with an individual about the right size in the second corridor where earlier reports had said the agent bunked, but there were two people in the room. The team moved to secure the area with the target until they could decide what to do. Damn, they could only take so many people out of here and keep them quiet, under control.

The team leader keyed up his mike. "We have to make a move here soon. We'll have to take our target and whoever else is in there as well. I think we can probably do this with no noise if we move quicklike. I want Miller and Romeo up here with me. We are going to go in fast, put both people on the floor before they know we're there. Fast and quiet and make sure they don't let out so much as a squeak. Tighten up the perimeter, everyone."

Gracie followed her babysitter down the hall and took a knee outside the room with the target. She watched as one of the soldiers picked the lock on the room and nodded to the others. He held up three fingers and got a nod of understanding from the team. He put one hand on the doorknob and held up a clenched fist with the other. Gracie held her breath while the trooper's fingers went up one-two-three. The door flung open and they burst inside. Gracie looked in as a kissing couple came apart and were taken down by the two special operators.

Holy crap!

That was her father kissing a flamboyant woman with their hands shoved up each other's clothes. Her absentminded professor dad was making his way toward a mattress with their target. The spy for the United Nation's IAEA—International Atomic Energy Agency. A woman wearing a skintight red dress and spiky heels that could put out a person's eye.

Well, he *had* been kissing a woman with wild hair and the reddest lipstick Grace Marie had ever seen— also smeared on her dad's collar.

Right now her dad was face-to-face with the carpet, a special operator's knee in his back. Another secured the woman to the ground as well with gags, plastic cuffs and no noise.

These guys were good.

And alert.

She nodded and confirmed. "My father."

At the whisper of her voice, her old man jerked on the floor, then went compliant. She was feeling damn lucky—shocked, but lucky. They weren't going to have to search for her father after all. They could slink right back out. The university would never suspect a military intervention.

Dropped clues would lead those in charge here to assume a late-night walk had gone bad. Big snake and a snack. It happened. Ugh.

Lucky as hell, she thought right up to the minute a door opened up into the corridor at three freaking o'clock in the morning.

Two people walked out into the hall.

Everything went totally still for one extended second before the Delta Boys gagged their latest two "guests." They were immediately dropped to the ground and secured in the same manner, gags, cuffs.

They would have been mighty fortunate to make it back to the meeting point with all the more bodies to manage. One false move from the extra people could draw fire from the reputably good security in this place.

So much for luck.

BOBBY FLEW the CV-22 in seemingly random patterns out over the boonies waiting for the team to report up.

His mind was so firmly on Gracie he didn't even toy around with some of his usual boundary-pushing maneuvers to test out the craft. With the terrain-following system on automatic, the pilots only had to monitor the radar terrain trace in front of the aircraft. They had to make sure the aircraft climbed appropriately to get over the hills and ridges in the area.

But all he could think about was Gracie.

The fear of not ever seeing her trek out of that jungle rocked him so hard he actually stopped moving for about half a minute. He hadn't been that still for that long since getting his clock rung in a bar fight.

The sensation was pretty much the same, and that scared him shitless and unmoving for another thirty seconds. When had this woman become so important to him?

Job. Think of the job. Watch the terrain. Things could go to hell in a heartbeat and he would need to take control and climb over the hills and mountains themselves. Gracie damn well would *not* die because he'd fucked up and not made it back to get her.

In theory, neither pilot should ever have to override the system. It would hold the aircraft right on the set altitude, in this case two hundred feet above ground level, until they turned it off. The team on the ground was supposed to be picked up before they required refueling, but just in case they had an MC-130P Combat Shadow capable of passing them gas on call.

Like now. *Damn it, Gracie, either get out here now or hold off for another ten minutes.*

"Face, we need to get some gas if they don't report up in the next five minutes," Bobby snapped, strung tight. Come on, Gracie, damn it.

"Yeah, I was looking at that and hoping to avoid it." Since that would be a really crappy time for the team, Gracie and "guests" to come out into the clearing. "Get them on the radio and have them head to the air-refueling initial point." Bobby changed from interphone to UHF radio number two and keyed it up. "Shadow four-five, Hornet one-five."

A voice answered him immediately. "Hornet, Shadow, loud and clear."

"Shadow, we will be at the refueling point at zero-three-one-five local, can you accommodate that?"

"We have two navigators and one of them is so old he learned his craft from Magellan. I think we can be on time."

"Magellan?" Bobby chuckled. "Those whacky National Guard guys. Face, give me a climb to seven hundred feet and come left to a heading of one-one-five. That will set us up for a little dog leg to get on track. Crew, we gotta get some fuel so get ready to meet the tanker. If anyone is cooking on a hibachi back there I would appreciate it if you put it out until we finish."

As they approached the tanker, Bobby finished the air refueling checklist and prepared the gas tanks to accept and distribute the gas while maintaining the correct center of gravity.

"Cleared to contact, Face."

Face drove the refueling probe into the basket hanging behind the MC-130 and got a green engage light on the overhead panel.

"Taking gas," Bobby reported.

Face held position behind the tanker until Bobby said, "Three thousand pounds taken, cleared to disconnect."

Face disengaged the toggles holding the two

aircraft together and backed away. "Thanks, Shadow. How much play time do you have left?"

"Shadow has five hours left, Hornet. We're heading back to our orbit. Let us know if you need us again."

"Roger that, Shadow. Thanks."

"Hornet, Snake needs a ride if you can accommodate." Bobby sighed in relief as the call came over the radio signaling that the ground team was ready to be picked up. "Roger that, Snake. Are you out clean?"

"That's affirm, Hornet. We have cleared the area and we are not being followed. Primary pickup point in nine minutes."

"Copy that, Snake. Face, come to heading three-three-zero. Your heading marker is to the pickup point. Looks like we are about four minutes early, so let's take a three-sixty to the left."

Face started a slow turn to the left and continued turning until he was back on a heading to the pickup. "How's that?"

"Pretty close, Face man. Slow down about fifteen knots and we will be right on time."

He had to be.

Bobby guided the craft toward the pickup point, scanning for threats and finding none. He pulled the airplane into a tight turn to align on a dirt road while slowing and transitioning the rotors on the wings to helicopter mode. He settled down onto the road just as the rear gunner identified the team coming out of the jungle. "I got them coming from the rear."

He counted, still not to twelve and still not seeing Gracie. They would have called in an emergency, right? She had to fucking be there. His stomach lining snacked on itself until he counted twelve…and more…too many more.

Face angled forward. "Looks like they picked up four new friends while they were out."

Four? What the hell? Questions later. At least they were out.

The team filed up the rear ramp guiding four re-strained prisoners into seats against the outer wall. They quickly belted them in as Bobby guided the aircraft up and out into the night. He took a precious second to look back and double-check…yes, Gracie. He couldn't afford to let relief stun him, but the explosion of emotion damn near blinded him.

He turned forward just as his radio cued up with a new voice.

"Hornet, you have a bogey at your one o'clock for ten miles," called the radio voice, a woman with a heavy

Jersey accent. "Appears to be a helicopter, five hundred feet moving towards you at a hundred twenty knots."

"Who the hell was that, Face?" Bobby asked. Crap, could this go any worse? Wait. Undoubtedly it could. If ever he needed to tap his boundary-pushing ways, this was it. He also noticed the seasoned instructor, Face, never once suggested taking over, so he must be hanging in there tight, fast and efficient.

Wiser, more experienced, Face shook his head, smile wry. "That, my friend, is the voice of God."

"What do you mean the voice of God?" And God was a female from Jersey? This wasn't a time for bullshitting.

"That's someone who does not want to be identified, or she would have led off with a call sign. Probably spooks of some sort or some sort of intelligence-collecting platform. Let's accept the blessing and turn forty-five right, see if the bogey turns with us. Chief, please get everyone in the back strapped in. We may have company here in a few minutes."

The voice chimed in again. "Hornet, the bogey's turned to intercept you. Now at your three o'clock for six miles."

Bobby gripped the stick and adjusted. "She is a

helpful little voice, isn't she?" Could this be a trap? They had very little evidence to go on. Only two choices and one would get them killed. Sometimes it all came down to instincts. And his gut told him that today, God was a female from Jersey. "Gunners, we have a bogey at three o'clock, six miles. He is tracking us somehow. All I have on the electronic warfare panel is some plain old air-traffic control. Suggest we drop down and see if we can shake those radars."

Face entered a hundred feet into the terrain following and turned farther away from the helicopter and waited for an update from their ghostly friend.

"Hornet, you have another bogey at your twelve for three miles hovering just on the other side of a ridge. Looks like they are driving you into an ambush cap."

"What the hell is happening here? Face, if my map-reading skills are as good as I think they are, then we are going to have to mess with one of these bogeys or fly over an international border." He turned to his pal, a pilot he'd flown with nearly his whole career. They'd pulled each other out of the fire more times than he could count.

Bobby couldn't help but think of the time they'd almost gone down in Iraq with a woman in back, a woman Face had feelings for. Bobby had known that had to be tough, but he hadn't had a damn clue how hellish until now. "Talk to me, my friend. What's your take?"

"Damn, Postal." Voice steady, Face's confidence shone even through the eerie green haze of NVGs. "You're going to do what you do best. Stoke up this baby and drive right past that one over the ridge. We have at least one hundred, maybe a hundred and fifty knots of speed on any traditional helicopter."

Great. A chance to justify all his crazy-ass antics in the aircraft. The payoff would be here. Now.

"What if it has some sort of heat seeker onboard, like a Stinger?" Hell, he already knew the answer. "Gunners, ready up. When we go over this ridge, there is going to be a helicopter waiting on the other side. There aren't any friendlies out there, so if it points at us, shred it."

Three wilcos—will comply—came over the interphone.

The CV-22 crested the ridge and everyone wearing night-vision goggles tried to find the problem on the other side. The bad guy was savvy and knew the area better than they did. The enemy helicopter was a Bell Jet Ranger, rigged up with some sort of machine guns.

The whole explosive encounter reeked of an ambush.

The Jet Ranger fired first, but the flash of his guns gave him away as huge blooms filled Bobby's goggles. Padre and Sandman both swiveled their miniguns and fired at the flashes. It was a matter of whose aim was better.

Here, Bobby firmly placed odds on his crew.

Rat, tat, tat like hail on a car roof, the echoing sound filled the ears of all on board. The enemy guns had made their hit.

But so had the CV-22's miniguns.

A huge flash filled the sky where the tracers from the rear and left gunners intersected, and as suddenly as the hail began, it stopped. Silence mixed with the cordite of the minigun rounds for three heartbeats before Bobby broke the spell. The fight was over. They were still in the air, unlike the enemy, but at what cost?

"Check in, all, with damage report and injuries," Bobby ordered, not even daring to think of silence from Gracie.

CHAPTER FOURTEEN

MATT COULD SAFELY SAY, after a lifetime of Bunsen burners, he'd never envisioned himself riding in the back of a military aircraft gagged and in handcuffs. What the hell was going on? And why was his daughter in the middle of it?

At least now that they were airborne, the soldiers began loosening the gags on the others, while Gracie freed him. Never once did her eyes leave his. He knew the look well. She was checking his state of mind.

Damn.

He knew he had to live with this disease, but he hated those times it made the child become the parent. He did his best to meet her gaze directly, calmly, and reassure her that for now, today, all was well inside his head, even if the outside world was in total chaos.

Once his arms were free, he pulled his daughter in for a hug. His heart did that inexplicable flip-flop thing that never ceased to astound him whenever he held his child. No science could explain it. But the first time he held her squirmy, slimy newborn body, his heart had done that same flip-flop.

Grace Marie could be six or twenty-six and it wouldn't matter. She was his miracle baby girl. Damn, he was proud of her.

The heart action made him remember somebody else who tugged at the edges of his emotions. Over his daughter's shoulder, Matt looked down the length of the craft and saw that yes, Felicia was unharmed. He would have to wait to speak with her though, because it seemed these uniformed fellas had very strong feelings about everyone staying seated.

Including the student Jiang Lee and the security worker Rurik Zazlov. What rotten timing for the two of them to decide to end their late-night rendezvous with a walk outside for snacks or whatever they'd been doing in the hall that late. Not that his and Felicia's midnight stroll followed by a stop into her room had ended as expected, either.

"Daddy, are you okay?"

No child should have to be that worried about the parent. It defied the natural order of things. "Other than being confused as hell as to why we left the compound, yeah, I'm fine. What's going on?"

Her eyes shone with tears and a hint of anger. "You haven't called or e-mailed in over six weeks. I was worried."

"And that leads you to do this?"

Gracie couldn't have possibly set up something of this level simply to lift him out. What explanation did that leave?

"Obviously I couldn't arrange this magnitude of help to get you out. But when I heard things were going squirrelly inside that compound, I was *not* leaving you in there. I simply did my best to wrangle my unit into the operation."

"You never thought to call?" He could tell her nerves were stretched, because she always chewed her nails when edgy, except he couldn't guess her motive. But then, reading people had never been his forte. He usually relied on her instincts where people were concerned. Even at ten, she'd been able to read a person's intent in a heartbeat.

"No calls were being accepted."

Odd. "I'm sorry you were concerned."

"At least you're out of there."

"I didn't particularly want out." His work had value. He couldn't take credit for his brain. His IQ could be considered much like a lottery win, but he felt an obligation to make the most of this strange gift he'd been born with.

"The place is a political snake's nest, Daddy. We had to get you out for your own safety."

His gaze slid down to Felicia again, Jiang and Rurik, too. "What about the safety of everyone else in there?"

"That will be Cantou's issue." Her attention shifted to the rear of the plane where the couple—Jiang and Rurik—were huddled together. "It's better if we discuss more later."

"I understand." As he replayed the events now he realized the couple had stumbled on them, leaving no choice but to bring them along. Therefore, they weren't to be trusted.

Yet he'd been studying, lunching, talking with these people and all the others on a daily basis. What about Felicia? He shuddered to think that if they hadn't been together she would have been left in that "snake's nest" when these big men garbed in black pulled him out. He might not totally trust her, but he couldn't stop the feelings that kicked him in the gut every time her high heels tapped into the room.

Gracie leaned closer, her voice a half whisper even though the drone of the plane engines drowned out most sound. "What about the woman? Is she your girlfriend or something?"

"Felicia? What bearing does she have on all of this?"

"She's the whole reason we went inside in the first place."

Felicia? He thought they'd come for him.

He really didn't like the uneasy feeling itching up his spine. "I'm not following."

"Just as you've been silent for so long, so has she."

"That's a problem because?"

"We had to make sure she hadn't gone to the other side."

Ah, shit, he started to see where she was going with this and he was pretty damn certain he wasn't going to like it. "Care to elaborate?"

"Daddy, Felicia Fratarcan-however-the-hell-you-prounounce-her-name is an agent from the United Nation's IAEA."

He could see her hesitation about revealing any extra information at all. He was damn lucky to have even gotten that much out of her, likely only because Felicia's cover was blown now, anyway.

Felicia. An agent doing her job looking for leaks, and what better place to start than mentally unstable Matthias Lanier.

Damn. He could have sworn his ex had hardened his heart against traitorous women long ago.

"The International Atomic Energy Agency. Well, hell." Not a student. He should have guessed by how much she already seemed to know on the topic. Which brought to mind a question even his lottery-winning IQ couldn't decipher.

What was her agenda for hitting on him? Because damn it, he could not deceive himself that she wanted him for any reason other than outside political manipulation.

BOBBY WAITED out behind the shower stalls for Gracie, certain she could come to him. Sorta certain.

Face had delivered the note for him, which made him feel like some freaking high schooler. But God, he had to see her alone and hold her for just a minute to feel her warm and alive against him after the stress of waiting and waiting and waiting for like a century for her to come back out of that university retreat compound alive.

He would hug her for three minutes, tops. Let her heart do that thump, thump against him and then he would feel it do the skippety bump when he kissed her. That would be it. There didn't need to be more unless she totally agreed.

Except where the hell was she? He was just strung tight after the mission, which was ridiculous since the thing had been an unmitigated success. They should be celebrating. Now. He narrowed his eyes and didn't see any more wildlife around than normal—birds and monkeys up high snoozing, owls hooting.

The moonlight was kind of romantic and, man, was he turning into a sap thicker than the stuff seeping from the tree he leaned against.

His mind raced with images of her tangling with a Sergio II in her shower stall, but sheesh, he couldn't go blasting through all the stalls. He'd never live that one down and Gracie really could protect herself. She was every bit as much a trained professional as he was.

Soooo.

His hand inched down for his knife anyhow. Just 'cause he liked to have it in hand to hack through the brush or peel some fruit if need be.

"Gracie?" he called out, not caring who knew they were hooking up since he was damned worried. He waited for the answer.

Silence.

And dark.

"Grace Marie?"

That should really shake her up since he never

used her full name. He walked deeper into the shadows as the foliage grew thicker.

He strained. Listened with his instincts honed from the streets rather than his ears. And he heard it. A low squeak. Not far away at all, but in the dense trees beyond the shower stalls.

Without another thought, he sprinted ahead, kicking aside brush. Whacking at bramble with his knife and arms, branches scratching at his face. He knew it, even if he didn't feel it. Too focused on Gracie.

No emotion. No room or time or thought for anything but following his instincts as they sucked him into the jungle like a buoy being winched up into a helicopter. Faster his feet carried him, he *would* reach his destination. His eyes adjusted to darkness and found…

Two tangling bodies. Gracie. And a man dressed all in black.

She was holding her own, by God, but he had his hand over her mouth. They rolled and tumbled. Her knee found purchase in his gut, just shy of pay dirt between the man's legs.

Bobby couldn't risk using his knife and possibly hurting Gracie, so he tossed it far away into a tree where it couldn't be snagged by the enemy. Silently.

Stealthily, he stepped forward. Waited for the right moment when the man was on top and…

And pounced.

He grabbed the man and hefted him off Gracie, landing a punch across his jaw, the man's garlic-and -onion breath a gagging stench of evil. The masked man tried to reach for a weapon, but Bobby struck again as Gracie swept her leg under her attacker's sending him flying backward.

He landed on the ground, his head hitting a rock with an ominous crack. He stared up with unblinking, sightless eyes. Bobby checked for a pulse just to be certain…

Dead.

"Gracie," Bobby managed to squeeze out past the lump in his throat, shifting from no emotion to too much.

Way too much on a night when he was already stretched to the max from worrying about her going into that university compound. He couldn't handle this…this…everything. He felt like a five-year-old again at the mercy of his ADHD, unable to handle everything catapulting at him from a thousand directions. Thinking of Gracie dying cut loose the constraints on his control until his brain couldn't contain it all.

Gasping, her cheek bruised, she held out a hand

for him to help haul her to her feet and then she tucked under his arm. "I'm okay. I'm okay," she repeated as if to reassure herself.

He couldn't manage more than, "Good."

"We need to notify the camp in case there are more like him out there."

Damn. He should have thought of that himself. Yet another example of how Gracie screwed with his head and not in a good way. He pulled her into his arms—hard, no control—and knew he was probably bruising her ribs and he couldn't stop himself. It felt so freaking clichéd, but how could something that felt so good be so very bad for him?

And more importantly, bad for her.

GRACIE TROMPED down the side steps of the C-17 cargo plane General Renshaw had used for a private debrief without their four "captives" from the compound, plus investigating the attack on her. They were being interrogated separately in tents by different officers. There didn't seem to be any other strangers lurking around, but security was tightened all the same.

Exhaustion pulled at her eyes and legs and heart. She wanted to find a bed, or better yet a broad Bobby chest to curl up against and sleep until she had her sea legs back under her again after two life-and-death situations. Then she would speak with her father.

Seeing the levelness in his eyes had been a relief, but she still had no idea what might have come before. She loved her old man so much, but the pain and worry that came with that love, well… Exhaustion tugged harder, heavier.

Yes, she wanted to find Bobby, but first she needed to speak with her dad. The General had given her the okay, and that okay was more like an implied order to see if she could find out anything more. She prayed nothing she heard would put her love for her father at odds with her obligation to her sworn vow to defend her country.

She tapped lightly on the tent flap. "Dad, it's me. Can I come in?"

"Sure, baby girl," her father's voice answered steadily.

She swept aside the green flap and entered to find her father sitting at a small desk. She ran to kneel in front of him and hug hard before inching back. The issue couldn't be avoided any longer.

"Daddy, are you okay? Because if you're in any kind of trouble, tell me now and I can help." She gulped down the fear that it would be something that could compromise her integrity. Worst-case scenario, she could lobby for a hospital.

He cupped her face in his hands. "Baby girl, I'm fine. As fine as I've ever been or can be. I'm sticking to the regimen. Look in my eyes. Deeply. You have a perceptive heart, part of why you're so good at this job of yours you took with the not-so-subtle need to cure your old man. Go ahead and sit in your counselor's chair for a minute if it makes it easier for you."

"Not cure." She placed her hands over his. "Understanding does help."

Their clutched hands fell on his knees. "Well, you can trot a slew of shrinks through here and I'm going to test out fine." He continued to meet her penetrating gaze without flinching. "And you know that in my right mind—hell, even in a wrong mind—I would never betray my country. I assume that's what this is all about."

Tears filled her eyes, the hot, burning kind of extreme relief as his words took hold and made sense. "I told myself that and hoped it was true, but Daddy, you brought up a very pragmatic daughter even before I became a counselor."

"That I did." He squeezed her hands.

She swallowed down the tears, refusing to let her

emotions control her. She shoved to her feet and sat on the edge of his cot. "I wanted to be sure that even in a worst-case scenario, you would be protected."

"Isn't it a father's role to protect his child?" A self-deprecating smile kicked up one side of his face.

"You took care of me and loved me. Love is a give-and-take and give-some-more kind of thing."

"I'm sorry you had to learn so young."

"And I'm glad that I learned." She owed him some peace. He'd truly done the best he could for a man given a heavy load in life.

"You're a better kid than I deserve."

"That's up for debate." She reached her hand out to meet his in their special handshake, two fists thunking, up, down, sideways, up again, then holding. She'd been five when they first started that.

She did love him so much.

Her father, sometimes her playmate and always her friend. "So tell me about this chick you were making out with. Things looked pretty hot and heavy."

Not exactly a high-ranking topic in her personal list of favorite conversations with Dad, but then, she couldn't deny a definite curiosity. He'd never been the kind of man whose head turned easily.

He went silent.

"No kissing and telling, huh? Interesting. Maybe I can get more out of her. I am a master interrogator, you know."

"I imagine it's a waste of breath to tell you to leave well enough alone."

"I did get Mom's stubbornness." The only good thing she'd inherited from the Machiavellian woman. Right now, her mother was sunning in Hawaii off the alimony Matthias had surrendered just to keep his child out of the woman's grasp.

A tap sounded on the tarp door. Since Gracie knew Ms. Fratar-what's-her-name had been cleared by the General, she said, "Ten to one that's her. Maybe I'll pump her for information now."

"And maybe you won't."

Jesus, she hadn't heard that stern a voice since she was a teenager. "Okeydoke, then. You're the parent."

"That's right, baby girl." He rose to his feet. "You'll be the first to know if there's anything *to* know."

He swept open the tent flap, ushering Grace Marie out while waving Ms. What's-her-name inside. Her father's private life had been such hell at times, thanks to her mother, and God knows his illness had brought grief. He deserved whatever happiness he could find and no way did she intend to tamper with that, no matter how curious she might be about the woman in the skintight red dress.

Damn. This woman had a good cover for her spy work, because she looked the least like a secret agent of anyone Grace Marie could envision, but the clothes could be a great disguise. She smiled and made a hasty retreat out of the room, closing the flap behind her.

Grace Marie slumped back against the tent feeling suddenly bereft. She couldn't escape the sense that her dad didn't need her anymore.

Had she allowed his dependence on her to be an excuse not to live her own life? A distinct possibility that any shrink worth her salt would consider.

Her eyes skirted the camp to Bobby's tent, then over to her van full of memories. Privacy was tough to find in this place, but she was darn near as smart as her old man.

Time to think about herself for a change.

FELICIA STOOD in the middle of Matt's private tent, wondering what he thought of her. Completing her debrief had been interminably long when all she wanted was to find Matt and pray the coldness of betrayal had left his eyes.

Best to cut right to the chase. "I couldn't tell you."

He finished securing the tent flap closed. "I realize that."

She twisted her hands together and waited for him to face her. Perhaps then she could read his eyes and know what to say next. She had training in communication and winning people over, yet all the knowledge felt jumbled inside her right now

Finally, he turned toward her, his face totally inscrutable, and cold, so very cold. "So you're with the IAEA."

"Yes." Keep the answers simple until she could determine his stance.

He stepped deeper into the tent, closer to her. "Your making contact with me was to ensure I hadn't turned to the other side."

"Yes again. I had to consider that possibility with everyone in the retreat."

"Did you kiss everyone in the retreat?"

Ah, he was hurt, too. She hated that even as relief surged through her. "No. Only you slipped past my defenses and wrecked all my professional training with a single absentminded smile."

"So you say. Or perhaps you were most concerned about me being susceptible to traitorous suggestion because you're well aware of my psychological history."

"What makes you think I knew about that?"

He raised an eyebrow. "I expect honesty from you, damn it, or you can take your pretty little ass and Cha-Cha Red lipstick right out that door."

She bristled at his tone and word choice, but then one of those Catholic school nuns, maybe Sister Magdalena Gail, told her the man had reason to doubt, reason to feel betrayed. "Okay, I knew. But I'm also smart enough to know we're all a little off in some way. And everyone has a skeleton in their closet. And I, of all people, understand the miraculous capabilities of medicine, so quite frankly, it didn't factor largely into my evaluation of you and your loyalties in the research facility."

He stayed silent, staring into her eyes and making her long to fidget. Matt may well have missed his calling as a CIA interrogator. The man had piercing eyes and patience down to a fine art. Something shifted in his gaze, signifying he'd reached a decision of some sort. Not that he seemed inclined to share. "You're allowed free rein to walk around this compound?"

She shrugged one shoulder, her breasts moving in sync. "Apparently so." She twirled on one spike heel with amazing balance. "Do you like the outfit?"

They'd talked a long time after the movie, about

insignificant things, both passing the time, reluctant to end the evening. So the next night they'd had a glass of wine and a walk. He'd taken her to her door, intent on leaving…then unable to do so.

"I would be a eunuch to say otherwise. Hell, we were three seconds from getting naked when the door burst open."

"Good thing they didn't come three seconds later."

He didn't even crack a smile. He simply stayed still, leaving those last few inches between them. "What do you want from me now?"

"To be your friend. To be more if you're still interested, and I think you are."

"You would be wrong. I don't do friendships or relationships."

"Then why haven't you asked me to leave?" She pushed ahead before he could argue. "That only leaves affairs. Are those taboo as well?"

His eyes widened, but he didn't back away or show her the door. "You sure do get straight to the point."

"You really think we can simply be acquaintances now?" Her body was on fire simply from sharing the same room with him and they hadn't even touched.

"I would hope we can," he answered, surprising the spit out of her. "I would miss very much the talks we've had, even sharing ideas and theories about our work."

"That sounds a lot like friendship to me. Perhaps you've been deluding yourself in spite of that lofty IQ of yours." Still, she had to press. "And what about the times we don't talk?"

"This isn't the time or place for that, there are guards only a few feet away."

"There is a time and place? Outside the reaches of these military people?"

"Maybe." For the first time he softened his stance, giving her a glimpse of the man she'd known these past months. "I've had a helluva shock today, Felicia, and I need some time to think."

"I can understand that." Even as she wanted to say, to heck with reasonable decisions.

He still didn't move but his green eyes took on that sleepy, sexy look that made her wobble on her heels.

"But I promise you'll be the first to know what I decide."

CHAPTER FIFTEEN

BOBBY COMPLETED his brief with General Renshaw and the rest of the investigative team with about two ounces of energy left. After the near misses in flight and the hell of watching Gracie stride into harm's way, well, he was officially done for the day.

He wanted to track down Gracie, check on her. Nothing more. He was committed to keeping his distance until he sorted out his head. God, he wanted to sleep. Just as he rarely stayed still, he liked white-noise-like jungle noise around him when he slept. Maybe a by-product of growing up in the city. If he could hear things, he knew what was going on.

The silences were often more fearsome because they usually foretold a surprise of some sort.

What was he doing thinking about that? He didn't want to remember those days. He was all about the here and now, no whining about the past. And right now, after those close calls in the air and her dangerous foray into the university retreat and outside their military compound, he wanted his eyes full of Gracie.

Striding through the tent camp full of snores of sleeping soldiers and crew members, Bobby damn near stumbled over Vegas sitting at the base of a tree with his cell phone clutched in his fist. The flight engineer simply stared at the portable phone. Not talking. Not moving.

Damn.

Didn't look like Vegas's last call home had gone well.

Bobby wanted to walk past and see Gracie, whose tent was only ten or so yards away, but hell's bells, he couldn't leave a crew member in turmoil like this. "Dude, you okay?"

"Does it look like I'm okay?" Vegas said softly, leaving off the "sir," which showed just how upset the man must be if he forgot.

"Guess not." Bobby crouched down beside him, pulled out his knife and started carving on a stray thick stick while waiting for the guy to spill all. And waited. How could anybody sit still for that long?

Halfway through carving a bird, Bobby figured the guy might need some prodding. "Something I can do for you?"

"Yeah." Vegas finally looked up and stuffed the cell phone in his pocket. "You can loan me your truck when we get home."

"Uh, sure." Bobby shaved the knife along the progressively smooth hunk of wood for another thirteen swipes. "Mind if I ask why?"

Finally, Vegas looked up from between his knees, his eyes expressionless, almost dead. "I need to move my crap out of my house on base by the end of the month."

Damn. He was afraid of that. Shane O'Riley's family troubles were common knowledge. Ten to eleven months on the road wreaked hell on any marriage. It was tough to pick sides, because the whole situation sucked for everyone.

"Sherry packed up the kids and left. I can't stay in base housing if I don't have a family."

Bobby wanted to offer hope for Vegas and, yeah, maybe for himself as well because he couldn't ignore these mixed-up feelings for Gracie. How could a woman kick a guy like Vegas to the curb when he had all the steady, stable qualities Bobby always figured went over big with the ladies? If Vegas couldn't make it work, then what did that say for Bobby's chances?

Suddenly way too invested in Vegas's marriage, Bobby searched for options. Solutions. There had to be something. "Hey, listen, you two have been through rough patches before. You'll go home, buy her flowers and some candy, romance her."

Steady guys knew how to keep their focus together long enough to make the big gestures.

"Not this time."

Bobby opted for a suggestion that even gave him the hives. "Have you considered marriage counseling?"

"Already tried it. No luck." Vegas shook his head.

The flight engineer, so competent at keeping the CV-22 running smoothly, looked totally lost now. "Divorce papers are already in the works. This has actually been a long time coming. She was just staying in the house while I was gone to save money so we could afford this move."

Flowers and candy definitely seemed like a lost cause if even counseling hadn't helped. How did one work CPR on a marriage sunk deep into code-red mode?

Bobby clapped him on the back, pretty damn sure he was the worst guy in the camp to be offering advice. "Dude, I am more sorry than I can say. Maybe we can get the squadron commander to work the schedules so your stateside time coincides with your kids' vacations."

"The kids aren't mine."

Huh? "What?"

Vegas shook his head. "They were adopted during her first marriage. Even though we married when the girls were one and three, I've got no legal rights to two amazing kids I've brought up as my own for the past seven years. The best I can hope for are whatever scraps Sherry chooses to throw my way to see my girls."

Vegas's head thunked back against the tree trunk. "Man, Sherry's fucking ripping my heart out with this."

Bobby's chest went tight with sympathy as he sheathed his knife back in his boot. He could see both sides of the hellish story. Shane O'Riley's wife was under intense pressure, not only taking care of the kids alone most of the time but also worrying about the man she loved until that love dimmed.

Bobby rested his elbows on his knees, bird carving cradled in his hands. Just what he needed. Another reminder why he shouldn't dig in any deeper with Gracie. As a Reservist, she understood his world well, but with their two jobs—hell, three if he counted her cop-profiler career as well—would they be destined to a few dates every nine months at best?

He couldn't give up his wings. He owed too much to the Lieutenant Colonel who'd had faith in him. He owed his grandma. And he owed all the people he'd hurt before he'd found his way.

The Air Force was his redemption. Without it, he was nothing, had nothing to offer anyone. Because of his past, he'd never planned on marriage or family.

And his crazy-ass self didn't even know what to do with those very normal dreams. His best bet? Steer clear of temptation, because he would never forgive himself if he hurt Gracie.

LATER THAT NIGHT, Felicia followed Matt along the trail out of the camp with some reservation. He'd said he wanted to continue their conversation away from the camp full of nosy people, and heaven knows she wanted to speak with him as well. Security was better than ever after Gracie's encounter. They had a spark between them beyond friendship. She couldn't bear to think the subterfuge of her job may have cost her a chance with this man.

When he'd said he wanted to see her, she'd spiffed up, sticking with what she'd been wearing when taken—a skintight red dress and spiky heels. Now nerves tap-danced double time. She hadn't done this since her smarmy ex. And sex with him near the end hadn't been all that great.

Even with a full moon overhead and a sky packed

with stars, the jungle canopy blocked most light. She could only hold on to Matt's arm, pick her way through the dark and pray she didn't step on—

Ew.

She'd worked with the International Atomic Energy Agency for over ten years now, much of that time spent in labs or at a desk. She'd only been out in the field twice before and they'd been in far more glamorous settings. Short-terms stints at a conference in eastern Europe and once in Beijing.

But never anything remotely roughing it like now. She didn't even have her ionic hair diffuser and cashmere robe, for heaven's sake. At least she and Matt both had been given the okay to freely roam the compound and beyond.

Relief shuddered through her over the affirmation she'd been right to trust Matt. He hadn't turned to the other side.

And about her job long-term? She'd done her best here, sent detailed reports right up to the time somebody apparently closed down all communications. She just hoped the info she'd given in debrief would be enough to help combat whatever the local terrorist cell had in the works for the upcoming election.

Seeing Jiang and Rurik taken together had stirred

her instincts, and so not in a good way, although their romantic connection couldn't be denied by anybody who spent four seconds watching the way they looked at each other.

Still, she had her suspicions, ones she'd passed on to the powers that be. She could do no more than that now. At least if they *were* undercover for the other side, the couple now was firmly in U.S. control and very much going to stay there until their background checks were complete.

She shivered. "I may be a super secret-agent spy, but I have to admit, trekking much deeper in this jungle gives me the heebie-jeebies."

"How so?" Matt asked, holding firm to her hand as he led her deeper into the dark terrain.

"I'm not much of a fan of snakes, especially the big, fat poisonous or hungry kind. I read this article about a snake trying to eat an alligator. I'm smaller than an alligator."

Matt gave her hand a reassuring squeeze while stepping over a downed, rotting tree that housed God only knows how much vermin life. "You're a helluva lot feistier. I have faith you'd give that snake his walking papers by fighting your way free with those needle-spike heels."

He'd noticed her shoes? Cool.

"Thanks. I think."

"You're most welcome." He continued down the circuitous path farther and farther from the tent camp. "I don't want to sound like an egomaniac, but it's rare for me to find a woman I can talk to who doesn't bore me shitless within ten minutes."

"You should really clean up your language." There, that should pacify Sister Esther Regina, who was still dogging her thoughts.

Matt slowed to a stop. "Clean up my language? See what I mean? There you go, surprising me again. That's not the logical response to what I said."

"What gives you a corner on the market as to what's logical?" She hitched her hands on her hips. "From where I'm standing, my response makes total sense. I'm a woman with tender sensibilities brought up with a Catholic-school education. I prefer that you not curse in my presence, please."

"Do you go around correcting everyone?" He leaned a shoulder against a tree, too far from the camp to see any of the tents anymore.

"Of course not. That would be rude." She sniffed, then admitted, "Only people I'm, uh, close to."

A smile spread wide over his face. "Now this is getting interesting."

She couldn't miss the sexual intent in his eyes. Had he finally reached his decision where she was concerned? "You barely knew my name last week."

"I lied."

He'd lied? Way cool! Now, back to one subject.

She needed to justify? Yeah, actually she did. "We're both very much adults."

"Are you calling me a COG?"

What? "COG?"

"Creepy Old Guy, one who happens to be losing his hair."

"Not even a chance." The man was so rangy sexy, smart and strong he made her curls spring to life. And she adored the way he trimmed his hair short. No comb-over in sight. Pure masculinity, aging with a grace and wisdom she found so much more enticing than some twenty-five-year-old boy toy.

"So you're attracted to me, secret-agent lady." His dark eyes were almost black, his pupils totally dilated in the dark.

Okay, time to make a move, since he'd taken the risk in bringing her out to this private place to talk. She stepped forward. "Very much so, super smart and sexy guy."

He reached over to pluck an orchid blossom from a bush, the terrain coming more into focus the longer her eyes adjusted to the stars and moonlight filtering through the lush green canopy.

Slowly, he traced her collarbone with the bloom. "I can promise you there are no snakes here."

"How can you be certain?" She shivered with arousal over that simple stroke, almost sexy enough to make her get over that snake fear ASAP.

"I did a little recon, tossed mothballs around, scouted the area, bribed a guard and deemed it as safe as anywhere else we might find even within the camp." He took the flower up the side of her neck, along her jawbone. "I promise no one will bother us."

Help. Her knees were losing strength fast. "Safe enough for what?"

"Safe enough to make out against that very sturdy tree directly behind you."

CHAPTER SIXTEEN

MAKE OUT against the tree? Behind her?

Felicia shivered in anticipation. She'd never made out against a tree. As a matter of fact, she pretty much hadn't done anything adventurous in the sex department, because her ex had been rigid—no pun intended—regarding his ideas about how a wife should act in bed. Apparently his ideas for his mistress had been far more acrobatic.

Right now, she wanted to banish those bad memories. She wanted to be audacious and spontaneous. And yes, she wanted safe. That timid teen couldn't be squelched altogether, and with Matt, she definitely felt safe, admired.

And very, very sexy.

The heat in his eyes left her with no doubts on that front. "So, Ms. Secret-agent-lady. Does the tree interest you?"

She struck a pose, hand on hip. "The man interests me. Anywhere. Anytime. But that tree certainly sounds like a good place to start."

He strode toward her one bold, unhurried step at a time. "And you trust me if we decide we want more than a kiss and a grope this time?"

Wow. He really meant they might go all the way. This was a pretty big leap from an adulthood of nothing but missionary sex that provided less satisfaction than her relationship with her shower massager. Bottom line, she trusted Matt and wanted him very much. "I believe I see that in your eyes already."

"Insightful as well as smart. I like that in a lover."

Lover. Holy guacamole, she was about to take a lover. Yet she could only think how she had darn good taste in men, after all.

He stopped in front of her, meeting chest to chest, not kissing, instead searching her eyes with a deep, penetrating gaze.

Still staring into her eyes, he walked forward, his leg nudging hers to move backward toward the trunk. His other leg moved, and so the dance continued until her back met the tree. A vague scent of bug spray clung to the air, making her smile as she thought of him coming here, planning, imagining.

Hopefully she could live up to those expectations.

Matt lowered his head to nuzzle her neck, whispered against her ear as birds serenaded in the background. "No one will come this way, so we're safe from intruders. But you'll have to be quiet, very quiet."

Already her nerves screamed with want. She whispered back, "That may be quite difficult."

"That's part of the fun," he assured her between kisses, fast nips, longer, deeper ones and back to the skimming, teasing kinds again.

Fun and sex had never been synonymous for her, but she liked the sound of it. The words rode the gentle breeze into her with a long inhale as he inched her dress down farther over her shoulders and cupped her breasts.

She fumbled with his belt, his pants, opening his fly until she had access to…the long, hot length of him. She explored with her fingers, her thumb rolling over the top, up and down. Loving that there were no boundaries in pleasuring each other, savoring the moment. He buried his face deeper into her neck, smothering his groan in her skin.

His hand withdrew from her breast and she whimpered her frustration until he pressed something into her palm. A condom. Of course. She so wanted to be as arousing for him as he was for her, but he had her beat in the sexual experience department. She felt on far more even footing in her secret-agent-lady persona.

And yet, he hadn't voiced a complaint yet.

So, just do it. Put the condom on him. Not that she had to worry about pregnancy. But at least she was smart enough to know that there were other dangers out there. Diseases that she didn't want to discuss now and ruin the moment.

The condom would take care of that. If one of them would just unroll it over the silky hard strength in her hand.

Get to it, girl.

She decided slow and careful would be best and hopefully he would take it as deliberately torturous, rather than inept. His drawn-out moan encouraged her.

His hands slid lower on her hips, to the hem of her short red stretchy dress. "You're going to need to get rid of some clothes, or at least adjust them."

She had to be grateful he wouldn't see some of the scars on her body from her surgeries and so many invasive procedures. She wanted this night to be all about the moonlight and mystery. "Lucky for you, I wore a dress today."

"For me?"

"For me, too. Because I like the look I see in your eyes when you want me."

"This dress worked like a charm."

He bunched the fire-engine red fabric up in his hands until he revealed her panties, a glitter-covered thong that glinted like stars in the moonlight.

"Rip them." She bit his bottom lip and said to hell with what they cost. The payoff would be well worth any price.

"My pleasure." He twisted one string side in his hands and pulled, the cord tightening an arousing pressure against the core of her, taking her close just before the thin strip of fabric snapped.

He swept the thong down and she slid her other leg free, kicking the underwear off. Matt snagged it in midair. He toyed with the panties in his hand in a timeless moment of masculine victory before he pocketed the scrap.

Night air brushed against her exposed and heated flesh. She'd never done anything like this, never expected Matt would be this uninhibited. The excitement sheered through her.

Her tight dress stayed gathered around her waist, giving him free access to stroke her stomach, hips, cup her buttocks while he stayed pressed intimately against her without entering.

"Are you okay?" he asked.

"Totally." She rubbed her cleft against his sheathed penis. "Matt. Now."

"Soon." He continued the gentle friction while he returned his attention to her breasts as well.

"Uh, you know there's not much to find there," she warned.

"There's plenty. Perfect."

He took the hardened peak of her nipple in his mouth and ever so seductively rolled it between his teeth, flicked his tongue over to soothe, adding a gentle suction, then started over again.

She reached up to yank the other shoulder of her dress down, greedy for equal attention.

He growled his appreciation. "I like a woman who knows what she wants."

Her hands ached to learn the feel of him. "I want to touch you, too."

"Feel free."

While he shifted his talented attention to her other breast, she slipped her hands up into his shirt and explored, learning the feel of him. Muscles and man and the slight slick of sweat caused by the heat and *her.*

She reveled in her power over him even as she knew she was totally mush for him. She might not be the most knowledgeable here, but instincts seemed to be working just fine.

Finally, yes, yes, yes, she felt the gentle prodding, the sensually slow thrust as he entered her. His hands slid around to her back, gathering her close. Her hands slipped lower, around and into his khaki pants to cup his taut rear and guide him deeper, harder. She wanted everything from this moment and him.

And he very wonderfully delivered.

Faster and harder, whatever she asked, as well as things she never would have thought to ask for at all. Sweat slicked her body, his, the air around them damp with the perfume of persimmon trees and raw sex.

Resting her more firmly back against the tree, Matt hitched his hands under her knees and lifted until she got the message and hooked her legs around his waist.

Totally opening herself to him.

Ahh. He filled her so deeply she could have sworn he touched her soul again and again with such pleasure as he reached a bundle of nerves up high inside her she'd never known she possessed. Apparently the G-spot notion wasn't bunk after all.

Rational thought shattered—such a rarity for her—as she let herself move and writhe to wring every ounce of pleasure from their coupling. Pressure built inside her as he buried his face in her hair, groaning the most amazing litany in her ear of how perfect she felt.

Perfect.

A word she'd never applied to herself since her imperfect body threw her life into such turmoil at fifteen. She blinked back tears. How silly to cry over one little word.

Especially now as everything inside her clenched, then released in an explosion of sensation that rivaled any reaction she created in a lab. She bit back the shout, since she knew she needed to stay quiet. Gasping for breath as aftershocks rippled through her, she let the tears flow while Matt found his finish with two more powerful strokes that wrung a second orgasm from her.

She kept her face tucked in his shoulder while he nuzzled her hair, stroked her shoulders, soothing her back to earth. The night air cooled around her, distant sounds from the camp filling her ears now that her heart rate had slowed.

As much as she tried to hide her crying jag, brought on by the implosion of emotion, a sniffle must have given her away.

Matt inched back, peering into her eyes as he stopped moving. "Okay?"

"Perfect," she answered with a peace and surety she hadn't felt in over twenty years. Yet what about afterward? She couldn't stop the niggle of fear, wondering if she could trust him beyond taking care of her sexually.

BACK IN HIS TENT, Matt held Felicia against his chest in a perfect fit as they reclined on his cot. A gentle rain tapped on the tent, adding an extra lazy air of intimacy. He wasn't enthused that folks might gossip about them together, but given how they'd been found in a lip lock by the Delta forces in the first place, well…the cat was already out of the bag, so to speak.

There'd been something so interestingly innocent about her lovemaking, he suspected she might need the reassurance of this postcoital cuddling more than some other women he'd known.

He wasn't quite sure exactly what words she needed and since his vocab skills weren't up there with his scientific acumen, he opted for silence while he toyed with her amazing hair, a flower tucked behind her ear. The same orchid he'd first touched her with. The practical scientist had a romantic side, after all.

She wriggled more snugly against his side, her

soft breasts a sweet temptation. "My hair hasn't always been this curly."

Not many women admitted to beauty-parlor enhancements. Where was she going with this? Best to toss some generic statements out there and let her lead the conversation toward whatever it was she needed to tell him.

Matt watched a dark lock loop around his finger, his eyes having adjusted to the dark, since he dared not turn on a light and have the whole camp see their silhouettes. "So you're a beauty-spa chick?"

"Duh." She grinned for a second, before her smile faded to something more sweet-sad. "Not for the curls, though. Those are for real now."

"Now?" An odd statement.

Her gaze fell away from his, her fingers toying with the vee in his polo shirt. "When I was fifteen I was diagnosed with uterine cancer."

What the fuck? That was the last thing he'd expected to hear. "Holy hell, Felicia, I'm so sorry."

She tipped her face up for a quick one of those sweet-sad smiles. "Thank you, but it's okay now. I'm still here, right?" She averted her eyes again as if looking at him made the telling more difficult. "I lost all my hair in chemotherapy. It used to be this supersilky long hair, all the way down my back, kinda swishy."

"That sounds beautiful, too, but no more so than you are now." Damn, he hoped that was the right thing to say.

"After chemo, it grew back in curly. I hated that at first. It was a constant reminder of all I'd lost. I looked different from me—from my family." She sighed a heavy breath over his chest while the rain tapped on. "Now, it's just a part of me, because of what happened. It's who I've become. More tangled. A little twisted and definitely a mess sometimes."

"Twisted mess? I beg to differ. I see an amazingly complex woman who has identified herself beyond the crap life threw her way and has come out a victorious Amazon warrior."

"I'm only five foot one inch."

"No one would ever guess. You're a large personality, lady."

She angled up to kiss him gently. "And you're quite a surprisingly romantic man."

"Whatever." He continued to play with her hair, sensing she had more to say.

"Since we haven't been totally naked together, I guess I should warn you there are some surgical scars."

"Not to diminish their importance, but Felicia, we all have scars. Some are just more visible than others."

"I realize that and I'm okay with it now. It's just that I haven't been with a lot of men, and I know that some—okay, one in particular—found them unpalatable."

Felicia sat up and swung her legs off the edge of the cot, her back to him. "My insides are fried from all the meds and chemo. I can't have kids."

Matt sat as well, beside her, unsure whether she wanted his touch or distance. "I'm so damn sorry."

"I was, too, for a long time, especially when the love of my life eventually took a walk because of that." Her head hung as if she was studying her painted toenails, but he suspected she was seeing the past instead. "Then I figured he must not be the love of my life if it mattered to him, ya know?" She straightened. "So I came up with a new purpose. Family and relationships were not for me. I can make a difference in other ways."

He had to touch her, this woman, so much more amazing than he'd even realized. He slung his arm around her shoulder and wished he could be a more sensitive kind of guy who could offer her the reassurance she deserved and quite probably still needed. "And here you are. You beat it and are still kicking ass."

"By luck, yes, I did." Her pep faded again as she picked at the hem of her dress. "They gave me the option of keeping my ovaries, but I figured they would be so damaged by the radiation, what would it matter?"

He tucked her closer, his chin resting on her head. "Did you have eggs extracted beforehand in case you wanted to go the surrogate route?"

She snuggled closer rather than pull away, so he breathed a sigh of relief that apparently he was treading through this terribly sensitive conversation without hurting her. Yet. He focused all his attention on her to try and be sensitive, something that wasn't second nature to him.

"My parents really wanted me to freeze some un-fertilized eggs. I'm an only child so they figured that would be their lone chance at grandparenthood."

Matt couldn't help but notice they'd been thinking of their wishes, not her needs. "What did you figure?"

"I could see their point and I totally support the notion…but for me?" She shook her head against his chest. "I just couldn't do it. I was at some kind of breaking point, I think. Too much to absorb, too afraid to think of the future when today already seemed in question."

He hooked a knuckle under her chin and tipped her face up. "And yet here you are. Any regrets?"

"I'm thirty-eight now."

"Plenty of women are mothers even later than that."

Her eyes held his. "Having a daddy for the baby is nice, too."

"I have to agree." His hand fell away as the past settled over him like a heavy blanket, tiring to carry around, but not a chance he would ever shrug it off. "The single-parent route is tough as hell."

"And you were so young." Felicia cupped his face in her soft hands, her long painted nails scratching ever so gently, soothingly up into his hairline.

"Grace Marie and I grew up together in some ways. In others, I fear too much pressure was put on her to grow up fast because she felt she had to take care of me." He worked to pull forth the happy memories, because if he let the others creep in too often he wanted to cry for his kid and he couldn't go down that emotional sinkhole.

"Because your wife left?"

"Because I'm bipolar."

She stilled beside him. "Excuse me?"

"I'm what others would call a manic-depressive. I thought you would have read that in my records before heading into the university compound."

"No. I mean, yes, I read your records and there was mention of occasional bouts of depression, but not this."

"Hmm. Guess I need to thank someone higher up for sanitizing my record." Could Grace Marie have had a friend in the FBI or CIA who'd adjusted his records? Possible, knowing his kid was so determined to protect him.

Except right now wasn't about Gracie. This was about Felicia and what they planned to do with the attraction between them. How far could this friendship tangled up with great sex go? "You hear of bipolar disease more in women, but that's thought to be because it's not as often diagnosed in men. We're not so great about going for help."

"Macho ego?" she said perceptively, her hands still massaging along his head soothingly, as if realizing how stressful talking about this was for him.

"I can't speak for other men, but for me, pretty much. They only caught it in me because so much money rode on the projects I was working on at the time, my bosses freaked when my productivity decreased." He couldn't keep the bitterness out of his voice. "Couldn't let their cash cow stumble."

"I never would have guessed." Her hands fell to his shoulders now, more massaging, reassuring, helping in a support he'd never had before.

"I take my meds. Check in with my shrink on a regular basis. But the thing is, there's no cure." He needed for her to understand fully. "I've done my damnedest to keep it under control and function. I had to, for my daughter, since I was solely responsible for her. Luckily, that dawned on me during one of my saner moments when I realized this demon would chew my ass all my life."

Her hands stopped moving and she grasped his shoulders with firm determination. "You're a strong man to have handled this amazingly well and brought up such an awesomely successful daughter."

A blush burned his neck. Sheesh. He didn't deserve praise for doing his job. "Gracie was a low-maintenance kid, pretty much an unbreakable model, ya know? I was lucky."

"Did she graduate early like you?" Felicia seemed to take the hint and shifted the conversation.

"A little early. She's smart, top-of-her-class bright and graduated at sixteen, but not freakland like me, thank God. She did manage to finish up her Ph.D. in psychology early. She's high productivity, but in a good, normal way."

"So you taught her lots?" Felicia prodded like a pit bull, determined to give him credit for a strength Gracie naturally possessed. She would have flourished anywhere.

"She hung around my computer and labs, but we

agreed on one hour of fun dad-and-daughter time each day." He thought back to those happier times and that heavy emotional blanket lost about ten pounds. "We alternated picking the activity."

"I hope there are pictures of the tea-party days."

"Tea party?" He snorted. "Not for my Gracie. More like basketball, carnivals, museums, movies, skateboarding and oh, there was the trampoline she wanted so much."

"You bought it for her?"

"Of course." He had money to burn, so he could buy his kid anything she wanted. Although he tried not to spoil her, it was tough to hold back. During a manic time, the spending could spiral out of control…wait. He wasn't going there today. "I would do anything for that kid to make up for the strange life she got stuck with all because I couldn't keep my pants zipped around a pushy lab assistant."

Felicia stiffened beside him. "Like me, you mean?"

"No, damn it." He held her tight, wanting his point to be strong and clear—and believed. Sometimes that was the toughest part of all. People doubted him because of the disease. He couldn't handle it if Felicia was that type. "I'm not a horny eighteen-year-old who can't see beyond the breasts anymore."

"Thanks." She glanced down at her perfectly pert A cups. "I think."

His hands moved to the stretchy sleeves of her dress and started to inch them aside. "If you don't mind, I would like to see those perfect breasts of yours again, while thinking about all the rest of the perfect parts of you, inside and out."

"God, you must have been the most popular stud in high school—oh, wait, you were only twelve. Ew. Scratch that thought."

"Thanks for the kudos."

She brushed her fingers over his chest, shaking her head. "You really are a freaking genius in places other than the bedroom. When did you finish your studies?"

"I completed my first Ph.D. when I was seventeen."

Felicia was as good at stroking his ego as she was his penis, which she seemed to be very occupied with at the moment.

"I seem to recall you have more than one." She rolled her thumb over the head, smoothing the drop of fluid easing free.

"Three," he said, surprised he could still talk with her hand on him and his hands now cupping her breasts. "It helps me blend the pieces of my studies, although I didn't get the second two until I was in my thirties."

"Why the wait?" Base to tip, she stroked again and again.

"I was busy with other things in my twenties."

"Solving world peace? Fixing the ozone layer?" She stroked faster.

"Bringing up my daughter." He grazed his fingers over Felicia's breast, teasingly. "And I have to confess I do not want to talk about my kid anymore right now."

She paused her stimulating hand job long enough to press a tender kiss to his mouth. "But that's so sweet about your daughter."

His hands dropped back to her waist. "Well, it's the truth, and the way things should be. I wish I could have been this level for her all the time, but it was a while before we realized exactly what meds I needed. Some of the meds now also work better for me."

He gently squeezed her waist and started his trek toward her breasts again. "Do you really want to keep talking about this now? Because if you don't start moving your hand again I think I may just die here."

She glided her fingers up. "Consider the conversation over."

Matt reclined her back against the cot, covering

her with his overheated body, more than ready for more of Felicia.

If only he could turn off those darker, heavier thoughts in the back of his mind reminding him it had been all he could do to hold himself together to bring up a child.

How could he ever guarantee Felicia anything beyond this moment?

CHAPTER SEVENTEEN

GRACE MARIE EXPERIENCED a temporary understanding of Bobby's twitchy boot. Bobby—who had been dodging her.

She suspected he was running scared, the fearless Bobby "Postal" Ruznick. She could see it in his eyes the few times their paths did cross. The fact that the feelings between them unsettled even *him* knocked *her* further off balance.

The two of them were a royal mess, and they both had too much time to ruminate about it.

The camp was in a holding pattern, waiting for the okay from the General to leave. Their part of the exercise was done, right? And then some. So what did he have in the works?

Instead, they were hanging around their tent camp playing "bonding games." Volleyball today, Air Force versus Army.

Damn. Wasn't putting your life on the line with each other a bonding experience?

At any rate, the guys did seem to enjoy the volleyball game. She would probably join in soon, because she couldn't wait to see the look on Bobby's face when she fed him a face ball in an over-the-net spike.

A shadow cast over her as she sat under the banyan tree. She didn't need to ask who it was. The woman's wild curly hair made a helluva shadow.

Grace Marie wanted her dad to have a normal life and relationships. However, she couldn't squelch the protective urge to make sure no one took advantage of him. What did this woman want? Well, Grace Marie felt no guilt over calling to the fore all her psychological training to probe around in this chick's mind to determine her motives.

The woman—Felicia Fratarata-sounds-like-a-Starbucks-drink swung around beside her, MRE pack tucked under her arm. At least she'd changed out of her red dress and darn-near-dangerous heels. Now, Felicia wore baggy BDU pants and a skintight T-shirt. Tough to imagine where she could have found one that small, but apparently this petite woman was determined to show off her assets.

Screw the fact this woman was a highly trained agent—Grace Marie's trust factor inched down.

For shoes, they'd scrounged her up some gym shoes—so small that surely no guy around here would actually claim them as his own for fear of scaring off potential dates.

The IAEA agent asked, "Mind if I sit with you?"

"Not at all." She definitely wanted to get to know this woman better.

Felicia plopped down on the blanket beside her and tore into the MRE, spreading the contents for a chili-and-macaroni meal out in front of her. She shook her water bottle with a powdered lemonade pack and pretty much ignored everything but the crackers. She reached up to unsnag one of her curls from a tree branch.

Grace Marie dug in her pocket and pulled out a hair scrunchie. She kept a couple on hand to ensure she always looked her most sleek in uniform.

The woman smiled. "Thanks. All my hair products are back at the compound and this mane of mine is fast going out of control in this humidity."

"Glad to help," Grace Marie answered.

Felicia nibbled her cracker and pointed to the volleyball match. "These men are so confident. I feel I'm backstroking through testosterone."

She watched Bobby in his shorts and sweat-stained T-shirt dive into the dirt to fish up a ball with as much determination as saving a life. He needed a shave and yet that only made him sexier. After spending more time with him, she now knew he had to shave twice a day if he wanted a clean-faced look. "They are a sexy crowd."

"Sexy? I was thinking overpowering." Felicia gathered up her mop of hair and secured it with the scrunchie into an abundant ponytail.

Overpowering made for an odd choice of word. Never once had Grace Marie felt afraid of Bobby, only of her feelings for him. Her eyes still glued to him, she answered absently, "They spend a lot of time on confidence courses."

"Confidence courses?" Felicia stopped her drink halfway to her mouth. "You're kidding. Aren't you?"

Grace Marie shook her head. "'Fraid not. Think about the things they need to accomplish and then tell me if they might need help in trusting themselves, their training, their instincts without hesitation."

"What goes into one of these confidence courses?" She swiped cracker crumbs from her lap.

"You might have heard it called an obstacle course but what it really does is build confidence. By running through a course of obstacles that require balance, strength and courage they gain confidence in themselves and each other. Say you have a fear of heights and you climb a cargo net to the top of a fifty-foot wall, swing over and descend back down the other side on a rope without killing yourself. That builds confidence. That's why so many of them think they can leap tall buildings in a single bound and all that."

"I've had some experience with survival training in my job, but since we mostly expected me to be a lab geek, I had to go through a crash course for this assignment."

"Then you've certainly got some sense of understanding for what these guys are put through. These Special Ops aviators have all been through not only the month-long regular survival-and-resistance training, but also what *we* call the Varsity Course. *They* call it 'Advanced Beating and Bleeding.' Either way, it's designed to help them learn how to resist if captured. They are finely honed for battle, without a doubt."

"Why would anyone choose to go through so much physical pain? I've been through training and served my country without risking my sanity or physical torture."

"Because of that, I consider my job all the more important, to make sure their humanity isn't damaged. The burdens they carry on their souls are heavy. These soldiers and airmen resent me, fear I'll take away their calling to serve, but in actuality my job makes them able to perform better, longer, healthier. In a nutshell, training their minds for combat is every bit as important as training their bodies."

"How do you keep them from being egomaniacs?"

"Some are."

"Their poor wives."

Grace Marie couldn't agree more and ohmigod, so not a subject she wanted to think about with Bobby on the brain—not to mention his sleek physique glistening with sweat as he threw everything into the game.

Grace Marie tried to explain this nearly inexplicable concept as best she could. "Aren't there personality repercussions in any career? Good and bad. What about a heart surgeon who shoves his hands inside a human being's body and squeezes life back into a heart? Wow. What power."

Mind boggled, Grace Marie shook her head at the magnitude of it all that she tried not to think of too often. It helped her to focus on the vulnerable, human quirks of each person she treated. "Truly, for the most part, they—" she jabbed a finger toward Bobby doing the electric slide while he cheered his point made "—are brave, self-sacrificing men who keep it all in balance by remembering to enjoy life."

"Okay, I see your point, and I even agree, but they're still not my cup of tea."

Felicia didn't think these guys were hot? Sheesh. Even being involved with Bobby, Grace Marie could still shiver a little at the macho factor of his crew members around him. "You're joking, right? That's like saying Godiva chocolates suck—a total sacrilege."

"Some women don't like chocolate."

Not like Godivas? What women?

And as soon as that thought hit her, she realized the shallow nature of her knee-jerk reaction. She couldn't miss Felicia's obvious attraction to Grace Marie's buff but brainy and balding dad. Not all women went for the guys who put themselves on the line physically. Some women thrilled to the genius factor. Which ought to make Grace Marie glad that someone could recognize her father as more than a meal ticket, but how could she be sure she could trust this woman—a globe-trotting sexpot secret agent of all things?

So upon further reflection… "All right, I see where you're coming from now. You'd think with all my training I would have known better. What kind of guy does it for you?"

"I guess in your psychological language of alpha males and beta males, I would be firmly in the camp that prefers the more laid-back betas," she took a deep breath, "like your father."

They *had* been kissing when captured, but in the back of her mind, Grace Marie had wondered if the woman was using her father. Now she wasn't so sure.

That took some serious mind shifting, thinking of her father in a real relationship with a happily ever after of his own. He deserved it, absolutely, but it would take an amazingly strong and unique woman. Did this woman, with her prissy ways and bright red lipstick, have it in her? In some ways her preoccupation with appearance reminded Grace Marie of her mother.

Except her mother *never* would have been a secret agent for an international nuclear agency.

People were complicated. She of all people should know that. Just because Bobby was alpha confident in his job didn't mean he wasn't vulnerable in relationships.

Shocker of all shockers, he was just as scared as she was of all this turmoil roiling between them. She'd seen the wariness in his eyes, but not the fear. Until now.

And wasn't that a liberating thought?

"Excuse me, Felicia," Grace Marie tossed over her shoulder as she shot out of her seat and sprinted toward the makeshift volleyball court as they rotated positions between plays.

She kicked up sand on her way over. "Hey, Bobby, your team looks like it's short a member."

His eyes went wary as she approached. "That it is, Gracie."

She stopped just shy of his sweaty chest. "Mind if I join you?"

Face ambled up, panting hard. "Sweet Jesus, please do. These C-17 dudes and their maintenance guys are kicking our butts and we'll never live it down."

"Bobby?" She cocked her head to the side, perspiration trickling down the back of her neck from more than the heat. "Do you need me?"

Oops. She hadn't meant to ask quite that way and, sheesh, did he ever look panicked, which panicked her as well because that meant things were going deep here.

Time to lighten the mood. "I've got a mean overhand serve."

Sandman swung around in front of her and fell to one knee. "A woman with an overhand serve. I may well be in love."

Taking their positions, the whole team laughed—except for Bobby.

Gracie settled into place, pitched the volleyball

into the air and slammed a clean, unreturnable serve over the net.

Too bad it felt like she'd launched her stomach right along with the ball.

INSIDE HER TENT, Jiang was pleased she'd managed to persuade the guards to let her and Rurik share quarters by insisting they were newlyweds. She unpacked the goods the Americans had given them to set up a room, bedrolls for their cots, pillows and a few extra of those brown packaged meals—MREs?

She'd lit some candles along with turning on the lanterns. Felicia had introduced her to Dr. Lanier's daughter. Grace Marie Lanier was a closet romantic, so easy to read. It hadn't taken much persuasion and a few welled-up tears to get the woman to find her some candles in the camp. Jiang had pretended such sadness over not having time for a honeymoon with her new husband, since now they were being held for questioning.

Rurik had actually sneaked out of the university compound with Jiang a couple of days ago, but not to get married. Rather to pass along the final bits of knowledge Jiang had stolen from Matthias Lanier, information they hoped would help their group be able to build a dirty nuke.

A dirty nuke wasn't a true nuclear explosion, but rather a conventional explosion that spread nuclear waste. Easier to build, less technology needed than for a nuclear bomb. Not as destructive but still grossly fearsome. Especially for its accessibility.

Slipping out had been simple. Rurik had become a security expert for a reason, even though he preferred science labs. He was a practical man. She admired that about him.

Elections were scheduled for four days from now. He needed to maximize the impact. Too close to the election and people would be too stunned for it to make a difference. They needed to give the country a couple of days to feel the impact.

The tent flap swept open and there he was, filling the space with his broad shoulders, his hair damp from a shower, his face freshly shaved, making his dark soul patch on his chin all the more prominent.

Sexy.

Wordlessly, he tugged the flap closed and sealed it tight. She hurried across the small tent, running right to him as he turned with his arms open.

"We have tonight all to ourselves."

She shivered in anticipation. They were nearing the time of making their big move. She just wondered what new plans Rurik had.

Backing her into the room, he shuffled her toward the cot.

His hands skimmed over her body with familiar knowledge, arousal, love, and oh how her parched heart needed affection since the murder of her family, her parents and baby sisters. But with Rurik she'd found a new family, connection, love.

Together, they could avenge the death of their cell comrades, and so many more who had become her new family. People called them terrorists, and she guessed that, yes, they often had to use fear to make people listen, to get their views across. But she preferred to think of herself as a freedom fighter.

Rurik had knowledge and connections she could never find on her own. She relished his strength and power outside the bed as well as in.

He'd made it possible for her to infiltrate the inner sanctum of the university retreat. They had passed so much data on to the new order. North Cantou. South Cantou. She didn't care which side. All she knew was their infighting had killed her family.

She and Rurik had lived under such immense pressure for so long. How amazing to simply be with each other. Even pretending to be married felt wonderful. Her dreams for forever were so close. Although first they would need to see this through somehow. He backed her to the cot, the edge hitting the back of her knees.

Jiang stopped him, too many questions piling up. She couldn't escape the sense he was using sex to delay—or even avoid—talking. "What are we going to do now that we're out of the compound?"

He lowered her to their musty bed, covering his body with hers even as he whispered their new plans. "We will simply adjust our plans and hit another target. Not a problem. Enough information has been sent."

To their cell that an explosive could be built, but how would they be delivered? And where, to make a statement without killing people? Would Rurik be content now to let someone else carry out the final stage?

She was adamant about that. She didn't want to be like the people who had taken out her family. Questions piled up in her head.

Jiang opened her mouth and he placed his fingers over her lips. "Shh. Enough for now."

Of course. They had to be careful of what they said aloud here among these American soldiers. He swore that after this mission he was through. Surely that meant he wanted a regular job and life, his obligation to world peace complete. They could share stories of their escapades with their grandchildren.

She snuggled more fully against him, tension

seeping out her toes. They were lucky to have this small tent to themselves, even with the guard posted. Her Rurik could slip past that paltry security in a simple breath.

What a strong life partner he would make. Never would she be alone, vulnerable again to marauding, abusive troops.

The cut of his muscles, the heat of his body seeped through her silky pants-and-blouse ensemble. She felt him stir against her stomach and knew his thoughts mirrored hers.

Time alone was a gift not to be squandered.

He rubbed his clean-shaven face against her cheek and whispered in her ear, "Let us turn out the lanterns, blow out the candles."

"You are not into voyeurism?"

"You constantly surprise me, little rose. The idea has merits, except I am too greedy to share even shadows of you with anyone."

"How romantic."

"Not at all." His hard face loomed over her, jaw flexing. "I am fierce on this. You will never be with anyone except me."

His possessiveness smoked through her much like the residual scent of candles, yet a tangy scent as well. Stirring and unsettling her all at once.

He, however, appeared totally focused, his eyes and intent clear. They would be making love.

They were able to have sex at will, thanks to her intrauterine device. No worries about making a baby until they were ready and safe.

Jiang dropped to her knees, huffing at the candles one by one, the acrid curls of smoke stinging her eyes and bringing tears. She sniffled.

He reached to shut off the lanterns—one, two, three—submerging the tent in darkness. Sounds from outside magnified, the soldiers standing guard, others using the showers or merely milling about.

She would have to stay very quiet while they made love.

Rurik scooped her up and placed her on the cot before covering her body with his. She accepted him inside, so deep he touched her womb as perfectly as he touched her heart.

They'd spent the past month reinventing the Kama Sutra, yet right now he seemed intent on making sweet, reverent love to her. How strange that it should turn her on more than any of their past intense, sometimes almost violent sex.

She rocked her hips and touched every inch of him, soaking in this special moment, wondering if anything could ever be this perfect again.

Jiang flew apart in his arms like a paper flower, fragile, crackling into thousands of pieces only he could put together again. Except his own release shook so brutally through him, she wondered if the pieces of him mingled with hers.

Rurik shuddered one last time before collapsing on top of her.

He brushed kisses against the side of her face and he stroked along her arms, legs, body during her aftershocks.

Such tenderness.

"I love you, little rose," he mumbled in her ear.

What an odd time to realize he'd never said the words before. She stroked her hands down his muscular, sweat-slicked back. "And I you. Always."

While her hands moved, her mind raced. So many things seemed…off. Yes, off. But her mind couldn't wrap around it all with so much pleasure still pulsing through her body as she slipped into the deep sleep of the replete.

Waking later—how much later, she didn't know, only that it was dark and cold. She stretched under the itchy blanket on her cot, rolling onto her side to look for Rurik on the other cot they'd pushed right up beside hers for a makeshift double bed.

Empty.

Where was he? Her eyes adjusted to the dark and she scanned the small tent, only to find him nowhere in sight. She sat bolt upright, switched on the lantern by her cot and searched, only to find herself alone. Completely. Sounds outside were still much the same as when they'd made love, a slight shuffle of guards.

So where was Rurik? The showers? She waited. And waited. And as the sun rose, she finally had to accept the truth.

Somehow he'd slipped out of the camp. He had left her.

She thought through their lovemaking and her sense of something wrong…something off.

In the clear cold of morning, alone, she realized he had not been celebrating a marriage of their hearts. He had been saying goodbye. Yet since she knew in her soul he loved her, she could only conclude he intended to carry forth their mission anyway.

He still planned to go forth but had not told her. That hurt. They'd been partners in this from the start and now he excluded her. Did he plan to go back into the university compound? But his credibility there would be compromised now.

She thought hard and long about options they'd discussed in the past, and what in the world could he want to blow up out here? There were no buildings that would have deserted wings at night.

Only American soldiers and airmen in tents, with his best method of destruction being the one he'd always sworn to her he would never use.

No. *No, no, no, no.* He couldn't be thinking of blowing up the American camp.

CHAPTER EIGHTEEN

BOBBY PLUNKED his butt down on the bench seat at the dinner table in the rustic mess-hall tent that had been erected yesterday.

For a group of folks who should be heading home soon, it sure seemed they were settling in deep. That happened sometimes in Special Ops. You're led to believe it would only be a little while…. He shook his head. *Little,* like Dumbo the elephant was small.

The troughs of food created a heavy smell in the room, not particularly pleasant when mixed with the body odor of this many people in a hot place with nothing but big-ass fans to stir the air. But hey, for a guy who'd known hunger, he wasn't complaining.

But he would have longer with Gracie. Good or bad? Definitely tempting.

Shoveling a spoonful of scrambled eggs into his mouth, he stared across the table at Rodeo, who forked his eggs and stared back silently. He should say something to the guy, especially since he knew now he had no reason to feel jealous. Except the dude was still giving him that, "Fuck with her heart and I'll cut yours out" look.

What a flipping perfect time for Gracie to show up with the rest of his crew. God, she looked good in the morning.

Silence stretched, unusual. Everyone could simply be tired or tense. He searched for something to say, but just his damn luck, Rodeo put down his utensil first. "Since everyone knows my secret shame about my call sign, what's the story with Postal?"

Ah, shit. What was the guy going for here? Gracie already understood him. Did the fella want to haul out a coffin and hammer some nails in it?

Not that he could stop the conversation. He had to be a good sport or suffer an even larger loss. "Face, why don't you do the honors?"

"We were TDY to Italy," Face said, while slathering grape jam all over his toast. "We'd landed late and there weren't too many places open to eat, just a fancy-schmancy sort of restaurant that included midnight dancing. So half the crew hit vending machines for snacks and crashed for the night. I opted for fancy-schmancy with Vegas."

Vegas glanced up. "No dancing though."

"How can you lie like that?" Face clapped a hand over his heart. "You made an exquisite dance partner. I'm crushed."

Laughter swelled around the table, tension easing for everyone but Bobby.

"Anyhow, there was this dive open across the street from us, so of course our thrifty pal Bobby opted for that. Probably figured he could score some peanuts off the bar." He smacked Bobby's hand reaching for a lone piece of ham on Face's plate. "After we finished up in fancy-schmancy, there's no sign of Bobby. I got a bit concerned, so we stopped in at the dive."

To this day, Bobby hadn't let them know how close a call that night had been. Those Marines had been pissed when he shouldered his way to the bar and gobbled up all the peanuts. But he'd needed to cut corners tight that month, so those peanuts were his protein for supper. Besides, he was used to fighting for food back in his elementary-lunchroom days.

Vegas interjected. "The whole place was full of Marines." His all-American-boy looks scrunched. "Big-ass Marines. Not the kind you mess with, a very stick-together-looking bunch who you wouldn't think would take to a new guy. And yet, they're all buddying up with Bobby."

Finally Face shoved aside his tray, surrendering that damn piece of ham. The least the guy could do if he was gonna pick on him in front of Gracie.

Face leaned his arms on the table, muscles bulging. "Here's the story we got from the Marines. Seems that when he first stepped inside, things were—how shall I put it…" He tapped his forehead then snapped. "Things were a *little tense,* military services' competition and all. A group of about thirty Marines circled him. And Bobby, being the whackjob that he is, pulled out his knife and challenged all thirty of the Marines, psycho style. One Marine at a time or all at once, he didn't care."

Bobby slowly chewed the rubbery ham, all the while watching Gracie's expression across from him.

Face finished, "As luck would have it, they admired his testicular fortitude. Right there and then they made him an honorary, gutsy Marine and paid for all his food and drinks."

Having his drinks paid for had been a lucky bonus he hadn't angled for, but he'd never been the kind of guy to look a gift horse in the mouth. The Marines had been good dudes that night, and for the first time Bobby got a real sense of the military personnel— *people*—he was protecting and saving. Every time he circled an enemy camp and Stones sprayed fire until troops could load up. He'd lost count of how many soldiers, Marines and airmen in distress, that he'd rescued, but he never forgot that night or the human connection.

Gracie smiled like everyone else, but with all the fallout from her mentally ill father, Bobby couldn't help but curse the luck of anything that made him look less than his best in front of Gracie.

Because he wanted to get her naked again?

Yeah, sure, but he couldn't delude himself. He wanted a shot at more, however much more they could work out with their insane schedules. These few days with her were a gift. He didn't intend to fuck them up.

Senior gunner Stones set his tray down as the story finished. "You think his call sign is bad? You should talk to Cheeky."

"Cheeky?" Gracie asked, looking around the room.

"Yeah." Stones shoved half a biscuit in his mouth. "He got his left ass cheek blown off by an IED in Baghdad."

"Ouch." Gracie groaned in sympathy, along with the rest of the table. "How embarrassing to catch shrapnel in the butt."

"Not just shrapnel. He got the whole damn cheek blown off. He wears a prosthetic now."

Gracie's forehead furrowed. "I'm having trouble visualizing—"

Figuring he was already screwed on the sensitivity factor, Bobby cupped his hand and molded it to his backside. "Fits right in his pants."

Gracie blanched, her breakfast tray joining others in the center of the table. "That poor guy."

Face shot his buddy a look that for some reason made Bobby think of when he'd told Face's wife about the same incident. Ah, hell.

He sensed payback time from his pal.

"This one time after a particularly squirrelly mission," Face continued, "a bunch of us got shit-faced and Postal decided it would be cool if we drank beer right out of the prosthetic."

"Run that by me again?" Grace asked. "I couldn't have heard correctly."

Face cupped his hand, this time lifting it to his mouth as if sipping.

Bobby grimaced. Fucking great. "Thanks. Now she'll never kiss this mouth again."

Dr. Priss would probably make him swallow a bottle of Listerine before sex, if he was even lucky enough to get another chance with her.

"Just returning the favor," Face replied, before turning his attention to Gracie. "He told Brigid that story at our wedding reception. I thought it would damn near ruin the honeymoon. I had to gargle before she would let me anywhere near her. Great way to start the romantic getaway, let me tell ya."

Bobby leaned in on his best bud. "Are we even now?"

Face grinned and slapped him on the back. "For this one, anyway. But never forget, my crazy-ass friend, I still owe you for so many more."

Bobby finally risked a look across the table at Gracie, only to find her face pensive rather than disgusted. Suddenly, she shot up from her chair and leaned across the table.

And planted the most unmistakably passionate kiss on his mouth, her hands cupping his face in the biggest PDA he'd ever seen, much less experienced, in his life.

The whole mess hall broke into applause and cheers, mingled with more than a few raucous comments. Not that Gracie seemed to care at all. She finished her kiss in her own sweet time, before pulling back, picking up her meal tray and heading toward the cleaning trough with a tie-ya-in-knots swish of her curvaceous hips.

And in that moment, Bobby lost it, totally.

How could he resist this woman?

GRACE MARIE made her way around tents and trees back to her quarters to grab some paperwork before heading to the van. Three days since the rescue, they were all in a holding pattern until the General gave them the thumbs-up to leave. They still had the election to worry about. They might be needed for extra security.

And yeah, maybe she needed an hour—or ten— to regain her balance after that impulsive kiss in the mess hall. What had she been thinking?

She hadn't, of course. Just acted, because at that moment all reason fell right into those disgusting eggs, leaving her with only a poignant feeling for a man who could make another man feel all right about a mutilating injury.

A few steps shy of her tent she stopped short. Of course Bobby was waiting for her. How he'd gotten here ahead of her—or even guessed where she was headed—she hadn't a clue. But figuring out Bobby Ruznick was a puzzle past even her comprehension.

He crossed his booted feet at the ankles as he lounged out front in a green fold-up yard chair. Where he'd found it she couldn't even imagine. He was the master scrounger, no doubt, but he could have been any guy hanging out on a camping trip getting ready to grill the burgers.

"Hey, Gracie." He smiled the welcome that never

ceased to tickle her stomach. "I'll never understand you, lady."

"Good." She nodded, grateful for at least some edge here with this man who knocked her off balance on a regular basis. "I like it better that way."

"Heartless wench." His face scowl morphed into a confused frown. "So why the kiss?"

She kicked her foot through the dust as she shuffled closer. "I thought the Cheeky story was sweet on so many levels."

"Levels, huh? Figures there would be levels for you when we guys were just getting drunk."

She stopped short of him, tucking his crooked collar down on his flight suit. "You were making Cheeky's injury into a badge of honor in a wonderfully unique guy kind of way. On another level, you were helping everyone shoot off steam in a job that demands more of you than anyone should ever have to give."

Bobby fidgeted, more like a schoolboy than a battle-seasoned aviator. "You're making too much out of a simple incident."

"That's my job. Finding the hidden meaning behind the seemingly insignificant things we do in life."

He stopped shuffling his boots in the dirt and transformed back into sexy, predatory male with a simple shift in his eyes, followed by a sprawl in the green-weave yard chair. "Speaking of quick events that might seem off-the-cuff...what was up with that kiss in the mess hall? I would think after learning I drank out of a guy's prosthetic ass, you wouldn't want any part of kissing me."

"Like I said, what you did was sweet. You're a good man who thinks of others' feelings. Your action touched my heart." And ohmigod this was getting way deep for the middle-of-the-morning bustle in the camp, especially when the guy had been avoiding her. "As for worrying about where your mouth had been, the alcohol in the beer kills off any germs."

He tipped back his head and laughed so loudly heads turned. "That's my Gracie. Practical to the end."

"So to speak," she quipped.

"Huh?" His laughter faded as he rose from the chair.

"To the end. Get the pun? Like his hind *end*." She slapped her leg at her own silly pun, enjoying the lighthearted moment.

Her gaze lifted to meet Bobby's and he wasn't laughing. Instead of humor, his eyes lit with such undisguised desire, she couldn't stop the ripple of want that rolled all the way from the roots of her hair to her feet.

Gracie scrunched her toes inside her shoes. "So why have you been ignoring me, you big dunce?"

"Because you scare the shit out of me."

"Ditto."

His eyes narrowed. "But wise or not, I'm losing the battle."

Her toes relaxed into a long, sensuous stretch. "Ditto again."

Standing, he stepped toward her or maybe she made the first move, but either way they were in each other's arms and doing a tango backward toward her quarters.

Bobby growled, "Anybody in your tent?"

"No. Gone into town to buy souvenirs at the open-air market."

"Two hours at least. Thank God."

Without another thought, she let this sweet, crazy, sexy man nudge her deep inside the tent and away from the rest of the world. Her mind rolled with a thousand other endearing moments with Bobby. She'd been so focused on his outrageousness she'd missed how those memories usually made someone else feel special or diverted trouble from someone weaker.

She didn't delude herself into thinking he was by

any means calm. But who said everyone had to be carbon copies of each other? She knew better than that.

So yeah, she was going to make love to Bobby Ruznick, right now, right here, with everything inside her. She would take what she could and everything he offered, because they would be leaving soon. Then she would face larger decisions.

Huge decisions.

She'd never considered herself a coward, but, me oh my, call her Chicken Little today. Just like nine months ago, she wanted him so much the unrestrained wildness of it scared her.

The difference? This time, scared or not, she wasn't running.

Once Bobby and Gracie ditched their boots, clothes made their way to the floor in a tornado of her camouflage, his flight suit, their socks, along with tossed dog tags and finally her scrunchie, so she could loosen her hair until it teased just below her shoulders.

Wearing only underwear, Bobby sprinkled kisses all over her face. "I can't believe you didn't go all prissy over Cheeky's story."

"Why would you ever think I'm prissy?" she said

with her straightest face possible as she rocked her hips against his.

"Never mind." He kissed her nose and cupped her bottom. "I guess my charm's busy snoozing right now. Although I do feel compelled to mention Sergio the Snake."

"An anomaly." She rubbed her bare foot up and down the back of his calf. *Yum.* "Besides, I couldn't fight that darn snake with my teeth and a bathrobe tie. I am a woman and soldier, but that takes nothing away from my femininity. I serve in the Army Reserves as a female and am damn proud of it."

"Amen, Flipper." He gave her a gentle smack on the bottom, which just happened to be sporting a thong. His eyes widened as much as his smile.

She swatted his fine tush right back. "Okay, to be fair, I am wired a little tight and enjoy my color-coordinated hair scrunchies, but I'm tough."

"Believe me, I know that." His hands gentled up her back, his forehead falling to rest on hers. "You're one of the toughest ladies I've ever met and it turns me inside out until I want you so much I can't fucking see through all the testosterone clouding my eyes."

His words floored her. She wanted to cry and

crawl all over him at the same time. "Wow, your charm woke up."

He clasped her hips and drew her against the erection straining at his boxer shorts. "I do believe another part of me has woken as well."

CHAPTER NINETEEN

INSIDE HER TENT, Bobby held Gracie in his arms and wondered how he could work his way past this woman's amazing mind and persuade her to let him stick around for a while.

Although right now, sex in her tent didn't sound too shabby and, as always, time alone was limited. They made their way toward her cot, only to have her yelp and stop short.

"Ouch!" She reached down and pulled up the bird he'd carved and stuck in his flight suit—apparently forgetting to zip the zipper. "Oh, how beautiful. Where did you find this?"

He scooped up the knife before she stepped on that as well and severed an artery, thereby prematurely ending their encounter. "I made it."

"No kidding? You whittle?"

"Passes the time. We spend a lot of weeks in foreign countries waiting for the world to explode again."

She cradled the simple carving that for some unknown reason she thought was special. "So you have other uses for your knife beside fighting and eating."

"Apparently."

"All those little toys you gave the children were *your* carvings?"

Yeah, but for some reason he couldn't define, he didn't want to admit it.

Gracie continued for him instead. "Again you prove my point. Battles can be won through the mind."

"I'm not an idiot," he answered, not liking this line of conversation because, damn it, Gracie always seemed determined to push him to think about things he would rather leave dormant. "I realize your job plays an important role, but eventually it's about the firepower."

He held up his knife between them, large and lethal. "Hell yeah, you can call it some kind of phallic symbol we guys have some deep-seated macho need to carry. Big knife. Big plane. Big firepower. That's who I am and the reason you wanted to leave in the first place."

Gracie sauntered closer to him again in her black lace bra and thong. She stopped inches away and ran her finger down the length of his blade, the side, not the edge.

All that talk of phallic symbols and her stroke had him throbbing like an oversexed teenager. Holy crap.

"Perhaps I can do more with my mind and with my words, until the size of that knife isn't as important as you seem to think."

Laughter rumbled, tighter than he would like, his balls pulled so close against his body with want he could hardly breathe. "So it all cycles around to size, does it? You women say it doesn't matter, but somehow it creeps into every conversation before you know it—"

"You know this thong I'm wearing?" She angled to whisper against his mouth. "It's edible."

He dropped the knife. The blade nailed into the ground, handle vibrating. "Where the hell did you get those?"

"There's nothing you can't buy in the wide-open-air market in downtown Cantou." She stared at his great big ol' phallic knife on the ground. "Point about the power of the mind made, my mighty warrior."

"You planned?" he asked.

"I hoped," Gracie responded.

She turned toward her cot, giving him a first-class view of her first-class ass.

"Gracie." He knelt to retrieve the blade from the ground. "Wait."

She pivoted toward him, standing like a lush goddess across the tent.

"Come here," he demanded of *his* lush goddess who was about to get a surprise of her own.

Four strides brought her back to him.

Carefully, so very leisurely that she could stop him at any time, he slid the knife's blade beneath the stringy strap of her underwear stretched across her hip—and cut the edible fabric.

"WE MISSED YOU at breakfast." Warily, Felicia sat on the bed behind stone-still Matt, wrapping her arms around his waist and resting her head on his shoulder. "Although given the level of the cuisine, I have to confess you weren't missing much."

No answer.

She could feel the low-down mood radiating off him like mist rolling across one of the Great Lakes. She'd grown up near Lake Huron, and that mist could be so thick you couldn't see your hand in front of your face, much less figure out which direction to walk. Her mind reeled with thoughts of that old Edmund Fitzgerald song about the boat sinking.

What a morbid thought, but she wasn't getting warm fuzzy feelings off Matt right now.

She thought of all he'd shared and she worried,

wondering if she should go get his daughter. "Do you need Grace Marie?"

He shook his head. "Already made use of the flight doc's bag of medical goodies."

Her hands roved a lazy rhythm over his chest while she stayed silent, just waiting. "Not a good day?"

"You could say that." His voice was thin, different. She would have noticed even if she hadn't known about his condition, but somehow she'd become attuned to this man. "That's okay. I like you on bad days, too."

He laughed, a dark sound unlike any she'd heard from him. "I don't think you know how bad the days can get."

"I'm an intelligent woman and perhaps have done some research on the Internet since you told me about your history."

That stirred a reaction from him as he looked over his shoulder at her with a half attempt at a smile. "Thank you." Then he turned back around. "I do a fairly decent job of juggling the meds, mixing a cocktail of sorts when needed."

"So you are cocktailing today."

He nodded slowly. "I took some Lamictal. It's pretty cutting edge, treats bipolar depression in particular so I don't swing over into a maniac fit instead. I'm just waiting for the meds to kick in and level things out."

She let the silence hang for a while since speaking seemed tough for him. Processing words would probably be equally difficult, so she gave him time to assimilate.

He didn't seem to mind her sitting behind him, rubbing his back, squeezing his shoulders then moving up to massage his scalp until the time seemed right to talk again. She slid her arms around his neck until her hands rested over his heart. She gauged his heart rate.

As much reading as she'd done, instincts still seemed her best bet. "Can I do something for you?"

He folded his hands over hers. "No, but thanks. Nothing more to do for this but wait now. I don't expect you to understand."

She put her chin on his shoulder. "I recognize pain when I see it."

He squeezed her hands on his chest.

"I've been in pain, Matt, torturous physical pain with my cancer surgeries and treatment. The emotional ride during those years wasn't all that great either. I understand how it can consume you."

"Explain?" he said as if he could only squeeze out

one word, but oddly enough the word sounded... hopeful.

Tears welled at just the memory of the aches and, worst of all, the terror. "I realize how it takes over your life. Yes, I'm cured, but I'll never forget. The fear of going out of remission still slips up on me sometimes after all these years, especially in the quiet of night."

He squeezed her hands again. "Thank you, but I don't have a potentially terminal disease."

She continued to rest her head on his shoulder since it seemed easier for him to speak this way, without making eye contact. The dreary tent full of shadows sure didn't lend a happy-mood setting. She thought of how she would enjoy filling his world with swathes of bright colors and light.

The future. She was actually planning for the future, something she'd always been wary of doing, just in case the worst happened. Going out of remission.

But this was about Matt. Felicia held him a little tighter to ground him in the here and now. "You have a disease nonetheless. The brain is every bit as much an organ as any other part of your body. How is this any different from someone who has diabetes and needs insulin? Perhaps the levels increase with time, but the person who stays in touch with his doctor for a good maintenance plan can live a full life."

He chuckled again, still dark and a bit thin, but longer this time. "Your 'people sense' IQ."

"Excuse me? I'm not sure what you mean."

"You're a wise lady."

Wow, a compliment that didn't have anything to do with her backside or breasts. "If I'm such a wise lady, will you please be honest with me if I ask you something?"

"I believe I can handle that."

Her stomach cramped at the fear of asking and being rejected. Being able to help him meant more to her than she could have imagined, but she refused to shy away. "Is it better for you if I stay or leave right now?"

She waited, her stomach gripping almost as tight as her heart.

Finally, he exhaled. "Stay, but no more talking."

"I can handle that and I thank you for your trust."

He angled around until she could see his face, such a sad and somber expression with eyes so full of agony she wanted to cry for him but refused to add to his pain. Matt gripped her waist and swung her around to sit on his lap, tucking her head under his chin and just holding her.

She'd always expected that if she ever found that romance novel kind of love she'd read about, she would be by a lake with fireworks exploding while the man of her dreams kissed her.

There was little light in this room to illuminate the olive green gear and shadows, but her heart brightened with the truth all the same. Light days or dark, she had found her man to love.

MAKING LOVE with Gracie blew his mind.

Sprawled on her cot, with her draped naked over him, a little sticky from the cherry-flavored underwear. He'd gotten dressed and run out to find them some food and get himself a change of clothes, comfy civilian duds for a low-key afternoon. He'd reentered her tent and promptly threw all clothes aside again.

Thank goodness her roomie would stay away. Apparently women had their "stay out—entertaining a guy" symbols like guys did. Her tent currently sported a water bottle resting right at the flap.

That she'd planned ahead for the two of them, the possibility…that, he liked to consider very much. Bobby traced his fingers up and down her spine, one vertebra at a time. "Shall we call that one a draw, Doc?"

"I'm too tired even to consider it anything else." She sighed over his chest.

"Why thank you, ma'am. We spent a lot of time making love…and talking." His booted foot started jiggling faster before he finally blurted, "I know we called the conversation a draw, but I just want to make sure you realize I'm not some whackjob for you to psychoanalyze."

"That never crossed my mind. The number-one rule of a relationship is for a shrink to leave that sort of mind-probing at the door. It's not fair to either of us."

"Can you honestly say you didn't look at me and think that I'm crazy, just like your dear old pops? Then you had your excuse to run. You never gave me a fair shake right from the get-go."

"There might be some truth to that, but you tried your best to scare me off. You may have spent a small fortune on a meal as an out-of-character gesture you say was meant to impress me, but every other move you made seemed determined to make me run, or at the very least, test me."

"See, there you go analyzing me." He pinched two fingers together as if grasping a pencil and writing. "Commitment phobic."

"So now you have your psychology degree?"

"You are a profiler. Is that something you can just turn off and on at will?"

She grasped his hips, his erection softening but still inside her. "I can when you're buried heart-deep within me."

"Wow, you sure do know how to shut up a fella fast." He throbbed to life again.

"But you're still talking." She wriggled her hips against his, inhaling the scent of cherry and sweaty sex.

He may have throbbed to life, but she knew neither of them was ready for round three of sex, and they would have to dress soon, anyway. How odd that she actually wanted to talk more right now than try to work in one more quickie, and her instincts told her he felt the same.

Even stranger.

He rolled off her and to his side, gathering her closer, which kept her from being able to see his face. "Okay, so we're talking as a couple and you've checked your degree at the door. Right?"

"Cross my heart," she answered, suddenly wondering how she was so fast losing control of that heart and who it belonged to.

Bobby continued to hold her, not rubbing, not even moving, so different for him, but almost as if he was anchoring himself in her intrinsic stillness.

"You want to hear what it's like growing up with a junkie mother? Never knowing if she's going to be there when you go to bed at night or wake up in the morning? The details aren't pretty but then you've probably heard worse with whatever sickos you deal with in your profiler day job when you're not doing your patriotic reservist gig."

His words shocked and hurt her, for him, for her as well, because they were so tangled up together now, his pain was hers. "Whatever I've heard in the past holds no bearing on this moment. This is just you and me, remember?"

His arms wrapped tighter with a slight tremor as if in a deeper trust rarely given. "I can fall asleep anywhere, so that wasn't a problem. The lack of food, however, was a big issue. You may have noticed I'm wired a little tight. Had a doc say once I'm borderline hypoglycemic so I need to eat frequent snacks. Kinda tough where I lived. My most common 'treats' as a kid? Mustard sandwiches or mayo sandwiches. Mayo worked better since it put some fat into the equation."

A gag built in her throat that she swallowed down for his sake. Only then did she realize that while he'd stopped stroking her, she'd begun rubbing soothing patterns along his back. No wonder he snitched restaurant and store freebies compulsively.

"I wish I had known you then and could have brought you to my house. Things may have been a roller coaster, but we had food."

She felt Bobby's smile against the top of her head. "Your father would have never let you play with a kid who lived where I came from."

"I would prefer to pretend otherwise if you don't mind."

"Sure, if it makes you feel better." He hugged her once and continued, "After a while, I learned to be charming and work the building. Little old ladies love to feed a kid a cookie or two. I'm a damn good liar so they never guessed that I was there because nobody else gave a shit. And yeah, I stole when I could. Slip on a sweater in a department store, rip off the tags and walk out. Shove precooked anything in my pockets. Beef jerky and granola bars were particularly easy to hide, and the jerky added some protein."

Her throat choked with tears far more burning than her earlier bile. She couldn't even push words past.

"One day when the Department of Social Services finally stepped in, I realized I had a grandmother. She'd disowned my mother, so she didn't know about me until DSS called her when I was nine years old.

It was that or foster care. Blessed luck and an over-worked, caring social worker dumped me on my grandmother's porch."

Finally, she could talk again and asked, "What about your grandfather?"

"Didn't have one, not that I ever knew about. Apparently Grandma and my mother both got dumped the minute the pregnancy test popped positive. Grandma just had a better grip on how to support herself and her kid. She worked double shifts and more if she had to. Problem was, that didn't leave anyone to watch over my mom, who already was hell on wheels. Grandma kicked her out for joining a gang, not knowing Mom was already pregnant with me. And voilà, Mom had me when she was eighteen, on the streets."

How could she have never known this? Because she'd never bothered to ask. Not knowing made walking away easier. "I'm so sorry."

"Her fault." He shrugged. "Not mine. Although Grandma about had a shit fit when she looked in the bag of my junk I'd brought with me."

"How so?"

"She found my switchblade."

"Oh, Bobby." At nine years old? She might have checked her doc credentials at the door, but she could still think of plenty of ugly reasons a nine-year-old would need to keep a knife.

"None of her perv boyfriends hurt me, but a couple of them tried. I figured they wouldn't expect a knife from a kid and they sure as hell weren't going to fess up to how they got the wound." He quieted for a dozen deep breaths in and out before continuing. "I almost killed one of them. That scared me a little, getting so close to the line between protection and vengeance."

She tried her best to stifle the welling emotion in a burning need to make sure he knew how damn well adjusted he was after living that kind of hell as a kid.

She sat up, needing to meet his eyes and let him see the conviction in her gaze. "But you didn't, even when you had every right to do that and more. You're a good man, Bobby."

He opened his mouth to answer—

Only to be cut short by a siren sounding blasting "assembly" through the camp.

CHAPTER TWENTY

RURIK HUDDLED behind a banyon tree, the camp's siren echoing through the jungle.

Undoubtedly they had now discovered him missing. He owed Jiang a huge thanks for delaying them, because only with her help could he have stayed undetected this long. Otherwise this perimeter would have been climbing with Army troops searching for him. They had been so concerned with keeping people from coming in, they'd missed him going out.

He had felt certain that even though he had not told Jiang of his plans, she would keep his absence secret as long as she possibly could. But he could not have known for sure until now.

He hated slipping from her bed that way; however, she would have insisted on coming with him and she wasn't as well versed in evasion tactics. For the safety of their mission, he had to leave her behind.

Hardening his heart was difficult at times such as these, but since he had entered school and been recruited by the underground he'd been taught this was his duty, his path. His old man's beatings only made Rurik all the more determined to find his own way in the world.

Pain meant nothing to him. He'd been honed by the master at torture. His father.

Now everything had come together for the final showdown that would send the country into a fear deep enough to affect the outcome of their election.

If anyone even dared vote.

His own people were close by, ready to help. Reaching them had taken less than an hour of running through the woods before he found the buried comm device. The information he had smuggled out two weeks ago had been implemented. His hand fell to rest on the innocuous-looking briefcase that carried a dirty nuke.

The explosives strapped to his chest had him sweating like a pig by ten in the morning, but were necessary. If anyone charged him, he only had to toss the briefcase and then he would take out his attacker with the explosive.

The briefcase was virtually indestructible—except for the ultimate nuclear explosive it held. And there was no way to disarm it. Their path, his role in history, had been set.

He wished he had been able to return before his absence was noted, but as the American saying went, "You can't win them all."

GRACE MARIE TOOK the emotional pulse of the camp and it was tense, to say the least.

How in the hell had Rurik Zazlov escaped? Surely Jiang must have known hours ago and helped him. The General was interrogating her now and would be calling Grace Marie in soon for lie-detector tests, psyche evals.

Sometimes things were as simple for her as watching for a good old-fashioned poker-game "tell" gesture, a twitch that betrayed intent. She'd interrogated Jiang Lee and Rurik Zazlov initially. Jiang Lee undoubtedly nurtured secrets but didn't have the spirit of a killer.

Rurik, on the other hand, she perceived to be capable of anything. He was so well trained the man didn't even have a tell. But trained by which side? That much she hadn't determined at the time.

His leaving the camp now confirmed her worst fears. Yet, why would he leave Jiang behind? Had he only been using her?

Not a very nice thought for a woman such as herself to have with relationship fears piling on like an overloaded backpack. And speaking of relationships…

For now, she stood with Bobby in the cluster of people outside their tent camp, planes parked to the side—the looming C-17 cargo plane Rodeo used to bring in her supplies, and the newer CV-22 Bobby had used to fly in her Delta troops, the craft that would be used for rescue if need be.

She needed to focus on her job, but her mind was still stuck on the conversation with Bobby, and the sense that there was more. Of course, wasn't that the whole point? There was so much more to this man than she'd ever given him credit for. She looked around at all the different airmen, mingling with the Army personnel, most everyone in civvies after reacting so fast to the report-in at the emergency siren.

Why had she been so hesitant about searching deeper with Bobby when she evaluated all the other aviators without a second thought? Even without their uniforms, she could see into their personalities. The way Face kept his life in a Palm Pilot. Organized. Dependable.

Vegas tucked photos of his kids inside his hat, along with a baseball card. Bobby had once told her

Shane—Vegas—always put his hat by his beside at night so he could see his family. And now that family was in jeopardy. God, there was still as much work for her to do for these service members once they got home.

With Bobby, she didn't even have to look at the window dressings. His wild eyes said it all. The uniform could barely contain all that energy.

Seeing them in civilian clothes, however, made the differences all the more apparent. Face in his bland blue shirt and conservative shorts. Hunky, no doubt, but that predictable fashion hinted a woman would always be able to count on him. A good thing. A very good thing.

But of course her eyes were inevitably drawn to Bobby in his plaid shorts as he sprawled in his green chair. She allowed herself to look, really look. The shorts could have been considered Ralph Lauren preppy and pricey if it weren't for the rest of his look—a plain white T-shirt and combat boots, for cripe's sake. She didn't doubt for a second he'd picked up those shorts at Goodwill.

The man was a serious penny-pincher.

A grin tickled her lips, loitered. She had to confess the practical side of her that struggled for dominance over her wilder impulses admired that trait. He was so darn funny, jamming free samples in his pockets, never passing up the last roll in the complimentary basket.

What would happen with them after this mission? The notion scared and thrilled her simultaneously. One thing she knew for sure, she wanted more time with him in the States. She wanted to give this relationship a chance. And if that were to happen, she had to stop shying away from digging deeper, getting to know each other, the real person and not just the social personality.

She closed the space between them. "Hey."

He grinned, reaching behind to pull out another matching green-weave fold-up yard chair he'd scavenged. "Have a seat, my lady."

"Ah, and what a lovely throne it is." She enjoyed his whimsy most of all. She dropped into her lawn chair beside him. "Where did you find them?"

"That day in the village, somebody tossed them out because a couple of the weaves tore. Hell, that's so easy to fix, why toss them? Anyhow, I gave them a couple of carved farm animals in trade and here we are. Now if we only had a little Weber kettle grill in front of us, we'd be an all-American couple."

The crowd moseyed farther away, giving them a wide berth with a decent amount of privacy. Still, an undercurrent of danger buzzed as everyone wondered what happened with that Zazlov fellow. "Would you prefer that grill scenario, or would you get bored in a week?"

"What do you think?"

She trod warily here. "I think you said I should respect your boundaries and not go probing in your head."

"How about this? You can ask whatever questions you want to get to know me better—as a boyfriend and girlfriend kind of thing—and I reserve the right to dodge answering if I so choose."

"Fair enough." Girlfriend and boyfriend? She couldn't ignore the kick of fun over the semi-high-school-sounding notion. Like going steady.

She stretched her legs out in front of her, covering herself with bug spray since she'd only been able to snag her exercise shorts and an Army T-shirt before heading out. "What's with the borderline kleptomania?"

"Why, Hot Doc," he answered while leering at her legs. "Whatever do you mean?"

She rolled her eyes and pitched him the bottle of bug spray. "Sorry, first question out and I break the rules."

"You're forgiven this time." He sprayed the insect repellent over himself in a haphazard pattern as if he didn't really care much but didn't want to reject her offering. "Remember the mayo sandwiches? Well, when you've been hungry, it's pretty hard to shake the feeling even if you've got a couple hundred thousand dollars in your portfolio."

Gracie Marie sat up straight. "A couple hundred thousand?"

"Give or take a buck."

She searched his eyes to see if this was more of his bullshit and found...ohmigod. He was serious. She struggled for something to say and could only come up with, "My grandpa lived through the Depression. He always had three freezers full of food out on his porch."

"There ya go, then." He waved one hand through the air, while the other pitched the insect repellant to Stones a good fifty yards away with the rest of the crew. "Not so crazy after all."

"Sure, except my grandpa periodically ended up throwing things out because of freezer burn." She tugged a hair scrunchie off her wrist and pulled her hair back into a ponytail, not even wanting to think how much it must have looked like "sex hair" before. "I've never seen you waste a thing."

He rubbed the back of his neck, a light scowl on his face. "Apparently you haven't seen that damn pile of boxes of salt and other wasted extra parts of MREs Face made me dump out behind the mess hall."

"Huh?"

"Never mind."

They settled into a comfortable silence for a while until she could almost smell hamburgers smoking away on a grill in front of them, hear the noise of squealing children rather than the deep timbre of adults.

Grace Marie had a sense of something heavy rumbling inside Bobby, something important. Maybe even something he preferred not to say. So her best course would be silence, ready to listen in case he chose to spill, but respectful of his boundaries if he wished to stay quiet.

He folded his hands over his chest, his eyes trained on the spot holding their imaginary grill. "Remember how I said I lived with my grandma after a while?"

"Yes, when you were nine." She tuned out the restless pacing of the other camp members so she could focus entirely on Bobby's words, the way he was opening up to her as he'd never done before.

"You're a good listener."

"I care what you have to say. I very much want to get to know you better, Bobby Ruznick."

He slid one of the hands off his chest and extended it for her to hold while they stayed in their mid-America suburbia seats, the rest of the camp far enough not to hear.

Bobby linked their fingers loosely. "My mother was a drug addict. My grandma found out from my mom that I was addicted to heroin when I was born. Grandma made it damn clear I'd better stay the hell away from drugs, because I needed to face up to the fact that I was already a recovering addict and always would be. The taste was in my blood."

Gracie Marie linked their hands tighter in support, to let him silently know she had no intention of letting go.

"I've always wondered if maybe there's a short wire in my system because of that early crap. Grandma said that even if that was true I had plenty more good inside me to overcome any of the rest."

"Your grandma sounds like a wise lady."

"A tough one." He smiled for the first time. No question, he must have loved his grandma and that love saved him. "She rode me hard, a good thing. She was determined I wouldn't turn out like my mother. Grandma felt guilty about that, which I always thought was total bullshit."

"There could have been many other factors in your mother's childhood that had nothing to do with your grandmother," Grace Marie agreed.

Bobby pulled his hands free and clasped them between his knees, leaning forward. "Then there are the choices we make as adults. She *chose* to shoot up while she was pregnant."

Grace Marie could envision the hellish scenario too easily and wanted to find the woman and kick her ass seven ways to Sunday. The image of Bobby as a baby going through withdrawal stabbed at her heart so hard she almost doubled over in pain. Only years of professional training enabled her to keep some semblance of control. Silence seemed the best course of action. Let him take the lead.

Bobby shook his head as if ridding himself of the dirt. "Anyhow, we were talking about my most-cool grandma. Things were better moneywise when I moved in with her, but we sure didn't have extras. We lived in a neighborhood that you probably wouldn't have been caught dead in, and if you made a wrong turn into it, you would likely lock your doors. But we always had plenty to eat."

Grace Marie noticed how it kept coming back to the food for him. Hadn't he mentioned being borderline hypoglycemic? It must be hell having your life ruled by food but being completely out of control where it was concerned.

"Grandma worked her butt off, though, and I really hated that for her."

The picture cleared for her. "So you brought home whatever freebies you could to make things easier."

"Pretty much." His smile surfaced. "I crossed the line once with her, though."

"What line?"

"I stole a package of steaks. I had stolen stuff when I lived with my mom, but I was so young then and truly hungry, somehow I could forgive myself for that. But this time, I was about eleven, solid weight. She'd sent me to the corner grocery store to buy milk and a box of corn starch."

"Corn starch? You remember the most interesting details."

"Important events paint a brighter picture in your memory so I won't slack off and forget. Anyhow, I saw this package of steaks on clearance and the sell-by date was right then. It was five o'clock in the afternoon, so I told myself, hey, they would just be tossing out those perfectly good steaks in about five minutes. Why let them go to waste? It wasn't like I was taking money out of the grocer's pocket. In fact, I was saving that butcher some time, which meant he could go do something else, which would actually *help* the business."

Interesting how a person could justify something and even more interesting that she saw so much guilt on his face even now, all these years later. Somehow, in spite of a hellish childhood, he'd grown into a strong and honest man.

"Grandma didn't quite see it the same way I did."

"You told her?" Grace Marie leaned over to whisper, even realizing there was no way the rest of the camp could hear them, tucked away in their green lawn chairs a football field away from the bulk of the activity.

"She knew I didn't have the money to buy T-bones, even on clearance."

"She punished you."

Bobby smiled again, guilt gone. "She blistered my ass with a switch." He held up both hands. "Before you go shrieking about child abuse, let me assure you the woman rarely resorted to corporal punishment—only three times in my life—and I had it coming."

"What were the other two times?"

"I back-talked a teacher in the fifth grade." He took a deep breath. "And my sophomore year in high school, I came home wearing a gang jacket."

She tried to picture that in her mind, a large teen and a tiny grandma. While Gracie Marie wasn't going to even delve into the whole to-spank or not-to-spank question, she thought more about how terrified that poor woman must have been to think her grandson was headed down the same road as her junkie daughter. "She whipped you in the tenth grade?"

"Yep."

"Weren't you bigger?"

"By about eleven inches."

"And you just took the whipping."

"Hell, yeah. That was my grandma."

His restraint combined with his love and respect for that little old woman blew Grace Marie away, after all her conflicting feelings about her father, who'd never once laid a hand on her, even at his absolute lowest points.

Bobby's face flooded with guilt again. "When I turned around, she had tears in her eyes. She told me she would rather see me shot dead in the streets making a stand for good than have me end up like my mother."

She couldn't stop her gasp even as she understood the desperate measures that drove his grandmother to say such a thing.

"Grandma said the measure of a person's character isn't in how many days they live but in having lived them honestly."

Grace sat in her chair, totally humbled. Here she'd been expecting to help him through some trauma and he'd been the one with all the depth. She felt so damned inadequate. For the first time she thought to wonder if she was enough *woman* for Bobby. "What an amazing lady your grandma was."

Bobby nodded his head. "Yeah, she was." His face went dark as if somehow he'd sensed her judgmental thoughts earlier. "So sure, I stuff my pockets with those free samples, I dance close to the edge, but I never, *never* cross the line."

As much as she didn't want to be the professional at the moment, her training told her well he'd stretched himself as thin emotionally as possible and needed space. He shoved up from his chair, bursting their mid-America fantasy and striding away.

She'd always thought it would be her choice whether or not to have a relationship with Bobby. She'd never considered the decision might be *his* and he would find *her* lacking.

CHAPTER TWENTY-ONE

STRIDING AWAY from the best damn thing to ever happen to him, Bobby held the pieces of himself together with emotional duct tape, the only way he could keep from falling apart in front of Gracie.

He needed to target practice with his knife or get in a bar fight, except Padre kept breaking those up for the good of the crew. Crew unity. It was everything. Maybe he just needed to hang with level-headed Face for a while to even out.

Eyes focused dead ahead, he didn't even see Gracie's dad until they brushed shoulders. "Sorry, dude. Guess I need to get my eyesight checked."

Although his vision was clearly twenty-twenty and working well now as he stared at Gracie's father with a skateboard under each arm. Really wicked-ass skateboards, probably contraband, that didn't come cheap, even over here. Element brand skateboards, the smile series, personalized.

Cool. And odd. He had to see what was up with this.

Matthias Lanier—Matt, as their U.N. spy called him—paused to look Bobby up and down. "I hear you're seeing my daughter."

"Yes, sir. When she'll have me."

"Any reason she shouldn't have you?"

"Honestly? About a hundred and seventeen reasons at last count, but I just can't stay away. I've tried. Didn't work." He swallowed hard. Shee-it. How the hell had men gotten through saying this to prospective fathers-in-law since the freaking beginning of time? Bobby inhaled deeply and let the truth flow. "I love her."

The older man nodded his head. "I pretty much figured that. My Gracie deserves much more love than she's been given in her life. Any man who can fill those spaces for her…well…" He swallowed as if overcome by emotion.

"Well, what, sir?"

Matt straightened to a height that topped Bobby by a good three inches. "I promise not to blow up that man's house with one of my experimental nuclear 'accidents.'"

He pivoted on his heel without another word to indicate he might be joking—the guy had to be joking, right? Bobby fidgeted double time as Matt made his way toward Gracie. Hmm…her father had called her Gracie, too. How interesting that now there were only two people in the world who used that name for her.

What a rush.

Bobby halted his retreat and turned back toward Gracie, watching her dad advance. Bobby figured his talk with Face could wait. Right now, he couldn't stop himself from watching the exchange between father and daughter. Parental relationships were still pretty much a mystery to him, but if he managed to find a permanent place in Gracie's life, this man would play a critical role.

"Hey, Daddy, how are you doing?" Gracie kept her gaze pinned to his as if studying his eyes.

Her voice drifted over and Bobby refused to feel guilty for eavesdropping. He probably—hell, definitely—had worse sins on his soul than that. And quite frankly, he wanted Gracie so badly he would take advantage of any edge he could get.

Like with her question about her father's mood. How early in her life had she learned to do that to determine her bipolar father's disposition?

"Doing okay, baby girl." He sagged to sit in the other ugly but functional green lawn chair, propping the two skateboards against the seat. "Much better than earlier, but I have to admit to being a little insulted that you felt the need to cross the ocean to make sure I'm eating my vegetables."

He reached down beside him and pulled up the hot pink skateboard. "I had one of these Army dudes drive me downtown to the open-air market and I picked something up for you."

Surprise flashed in her eyes as she reached for the board with her name scrawled in hot pink with a smiley face over it. "It's not my birthday."

Regret creased the older man's face as he watched his daughter with undeniable love. "I've probably missed a birthday or two at some point in time."

She stayed diplomatically silent for a few seconds, staring at the gift in her lap, tracing her cursive name. "We did grow up together, didn't we?"

He pulled up the second board and rested it across his knees, his name painted in midnight-blue. Matt stroked his hands over the varnished skateboard. "Yes, my little Gracie, we did. I wished better for you than I could give."

She looked up with an expression of such total peace Bobby envied her. "And, Daddy, I thank you for giving me the very best you had."

Gracie leaned to kiss his cheek before straightening, quirking a brow and lifting her skateboard.

Without a moment's hesitation, they both sprang from the butt-ugly chairs, boards under their arms as they raced across the camp. Luckily, no Army dudes loitering about tackled them. Instead, everyone backed up to see how far this skateboard gig would go.

Gracie nodded toward the lowered C-17 load ramp. Her father smiled in return and jogged alongside, their feet thunking all the way up the metal ramp into the belly of the cargo plane. Bobby leaned back against an overgrown persimmon tree and squinted to see deep into the plane.

Their ride down the ramp, then the cement path to Base Ops would be bumpy, to say the least. Almost certainly there would be scraped elbows, if not broken bones, but this ritual seemed worth it to the two of them.

Bobby waited, mesmerized by this playful side of Gracie he'd never seen before. What he wouldn't give to have her let go this way with him. How could he find the key to this footloose side of her? He'd learned long ago not to want anything unless he was damn certain he could have it. Saved disappointment. But right now, he wanted Gracie enough to risk everything.

So he watched her with her father to learn whatever he could about the multifaceted woman who'd nabbed his heart.

Matt placed his foot on the board and shouted, "That which cannot kill me will only make me stronger."

"Amen, old man," Gracie concurred, settling her foot on her shiny Element board. "Amen."

"Ready," Matt called.

"Set," Gracie answered.

"Go!" they shouted together.

Her foot launched her into action down what must have been a teeth-rattling ride alongside her father down the cargo plane load ramp.

Whoops and hollers echoed from the growing crowd of crew and support personnel gathering around the base of the plane and lining the cement walkway to Base Ops. Money even started exchanging hands as to who would last the longest.

At the base of the ramp, with a kick at the back of the board, Gracie catapulted herself airborne to take the slight bump. She landed with unmistakable skill on the hill toward Base Ops.

Holy crappola. She'd really done this before. She pushed harder with the other foot, even working a slight sway from side to side to keep her father from passing her. NASCAR drivers had nothing on this woman when it came to defending her lead. The wind tore at her hair, pulling unruly locks from the scunchie until the hairband gave up and dropped off behind her.

Gracie's full mass of blond hair trailed behind her, her T-shirt plastered to a poster-girl perfect chest as her arms splayed out for balance. But all Bobby could see was her smile of unfettered happiness.

He wanted to be around to see that smile for the rest of his life.

The cement path neared its end, Gracie still in the lead with Matt only inches behind. At the last second, he veered off the path onto a jutting rock, his rangy body taking flight, totally in control as he hooked an arm around his daughter's waist and landed them both on their feet in front of the Base Ops door.

Applause exploded. How could it not? Who would have expected this?

Over the chaos, Padre shouted, "How do we decide the bets since they finished at the same time?"

The masses parted to reveal the Felicia chick—who the hell could pronounce her last name, anyway? She perched her hand on her hip in a way that made cammo pants on a woman look more than a little risqué. "Uh, excuse me, but I do believe I was the only one to place a bet on a tie, so hand over the cash, boys."

Her audaciousness made her winning fun even if it cost money.

Sandman strode forward—apparently the bookie for this operation—and passed her a stack of bills. "Interested in letting me buy you a drink?"

Felicia patted his cheek. "Thanks, little boy, but I'm already taken."

She strutted right past the crew's well-known player—currently slack-jawed over the rejection—and made her way to Matt. He released his daughter and strode through the crowd to Felicia. She reached to cup his face and planted a big kiss on his unshaven cheek.

Catcalls ripped through the air, only to grow louder when Matt looped his arm around her waist and pulled her closer for a full-out, old-fashioned dip kiss that would have done Bogey proud.

Bobby searched the crowd to find Gracie, but she seemed to have momentarily disappeared from sight. Had she fallen when her father left? Was she taking her skateboard ride deeper on her own to air out her brain? He certainly understood the need for solitude sometimes. Still, with that Rurik Zazlov dude on the loose, Bobby didn't feel he could let down his guard for even a second. He sidled through the crowd, still enjoying the hell out of that unexpected lip lock.

And in the middle of those whoops and hollers and a kiss that seemed never ending, a piercing whistle sounded. Gracie? Bobby pushed through the crowd to follow the sound...

Only to find Rurik Zazlov standing at the edge of their camp, his coat flapping open to reveal explosives strapped to his chest. With one hand, his thumb depressed a plunger attached to wires leading to a suicide vest.

However, it was the other hand that worried Bobby more, the hand that held a briefcase full of God only knew what.

But Bobby had a damn certain, deadly notion.

STANDING IN the agitated crowd, Jiang looked into the eyes of her lover and could see that he was already dead inside.

How could she have so deluded herself that he only planned to blow up some factory or military munitions tent in the middle of the night? She had told herself what she wanted to believe.

That he was honorable.

That they would have a future.

That finally she would have a safe haven.

Instead she saw the blankness in his dark eyes that she could have once sworn held love for her as he cradled her body to his. She knew he was talking, shouting even, at the crowd to hold their positions.

To shut up. A ramble of other orders that bounced off her stunned psyche.

Had he only used her for sex? Certainly she had given it to him any way he wanted it, anytime they could steal away.

No.

She could not believe it was all a sham. She had felt his emotion when he plunged inside her. Heard the yearning when he discussed their plans for the future with children. Although now she understood the yearning came from his belief they would never realize those dreams.

The tension around her built even as her heart crumbled to her feet. She could feel their need to act. Her ability to sense emotions, honed through her meditation, told her these people would do their best to murder Rurik before he could kill any of them. As much as she believed in hope to the end, she could see no way out of this.

Where were the Army soldiers? Had Rurik in his zealous rage noticed their absence?

For the first time since she'd seen Rurik and given him her heart, her body, her soul, she realized he was wrong. Killing all of these people—military and civilians—in such a way that defied humanity made him no different from the people who had massacred her family simply because of her father's outspoken ways.

A part of her raged at Rurik for what he was doing. She wanted to hate him and a part of her did. But she also didn't hand over her heart lightly. She couldn't change where she'd poured her love, even as she knew she had to do everything in her power to stop him from following through with his plan, a murderous plan.

Rurik thought she was weak and needed protection. He was wrong. She understood full well what had to happen in these next few minutes. Her body and heart might be broken, but not her soul. She would try her best to save these people around her.

And as much as she grieved over ending her life, at least she knew she and Rurik could realize their dreams and love in the afterlife.

GRACE MARIE CROUCHED from her hiding spot in the bushes beside Bobby and whispered in a voice she was surprised as hell didn't shake with fear, "Bobby, don't look down. I'm here and I can help."

Thank God Bobby didn't so much as flinch when she spoke, his nerves of steel apparently in full working order. She envied him that. This was scary stuff going down with Rurik only about fifty yards away with death strapped to his chest.

She continued, "I'm in radio contact with the Delta team. Thank God they were already out running an exercise. They've surrounded the camp and captured or killed Zazlov's band of merry men. Hopefully he doesn't know this since one of the captured men seems willing to keep reassuring Zazlov over their radio in exchange for not being turned over to local authorities."

How damned ironic he would rather defect than deal with his own country's interrogation techniques.

Gracie tapped Bobby's boot, praying with everything inside her that somehow he could survive this hell. She would give him any edge she could. "Let me know what you need."

Once she'd seen Rurik step out with his suicide vest—five minutes ago, although it felt like hours—she'd known immediately what was about to happen. Death. She had the skills at least to try and talk down a person in order to gain time, positioning.

But she doubted the maniac would listen to or respect the opinion of a woman.

Bobby was standing the closest to Zazlov—and the closest to her. Unpredictable "Postal" Bobby, who'd gone rogue nine months ago without bothering to speak to anyone, much less her.

God, she needed his fearlessness now, along with some logic she hoped to offer.

But to make matters worse, they probably only had about five or six conversational exchanges between her and Bobby before Zazlov would make his way over to the fuel tanks in the wings of the CV-22 or C-17. If the explosives on his chest went off and ignited those parked ariplanes, this whole camp and everyone here would go up in uncontrollable flames.

No question, Zazlov likely had planned that very scenario.

They couldn't risk a sharpshooter because there were still too many people close enough to catch the shrapnel when Zazlov released the thumb plunger.

Bobby shuffled his foot in the dust, nudging dirt her way. "Hey, Gracie," he said, doing a fairly decent job at ventriloquism, "any shrink-type suggestions on how to handle this guy would be really appreciated."

He actually wanted her advice? Praise God and a great big sigh of relief for Bobby's crew, who were suddenly having coughing fits, slapping bugs and a thousand other minor sound effects to cover her discussion with Bobby. "First thing you need to do is keep him busy talking."

Bobby's shoulders went back, his face trained right on Zazlov. Not one part of Bobby's body twitched or moved and he held eye contact with the suicide bomber. "What is it you're trying to accomplish here, Zazlov? What's your cause?"

The man with dead eyes and hands full of destruction ready to go off threw his arms wide. "We want to save this country from Western influences and immorality."

Come on, Bobby. Stay focused. Keep him talking. She couldn't help but be complimented he wanted her advice. They'd come a long way emotionally in nine months, both of them. Not to mention she'd finally realized crazy Postal wasn't nearly as off balance as she'd first thought. She'd been evaluating him from a position of personal fear rather than detached professionalism.

Not surprising, since Bobby touched places so deep in her heart.

Bobby cocked his head. "Who is this *we* you're talking about? Does the group have a name or home base?"

"People's Revolutionary Council," Zazlov said with a proud tilt of his chin as if they all didn't know it was just another offshoot of the terrorist spider network. "You egotistical Americans spread your immoral culture to the world. Defiling women and poisoning the minds of the young. Drugs, movies, television, music, and we will not rest until you are all dead."

He continued to ramble about his cause and his council's plans to rule the world or fight to the death of every last one of their followers. His voice gained speed and volume, setting the whole camp on edge until finally Zazlov tossed the briefcase toward where Matt and Felicia stood close together. They would have to move closer to pick it up. A risk worth taking? They both waited with defensive eyes.

"Here, Professor. Really. Have fun with this dirty nuke my people have built. I'll even give you the code to unlock the case." Zazlov spouted off a series of numbers. "Of course, you'll have to wonder if I've set it to blow up when you lift the lid."

Matt extended a hand, holding Felicia back while he went to retrieve the briefcase. Grace Marie held her breath, her heart screaming, no, no, and hell no, her father couldn't be about to… He picked up the case in cradling hands as gentle as the ones that had held her as a child.

Nothing happened.

Her father strode back to Felicia and looked to her for her input as well. She studied the hinges and lock.

Rurik laughed low. "Really, you can open it. In fact

I want you to see how Jiang, our people and I were able to build this based on knowledge *you* gave us. You made this happen. How does that feel Dr. Lanier?"

Matt's hands clenched in fists as he barked, "Ah, to hell with it. We're likely screwed no matter what we do so I'm going with my gut."

He spun the lock numbers and flipped opened the briefcase lid. Again, nothing.

This Zazlov bastard should have known better than to mess with her genius father.

Grace Marie could only see so much through the sculpted branches of the bonsai, but when she heard her father mumble, "Fuck," she guessed that meant they were all very close to glowing in the dark—if they didn't vaporize.

And where was this dark humor within her coming from at such a time? She sounded like Bobby. With that realization came a smile. Learning to laugh in hell made the underworld a bit more bearable. If only she'd realized that soon enough to appreciate the quality in him.

Zazlov sneered. "Good luck trying to defuse it. You were such a good teacher, that weapon is indestructible. What does the timer say right now? I am unable to check my watch without blowing myself up."

Grace Marie figured she could talk herself blue in the face. This man didn't intend to give up, and time was ticking away to determine what to do with the nuclear weapon.

Her father straightened quickly, a smile she'd seen many times before spreading over his face. Total victory. Yet she didn't dare step out to ask.

Felicia grinned as well. "Ohmigod, Matt! You've fricking done it." She glanced skyward. "Sorry Sister Martha Michelle, but ohmigod again. You did it, Matt!"

"Damn straight, I did."

Zazlov's body shook with rage at the announcement, his soulless eyes turning to pure evil determination.

Don't! Grace wanted to scream. Now there would be nothing to stop the man from blowing himself up. Or was that what her father and Felicia were saying?

Grace slipped her hand through the bush and tugged Bobby's knife from his boot, whispering, "Zazlov's just another crazed and brainwashed terrorist. You can't reason with him. It's time to stick him."

"That, I can fucking well handle," Bobby whispered, his breath heavy, his muscles bunched as if finally he could act after torturous restraint. He'd learned to control himself and offer up calm talk, but Bobby would always be the sort who preferred to toss knives.

God help her, she'd just told him to kill a man. There wasn't a choice, but that didn't make the burden any lighter.

Bobby's hand slid down and behind slowly to take the weapon from her and position it in his palm. He would only have about two seconds before Zazlov figured out their intent and tried to launch himself at the airplane fuel tanks.

Once Bobby's fingers clasped around the knife handle he moved so quickly Grace only saw the flash as he shouted, "Take cover!"

His knife went airborne, end over end over end…

As fast as Jiang ran past screaming, *"No!"*

For a moment Grace feared the knife would embed in Jiang Lee's back, but it whizzed past the woman with perfect aim, nailing Zazlov's free hand to a tree. The knife vibrated from the impact and held firm the man's hand, blood gushing.

Zazlov screamed in agony or rage or both, while Gracie blinked her surprise.

Why hadn't Bobby just killed Zazlov? Because now everyone had a few seconds longer to protect themselves from the blast as Zazlov made his decision. In an act that was as merciful as it was clever, Bobby left it to the man to kill himself. Bobby was the clearest thinking, sanest one here.

Grace Marie flattened her body to the ground by the cover of her tree, her eyes caught in a macabre inability to look away from Jiang Lee and Rurik Zazlov. His thumb had already begun sliding off the plunger. There was no going back.

The crazy woman would not stop running, her eyes locked on her lover's. Jiang flung herself on top of Rurik Zazlov just as—

Boom.

Jiang Lee absorbed the bulk of the blast. Body parts flew in a hideous spray of death. Gracie hadn't even realized Bobby had dropped to cover her, to protect her.

She couldn't breathe anyway, so his bulk didn't matter as long as she could feel his breaths go in and out. He was alive. Heaven forgive her for being selfish, but she could only care about Bobby and her father staying alive.

Once Bobby levered off and she caught a full glimpse of him, the pressure exploded inside her. She screamed.

Blood bathed Bobby in a crimson wash.

"Not mine," he assured her. "Well, most of it isn't

anyway. A few shrapnel bits here and there, but nothing lethal."

He yanked her to him for a life-affirming hug he seemed to need as much as she did. Now that she could put her mind at ease about him, she scanned the camp. She saw her father and Felicia embracing and pressed against a bulky tree, still preoccupied with keeping that damn briefcase closed.

Bobby's crew members all moved as if unharmed, scratches, scrapes and so much blood from the two ill-fated lovers. Everyone else was fine.

Except ever-ballsy Stones throwing up in the orchid bushes.

Vegas crumpled his hat with his family photo in a white-knuckled grip.

Face sat stunned silent, eyes closed undoubtedly in prayer.

None of them would get over this day with ease.

Her father stood, briefcase cradled in his hands. "I hate to break the thank-God-we're-alive mood here, but, uh, I lied about being able to disarm this sucker."

Silence thudded through the whole camp in time with Gracie's heart hitting her feet.

Bobby released her, his eyes going wide. "What the hell are you talking about?"

Already Grace Marie saw the path of her father's reasoning and heaven help them all now. No knife or shrink talk would save them.

Her father shrugged. "It was the only way I could think of to get him to take himself out quickly so we stood a real chance of getting rid of this thing. Because he was right. The notion that we can disable something like this is just Hollywood-movie hype."

Bobby exhaled long and slow with a stillness she'd never seen before, even when he'd taken down Zazlov, which worried her more than the bomb. "So, Dr. Lanier, what do you propose we do to keep from wiping out the city as well as ourselves?"

Her father started walking toward Bobby, passing the man she loved a lethal briefcase instead of a bride. "Well, son, you're going to need to fly this dirty nuke out as far as you can over the ocean and dump it into the water. According to the timer, you've got about twenty-seven minutes to play with."

CHAPTER TWENTY-TWO

"HOLY SHIT." Bobby held the open briefcase full of nuclear material and high explosives in his hands, mind completely blown by the fact. "Let's get the aircraft cranked up so I can fly this damn thing out of here."

Face looked Bobby in the eyes for a heartbeat. "What do you mean *you* are going to fly this thing out of here? We're a crew, you and me, pal. We've been a team since you were a baby copilot. We most certainly will fly it out of here together." He turned to the rest of the crew. "Get her ready to fly, ASAP."

The men turned and ran to the aircraft, readying it for flight, pulling covers and cranking up support equipment.

Bobby and Face started toward the hustling crew members and Bobby took one last shot at dissuading Face. "You know I should do this alone, Face. I'm not married and you are."

Crap.

The reality hit him full in the face.

He couldn't make that argument anymore. He turned and looked at Gracie standing with Felicia on one side of her, Matt on the other side, her face pale with acceptance, fear and tears sheening without falling.

Gracie changed everything.

Blood dripped from his forehead down his temples with a gruesome reminder of mortality. He didn't dare swipe it away. Cleaning up could come later—if he had a later. Oh God, Gracie. He couldn't think of all those dreams he'd only just started to dare allow himself to have with her.

Crap, crap, crap! He loved her so damn much.

"Really, Face." Bobby swallowed hard. "Let me do this. I can fly it alone, put it on autopilot and chunk it out the back. There is no reason for both of us to take this risk. Think of your wife."

Face kept right on charging ahead as if he hadn't even heard the argument. "I'm the senior pilot in hours. Shut the fuck up and be my copilot this time."

"Fair enough." *And thank you, my friend.*

Bobby's boots pounded dirt toward the plane, but his eyes and heart were tugging him to the left.

Shit. He didn't have time for this and still he couldn't resist the insane urge to steal thirty seconds.

Bobby veered toward Gracie, hooked a hand behind her neck and kissed her hard and fast. "I've loved you since the first time I laid eyes on you. Don't ever doubt it."

Before she could even respond, he pivoted and sprinted away. He didn't think he could take hearing her answer right now, either way.

As he entered the side door with Face, they bumped into Vegas, the flight engineer, standing in front of the three gunners.

Vegas took the lead. "You guys are *not* going it alone. I don't even want to think about facing Brigid or Lieutenant Lanier if you don't come back. Hell, I don't even want to think about the survivors' guilt we'll have if that happened." Flanked by the gunners, he pushed deeper into the CV-22. "We don't have time to argue about this, so sit down in your seats, sirs. We are ready to roll."

Stones stepped up. "Give *me* the case, sir, and I'll make sure she falls out the back with style."

Both pilots shrugged, and Bobby handed the case to Stones, certain in the man's steadiness. "Don't hold that too close to your enormous 'nads, dude. You don't want your little jumping beans inside to glow in the dark."

Stones winked with unshakable bravery, as if he

hadn't been hurling in the brush just minutes earlier. "Not a chance, sir."

The pilots bolted toward their seats, strapping in faster than ever before. "Hey, Face," Bobby said, "you know what we're missing here?"

"What's that?" he responded with sweat dripping down his neck, mingling with blood from shrapnel dings and scratches.

"How far we need to get off the coast, and how far we need to get away before it goes boom. You finish starting the engines. I'll scope out some math." Bobby leaned out the window and gestured for Matthias Lanier.

The older man sprinted over to the aircraft at a truly honed runner's pace. "I'm going to assume you want to know how far to go and how far away you have to be at detonation, correct?"

Bobby grinned in spite of the tension searing the air hotter than the summer sun. "You really are a genius, aren't you?"

Dr. Lanier smiled back, perspiration beading on his slightly balding head. "It does come in handy every once in a while." Without consulting even so much as a notepad, he recited, "You need to get twenty-five miles off the coast—at least—but the farther the better if your craft's got the juice. Then you'll want to get that case in the water. If you can weight the case to sink faster, go for it. As far as a safe escape distance afterward. Well… I am guessing, try for at least two minutes to haul out, but in a pinch, a mile will probably do it."

Bobby wrote every word, no room for screwing this one up. He didn't much like probably and maybe, but he trusted this man's certainty on the subject probably more than anyone else's.

Gracie's father continued, "The water will eat up most of the explosion and I'm damn near certain the nuclear material will also stay in the water if the case sinks deep enough. And no worries about the timer's accuracy. That much I could determine." He reached through the window and squeezed Bobby's arm just as the engines roared to life. "Good luck, I *will* see you back here in about an hour, because you and I have some talking to do about my daughter."

"Yes, sir, we do." Bobby pulled his helmet onto his head and plugged into the interphone system. "Anyone who wants off needs to go now. How long do we have left on that ticking timer?"

Stones reported up. "We have twenty-two minutes so let's haul ass, sir."

Bobby looked at his instructor pilot, his best

friend, and gave him a thumbs-up. "Ready on this side, Face. Everybody ready in the back?"

"Left gunner ready," Padre, the king of bar fights, answered.

"Rear gunner ready," Stones of the fearless nerves reported.

"Right gunner ready," Sandman, the lady charmer, said.

"Engineer ready," Vegas, a family man at heart, concluded from between them.

Face applied power and lifted the tilt-rotor off the ground and into the air. The aircraft transitioned to forward flight and accelerated over the trees until it was at top speed, foliage bowing in farewell as they sped away.

Bobby pulled out a map of the area and gauged the fastest route to the water. "Come left ten degrees, Face. That will get us over the water the quickest. I wish these aero charts had water depth on them, but other than this odd-as-hell situation, who would use that data?"

Bobby dialed up the emergency frequency and announced, "Attention all aircraft. Hornet two-one is an emergency aircraft. Ten miles south of Cantou proceeding out over the water."

That should hold them through. Nobody around

here would really care if they were leaving. He would deal with returning when the time came. And damn it, they would return. Thank God for the Delta dudes on the ground clearing the area to eliminate risks of that freaking Council shooting up with antiaircraft fire.

Crystal-blue water soon became visible on the horizon. As they crossed over the sandy beach and palms, Bobby came over the interphone. "Feet wet, crew. How long, Stones?"

Stones cracked open the lid and replied, "Fifteen minutes."

Bobby answered, "Okay, now let's see if we can weight the thing down. Gracie's old man said that would help sink it faster. Anything you can work with back there?"

From the rear, Padre answered, "I think so, sir. How about an A-three bag and some full ammo cans? That ought to sink the case like a rock."

"Outstanding," Face agreed. "Make that happen, but don't put the case in there until we are ready to get rid of it. We've got to keep an eye on that timer."

The miles clicked off as they headed out to sea, the crew unusually quiet. No music, ribbing, overall chatter. Instead Bobby's mind channeled through what-ifs with Gracie. The possibility of taking the eternal dirt nap. He needed to shut up his ADHD brain.

Who knew silence could be so heavy?

Bobby switched on the interphone. "We're twenty-five miles out. Give us a heads-up when you've got it weighted or when we've got five minutes left, whichever comes first."

"Roger that," Stones clipped.

Time passed along with the ripples of water beneath them and trickles of perspiration tracing down skin. Bobby started to seriously sweat it for the first time when finally—thank God—*finally* the interphone crackled.

"Sir," Stones called. "Five minutes."

Bobby measured his breaths. "All right, get it in the bag and zip it up."

Face nodded. "I'll slow to a crawl here to cut down on the wind when you drop the hatch."

Stones reported, "Thanks. I'm tied down and ready, sir."

Everything happened so damn fast, calls shooting back and forth. He couldn't remember a shorter twenty minutes in his life. Face slowed the aircraft down while Bobby called out airspeeds and altitudes, thank God for training, the only thing carrying him through.

When he was down to twenty knots and three hundred feet he called back, "Get rid of it. Now."

From the back he heard, "Package away."

The thing couldn't have weighed more than forty pounds and yet the plane seemed buoyant from the release of the threat of death.

Gracie. Bobby tried his damnedest to swallow, but his throat clogged with thoughts of seeing Gracie when he landed.

Face accelerated, all-out. "I don't care what the doc says. Let's get miles and miles between us and that thing."

Clearing his throat enough to speak, Bobby monitored the panel. "I couldn't agree with you more, dude."

CHAPTER TWENTY-THREE

Cantou
Three months later

GRACIE COULDN'T believe she was hanging out in a crappy ol' bus with Bobby again.

She glanced out the windows at the familiar roads and stores, the beauty of the sculpted landscape so exotic and lush. Pedestrians ambled along the streets, looking straight ahead and relaxed rather than over their shoulders, tensed for danger.

Today, the CV-22 and C-17 crew members, along with the Delta forces and psy-ops team, were heading to a command appearance from the newly installed president of Cantou, a great friend of democracy. A banquet was being thrown in their honor, complete with medals and some seriously rocking good face-time with General Renshaw.

The new leader of Cantou was also grateful beyond measure to have that dirty nuke explode ineffectively way the hell deep on the ocean floor. Just as Matt predicted, the water and the depth worked to disperse the lethal possibilities. Like a cup of sugar seemingly disappearing in a pool, the nuclear waste dispersed in the vast ocean, one of those odd quirks of nature, but one that enables underwater testing of nuclear weapons. And even if it hadn't, bottom line they still wouldn't have had a choice when it came to all those lives in the village.

They'd saved a town. Wow. Unbelievable.

The new president wanted to thank the Air Force and Army service members responsible for shutting down the terrorist group who called themselves the People's Revolutionary Council.

Gracie hadn't lost much sleep over Rurik Zazlov's death, but Jiang Lee's face had haunted her dreams more than once. The woman had been a part of the organization, yet she'd saved them by absorbing the blast with her own body. Her love for Zazlov had been undeniable, yet her sense of humanity stronger. The woman deserved to be remembered for that final act and sadly, it seemed Gracie would be the only one in any position to honor that sacrifice.

And yeah, she thought of herself as Gracie these days. Bobby had brought a lightness and informality to her life she had to admit she enjoyed on occasion. And she'd straightened his crazy ass out just enough to keep him safe and on this planet, but not so much to take the fun out of him.

After all, Bobby really did know how to have fun.

Her father most certainly was happier these days as well. Felicia's organization was based out of Zurich, Switzerland, so her father had taken a sabbatical to write a book and guest lecture. Their lives fit, and her father finally had a partner who loved him. Best of all, she understood him. Gracie didn't have to worry so much about him with Felicia to look out for him. For all Ms. Fratarcangelo's outward fluff, Gracie's personal and professional opinions agreed. The woman was rock solid and loved Matthias Lanier.

Besides, Felicia made her dad happy, and that was truly a wonderful sight to see after so many years of him busting his hump searching for balance.

The bus rattled along the pocked road toward the capital, worn-out shock absorbers throwing her against snoozing Bobby with a regularity that tempted her with teasing brushes against his rock-solid body and bouncing knee. A body that looked particularly tempting in his full mess dress uniform, with more medals than a military aviator should have earned in a whole thirty-year career.

Her heart squeezed at the thought of the dangerous missions attached to each medal, but she had to let it go. She understood him and his call to serve. More than that, his call to the sky had saved the son of a junkie.

She also understood her calling could be fulfilled just as easily in his town of Fort Walton Beach as a profiler for the police. She'd already turned in her paperwork to resign her commission as an Army Reservist.

"Hey, Gracie?" Bobby opened his eyes, a gaze so full of love for her she never doubted for a second he was hers for life.

"Yeah, Bobby?" she asked as lush trees whooshed by the open windows, letting in bugs and the cacophonous sounds of a symphony of jungle animals in the distance.

"You sure do look hot in that uniform of yours."

"Why thank you. Right back atcha, my love."

He smiled at that with such peace, this man who hadn't been loved nearly enough, but accepted the gift of her heart with such tender care. "You're gonna look hot in the cop uniform of yours, too."

"Thank you, again."

His eyes twinkled that wicked warning. "Will you have handcuffs?"

"Yeah, and a Taser, too, so watch your butt, Captain." She pressed her lips together primly because she knew it drove him crazy and would most definitely earn her a kiss.

They'd spent a large chunk of the past three months seeing each other. They took week-long and weekend vacations together and even wrangled a second assignment together. Soon, she would be living in Fort Walton Beach near his Hurlburt Field base for good.

"Taser?" He waggled his brow. "I'm always up to try something new. Face it, Gracie, I'm not ever gonna be able to stop admiring that amazing rack of yours. And holy shit, just think of how amazing it's going to look once you've had a couple of kids."

Gracie's throat closed up. Kids? "Is that a proposal?"

"Well, duh," he said, tone light, face serious. "Otherwise my grandma would trot down from heaven and whup my ass."

"Such a romantic proposal it is." She couldn't resist a hint of sarcasm even as her heart jumped in response.

He splayed his hands. "Gracie, I am the man that I am, and for some reason beyond my comprehension, you love me. And that is something I thank God for every morning of my life."

"Oh." Her eyes filled with tears and her heart, well, it went mushy. Even women who could kick butt seven ways to Sunday were susceptible to mush. "That was good."

"Does that earn me a yes?"

She threw her arms around his neck in a flagrant PDA. "A most definite yes, forever yes, all my heart and love yes. My father will adore being a grandpa. Ohmigod, what a big family all of us loners will put together. I want everything with you."

The busload full of airmen and soldiers burst into a round of applause.

Face shouted from the front seat, "Give her the ring, you dumb ass."

A ring? How fitting that this relationship started under the noses of all their military friends, and now she and Bobby would cement it under their watchful eyes as well. No matter how much time she spent on the police force, she knew these guys would always be her brothers.

Bobby thunked himself on the head. "Ah, yeah. The ring. Sheesh. I hope I didn't forget it. I really wanted Gracie to be able to bling up her uniform for this whole awards ceremony."

He fished around in his formal jacket while Gracie waited, touched that her tightwad true love would even buy a ring. She would have been happy with a simple gold band exchanged in front of a preacher.

"Okay, whew." Bobby tugged his hand from his pants pocket, a small blue box cradled in his palm. A ring box.

She saw right through his pretended worry and knew how carefully her crazy lover, friend, soul mate must have planned to make this happen for her.

Slowly, he creaked the jeweler's box open.

"Holy shit!" Gracie exclaimed, her eyes surely about as big as the diamond, a princess-cut rock in a fourteen-karat-gold-pronged setting that Bobby had picked out.

For her.

"Bobby, really, this is gorgeous." And expensive. Like it must have cost a mint, but she wouldn't be tacky enough to say anything. Her hand trembled as she reached toward it. "But really, are you sure—"

"Gracie." He plucked the ring out. "I'm positive this is exactly what I want on your hand to make sure every man knows you're officially off the market."

He slid it on her ring finger and sealed its placement with a kiss. "You know what a thrifty guy I am. I was just waiting for someone I love to spend it on."

"You really can be so sweet when you let yourself." She locked her arms around his neck again and kissed him again to another round of whoops and hollers from the rest of the riders.

Pulling back, she extended her arm to study the look of the engagement ring on her hand as the sun glinted off the jewel. "Where in the world did you find this?"

"Well, Gracie, like you once told me on a very memorable occasion that included a tasty treat. There's nothing you can't buy in the wide-open-air market in downtown Cantou."

* * * * *

Look for Catherine Mann's next release, a **WINGMEN WARRIOR** *story, available in November from Silhouette Intimate Moments.*

CATHERINE MANN

77049-9 CODE OF HONOR   ___ $5.99 U.S. ___ $6.99 CAN.

(limited quantities available)

TOTAL AMOUNT	$ _____
POSTAGE & HANDLING	$ _____
($1.00 FOR 1 BOOK, 50¢ for each additional)	
APPLICABLE TAXES*	$ _____
TOTAL PAYABLE	$ _____

(check or money order—please do not send cash)

To order, complete this form and send it, along with a check or money order for the total above, payable to HQN Books, to: **In the U.S.:** 3010 Walden Avenue, P.O. Box 9077, Buffalo, NY 14269-9077; **In Canada:** P.O. Box 636, Fort Erie, Ontario, L2A 5X3.

Name: _____
Address: _____ City: _____
State/Prov.: _____ Zip/Postal Code: _____
Account Number (if applicable): _____

075 CSAS

*New York residents remit applicable sales taxes.
*Canadian residents remit applicable GST and provincial taxes.

HQN™
We *are* romance™

www.HQNBooks.com   PHCM0706BL